merging magic and history. The result is a wonderfully dark, delightfully well-written [series]. Readers will eagerly await the next Dark Sword book."

—RT Book Reviews

"Another fantastic series that melds the paranormal with the historical life of the Scottish highlander in this arousing and exciting adventure."

—Bitten By Books

"These are some of the hottest brothers around in paranormal fiction."   —Nocturne Romance Reads

"Will keep readers spellbound."

—Romance Reviews Today

Also by
DONNA GRANT

THE SONS OF TEXAS SERIES
The Hero

THE DARK KING SERIES

THE DARK WARRIOR SERIES

THE DARK SWORD SERIES

From St. Martin's Paperbacks

THE
PROTECTOR

DONNA GRANT

St. Martin's Paperbacks

This is a work of fiction. All of the characters, organizations, and events portrayed in this novel are either products of the author's imagination or are used fictitiously.

THE PROTECTOR

Copyright © 2017 by Donna Grant.
Excerpt from *The Legend* copyright © 2017 by Donna Grant.

All rights reserved.

For information address St. Martin's Press, 175 Fifth Avenue, New York, NY 10010.

ISBN: 978-1-250-08340-1

Our books may be purchased in bulk for promotional, educational, or business use. Please contact your local bookseller or the Macmillan Corporate and Premium Sales Department at 1-800-221-7945, ext. 5442, or by e-mail at MacmillanSpecialMarkets@macmillan.com.

Printed in the United States of America

St. Martin's Paperbacks edition / January 2017

St. Martin's Paperbacks are published by St. Martin's Press, 175 Fifth Avenue, New York, NY 10010.

10 9 8 7 6 5 4 3 2 1

To Dad—
Because I've never known a better man

ACKNOWLEDGMENTS

It takes a dedicated team to get a book ready to hand to a reader. My deepest thanks to:

Julia for the Russian translations, the SMP art department for the amazing cover,

Brant, Marissa, Justine, Jordan, and the others in the marketing and publicity departments, Monique Patterson for her expert editorial input, and Natanya Wheeler for believing in this series.

CHAPTER ONE

Florida

"You double-crossed me," came the heavily accented Spanish voice.

Mia looked into black eyes and saw nothing but death reflected there. Thunder rumbled right before lightning flashed and sounded with a crack that reminded her too much of the pop of a gun.

She wanted to take a step back, but she was surrounded by Colombians with no way out. Her gun was on the plane. A show of faith between her and this unsavory party.

But she wasn't exactly weaponless—never would be again after. . . . She stopped that train of thought. She needed to focus on the here and now.

She took a deep breath and lifted her hands. If she didn't get control of this situation, it could go from bad to worse. "You've got it all wrong, Camilo."

"Really?" He smirked and looked at the three men around him. Camilo ran his thumb and forefinger along his thin mustache as he regarded her.

He took a step closer, bringing him within reaching distance of her. His reputation as a lady's man was one he embodied in everything he did, from the Armani suit to his perfectly styled hair.

"Yes, really," she said. "You hired me to fly to Panama and retrieve your boxes. I've done that."

His eyes narrowed. "But you don't have my merchandise."

She kept her gaze on Camilo, but she was aware of every move his men made. They might not have guns, but, like her, they weren't weaponless. "I'm not to blame for the authorities checking my plane and confiscating what they found."

"I was told you were the best. That you could get anything into the States."

"This is the first time in hundreds of flights that I've been caught with anything. Perhaps if you'd told me I'd be transporting reptiles for the black market trade, I could've determined what airfield might have authorities searching planes for just such cargo and diverted to another."

"You didn't need to know," he said.

She shrugged. From the moment the reptiles had been taken from her plane and she was arrested, there had been no other outcome. She was in serious trouble with the law—not to mention the sanctions that would be placed on her by the military.

Her only hope had been leaving Florida before Camilo and his men found her. If they had only arrived five minutes later, she would've made it home.

"A shrug," Camilo said with a grin that held not an ounce of humor.

Shit. This was about to get very bad. If only she'd listened to Sergei, but the old Russian was always telling her to stay away from bad men. Never mind the fact that he was such a man.

Camilo walked around her. "You give me a shrug when I'm out two million dollars."

She turned her head to keep him in her sights. "These things happen."

"Not to me. I've promised those animals to someone, and he doesn't take a shrug for an answer."

"I'd be happy to make another run to Panama for free. However, my plane will be searched every time from now on."

"That's not my problem." He stopped before her, closing in on her. "You agreed to bring me my cargo. I want it. Tomorrow."

Mia hated when people got into her personal space. The creep did it because he thought he'd intimidate her—a common misconception with men.

"I can't be clearer if I spelled it out for you. I'll be lucky to retain my pilot's license after this. I can't help you."

"Then you'll pay me the two million."

She lowered her hands to her sides. Then she said, "No."

"You obviously have no idea who you're messing with," Camilo said before taking a step back.

Mia ducked and spun around as she felt one of the men come at her. When she straightened, she fought the desire to release her hidden knife into her palm.

She moved back to keep all four men in sight. They would come at her all at once. They had the numbers, but they would underestimate her.

"You'll die tonight," Camilo said with a laugh. "Or perhaps I'll take you with me and give you to my men. It'll be fun seeing what they will do to that nice body of yours. I doubt you'll last a week."

No one would ever keep her chained again.

She smiled at the men and motioned them to come at her. The first to reach her was the biggest of the group. She dodged his meaty fist by ducking.

This time when she straightened, the hilt of her knife

slid into her grip. It felt good to have a hold of the weapon. She kept it hidden so that none of the men saw it.

The next time the big guy came at her, she leaned to the side to evade his punch. Then she twisted as she reversed her grip on the hilt of the blade. Swinging her arm wide, she sliced the big guy's chest.

The next instant, she spun back the other way and stabbed him in the gut. When he attempted to grab her with both hands, she used his momentum against him, sticking him in quick succession.

He stood still, swaying. She took a step back before kicking him in the chest. By the time he hit the ground, he was dead.

"Get her!" Camilo yelled, spittle flying from his mouth as he rushed her.

She was good in hand-to-hand combat against one. Against two, she could hold her own. Against three? Well, she wasn't going down without doing some damage of her own.

Right before one of the men reached her, a knife embedded in the back of his throat. He fell at her feet, gurgling blood. She looked around, trying to figure out where the blade had been thrown from, but she couldn't see anyone.

Then she didn't have time to keep looking as she was fighting Camilo and his last man. She gritted her teeth as her upper right arm was sliced.

She took a step back and eyed Camilo and his man, each holding a long blade. Out of the corner of her eye, she saw movement. She caught a glimpse of a man in all black right before Camilo raised his weapon and came at her.

Mia held her stance as he charged. She saw her advantage and took it. Using the big guy's dead body as a vault, she launched herself, feet first, at Camilo in a double leg grapple.

Wrapping her legs around his neck, she used her momentum and swung to the side, bringing him to the ground. She felt his neck break as she twisted.

Rotating midair, she landed on one knee with her left hand on the ground. With her combat knife still in hand, she turned to the last of Camilo's men—only to find him lying on the ground with a knife in his chest.

A man in all black walked from the trees and retrieved his blades. Without a word, he made his way to her. As he closed the distance between them, she let her eyes run over this unknown man.

Tall, muscular, and . . . hard. He walked with purpose, as if assured that he would get whatever he was after. He had the appearance of a military man with his dark hair cropped close on the sides and short on top.

The hint of whiskers graced a strong jaw and chin. His wide, thin lips tilted in a half-smile that made her stomach feel as if she'd just been on a roller coaster—and wished for another ride.

Thick brows slashed over hazel eyes that watched her with interest. He stopped a few feet from her and let her look over him. She slowly stood, taking in the black fatigues and black tee shirt.

"We've got company," he said and jerked his chin as he looked over her shoulder.

She turned her head and saw the six men rushing toward them. A second later, bullets began flying around them.

"Go!" the man said as he grabbed her arm and tugged her toward the plane.

She didn't need to be told twice. In moments, she was inside the plane and starting the engines. With every bullet that pierced the Valkyrie, she winced.

The sound of the engines roaring to life made her smile. She started forward, glancing back at the open door. Whoever the stranger was who'd helped her had little time to reach her before she left.

She closed her eyes briefly, because she knew she wouldn't leave him. It wasn't in her nature. Impatience filled her as the plane began to roll forward away from the gunfire.

There was a grunt. When she looked back, the stranger was in her plane, pulling the door closed. Without a word, she throttled the aircraft, speeding down the runway.

The flashing lights of police cars halted the chase of Camilo's men, but for how long? They didn't know where she lived. With Camilo dead, they might leave her alone. But it was a big "might."

When the stranger came to sit in the seat next to her, she glanced his way. He buckled the seat belt and leaned his head back, closing his eyes.

"Who are you?" she demanded.

"Not even a thank you?" he asked with a grin, his eyes still shut.

She held back a sigh. "Thank you. Now. Who are you?"

"I thought you'd know." His head turned, and his eyes opened to stare at her again.

There was something about him that looked familiar. It took her a moment, but she pieced it together. "Which Loughman brother are you?"

"Cullen," he said with a smile.

Cullen. She stared at him with a bit of surprise. She knew from talks with Orrin, as well as from reports she'd read, that the Loughman boys were some of the best around—military or private sector.

She also knew the middle brother, Owen, was the peacekeeper, who was quiet as he listened to everyone and everything before reacting. The eldest, Wyatt, was the intense one with barely leashed violence beneath the surface.

But it was the youngest, Cullen, who set her back on her heels. Each time she thought of him, chills raced over her skin—and that was before she knew he was heart-stoppingly good-looking.

He made her . . . ache . . . in a way she hadn't experienced in a very long time.

Why did it have to be him that came to her? Why couldn't it have been Wyatt? She could've handled the eldest Loughman with ease.

Cullen held a combination of both his brothers. There was a heavy dose of lethal brutality just waiting to be released on those who stood against his country—or his family.

But he was also patient. To some, he might seem indifferent, but she'd seen the look he currently wore on Orrin's face before. There was no indifference. Only planning and preparation down to the very last detail.

She briefly closed her eyes. The attraction couldn't be denied. But it wasn't just that. She'd felt desire before. This was something . . . more. It was deeper, fuller.

More acute.

It left her with a yearning that rocked her, a hunger that consumed her. She might've heard stories about Cullen, but she didn't *know* him.

Her gaze locked on him as if magnetized. His hazel eyes watched her like a predator, but she wasn't afraid. No, it was more exhilarating than anything.

Forcing her attention back to flying, she set a course for Dover. Back to the place that hadn't just altered her life, but the Loughman boys', as well.

"I've been expecting one of you," she finally said.

He looked out the windshield. "There are answers to

questions about my father's kidnapping at Dover. And with you."

"Nothing is going to stop me from finding him. Orrin is one of the best men I know."

"Then start at the beginning. We've got a little time before we reach the base."

The beginning. No. Not so far back as that. There were things Cullen didn't need to know, things that were better left in the past.

She may be in an unsavory situation, and he might have just saved her, but that didn't give him the right to her secrets.

"It was Orrin who approached me," she said.

CHAPTER TWO

Cullen hadn't expected Mia Carter to be so . . . amazing. He'd never seen a woman fight with such passion or with movements so beautiful that he'd found himself watching her instead of finishing off the Colombian.

For the first time in Cullen's life, he couldn't find words. He could only stare at the beautiful woman with one thought—Valkyrie.

She was the epitome of what he imagined the winged creatures of Norse mythology would look like. All she needed was armor and a sword to complete his vision.

Now, as he sat in the cockpit of the British WWII Bristol Buckingham C. MK 1 plane, also known as the Bristol Type 163 Buckingham, he couldn't keep his eyes off her.

Beautiful didn't begin to describe this incredible woman. Every time her steely black gaze fringed with impossibly thick lashes turned his way, he became entranced. Her eyes were large and slightly tilted up at the corners.

He forgot to breathe as he took in her unblemished, sun-kissed face. With high cheekbones and wide, full lips, he was smitten.

Wisps of inky black hair escaped from her ponytail to fall along the narrow column of her neck. An olive tee skimmed her torso to show mouthwatering curves, and black denim showcased her lithe legs to perfection.

"It was Orrin who approached me," she said.

That didn't surprise him. His father had always had a gift for finding talent and using it to his advantage. "When?"

"A few years ago."

It made Cullen wonder what else his father had been up to. While he and his brothers were off building their lives, Orrin Loughman had been setting up a team of Black Ops members to do some of the dirtiest jobs.

One of the missions, put together by the DOD, had sent Orrin and his team to Russia to steal a bioweapon.

Except something had gone terribly wrong. Someone betrayed Orrin Loughman. In the process, he'd been kidnapped, and his team was executed.

The last person to see his father was the woman sitting next to Cullen.

The years he'd spent as a Marine Force Recon captain had taught him many things. He knew how to fight his way out of various situations using his hands, body, and mind. He knew how to spot lairs and traitors. He also had dozens of rescues to his name.

He was damn good at his job. But he had to be more than good now. His father's very life depended on it.

"How did you find me?" Mia asked.

"I went to the Air Force Base. When you weren't there, I went to General Davis's office. It seems they keep a record of every flight you make."

Her lips compressed. "That they do."

"To my benefit. If I hadn't arrived, you would either be dead or in Camilo's care. Neither of which sounds appealing."

"I already thanked you."

"Yes, ma'am. You sure did." He linked his fingers over his stomach. There was something about Mia Carter he found compelling, and it had nothing to do with her beauty. She was very much like him, he suddenly realized.

Wary of the world with a look of cynicism she didn't bother to hide.

"Tell me how a pilot with your skills is able to have a hangar on a base, work for the military as a contractor, and still be able to take jobs with criminals. Because let's be honest . . . Camilo was a criminal."

"It won't matter what I give you as an explanation. You've already formed an opinion," she replied coolly.

In fact, he had formed an opinion. He suspected that she liked danger. She also loved to fly. Combine the two, and she was in heaven.

"You were telling me about how you and my father began working together," he said, getting them back on topic.

She cut him a look with her black eyes. "What you really want to know is if I betrayed him. As I told Callie—and everyone listening on the phone that day—it wasn't me."

"I do remember that call. Though I've learned that people say a lot of things that aren't the truth."

"You want the truth?" she asked, turning her head to him. "I'll tell you the truth. I hated taking orders, so I left the Air Force as soon as I could. But I wasn't ready to give up flying. It's my life."

That much he could tell. It was in her blood.

"Lucky for me, the Air Force wasn't quite ready to see the last of me. My skills as a pilot come in handy. I came up with the idea of contract work in exchange for using a hangar and obtaining parts for my plane. It's a mutually beneficial situation."

He nodded, impressed. "Smart move."

"I was taking . . . other jobs when Orrin approached me to fly one of his missions. I never flinched at the work, and I never let him down."

Cullen looked out the window at the cities below. "And the Russian job?"

"Orrin contacted me about flying the team. The money was good, and I didn't mind the trip. I explained to him that while my plane is sturdy, she couldn't make the entire trip without stopping in Ireland to refuel."

"He agreed to that?"

"There was no other way," she said with a slight shrug. "But we got to Russia without incident."

"Did Orrin mention anything about having any doubts about the mission?" he asked.

She thought for a moment before she shook her head. "He acted as he normally did before a job. Quiet, thinking over everything. An hour before we arrived in Moscow, he and the team went over the plans."

"And after?" Cullen pressed.

Her forehead creased as she glanced out the front window. "I was in a hurry to get refueled and do my preflight. The team arrived earlier than expected. It wasn't until we'd taken off that I realized how silent they were. In the past, they usually celebrated."

He wasn't surprised by the news. The fact that they had stolen a bioweapon from another country without being told that's what they were after had a way of putting things into perspective. "When did Orrin tell you what they took?"

"When I had to stop and refuel in Dublin, I knew that Orrin and the men were anxious. They had their guns out as if they were expecting trouble."

"Did anything happen in Ireland?"

"No," she said with a shake of her head. "Not at all. Once we were airborne again, Orrin came to the cockpit and showed me the vial. He told me what it was. I asked him who he'd stolen it for, and he answered 'the government.'"

Cullen crossed his ankle over the opposite knee. He'd wondered when his father had mailed the vial since he'd been taken as soon as they landed in the States. Now he had his answer. He just needed Mia to admit it.

"What did you do to earn my father's trust so completely that he handed over such a weapon into your hands?"

"I keep my word," she replied instantly.

He wasn't buying it. He knew Orrin well enough to know that something had happened between him and Mia. Whatever it was, she wasn't going to part with the information easily. "There's more to it than that."

She sighed and looked straight ahead. "It was my second time flying Orrin. We were in South America, and he missed the time of departure. I remained hidden and waited another hour for him. When he still didn't show, I had a choice to make. Leave, or find him."

"And you went looking for him?" Cullen asked. "How did you even know where to go?"

"I knew his course. He had to go through the jungle at one point. I flew over his route and found him pinned down by a group near a river. I circled back around, hoping Orrin had seen me and would get clear. On my return approach, I opened fire."

"Clearing his path?"

"Most of it. More gunmen arrived. Valkyrie's wing was shot, as was the fuel line, which caused my left engine to stop working."

He looked at the vintage British World War II plane and

wondered at Mia's sanity. It was one thing to go into a battle like that with a jet or chopper, but her aircraft? It was suicide.

He turned his gaze back to her. "What happened?"

"I circled back around for another go."

"You knew the plane couldn't fly much longer. You barely even knew my father. Why would you risk your life in such a way?"

She cocked her head to the side and looked at him. "Did you miss the part where I was in the military? I might not have been in Special Forces, but I know what it means to be in battle. I did a tour in Iraq. There was no way I was leaving Orrin. He was resourceful. I just had to give him time to get out."

The more he was with Mia Carter, the more she surprised him. She was nothing like he'd expected. "What happened?"

"I took out more men. On my turn, I saw Orrin make it to the trees. I flew as far as I could before I had no choice but to land the plane in a clearing. Then I hurried to fix the damage to the fuel line."

"A mechanic, as well?" Was there anything this woman couldn't do? She might damn well be the perfect female.

Which might be a very bad thing since he was positive one didn't exist for him.

She lifted one slim shoulder, her olive shirt with its wide neck moving just enough to give him a glimpse of a black bra strap.

He clenched his teeth as he fought the growing hunger to taste the beautiful, daring pilot.

"A pilot should know how to fix their own plane for just such situations," she replied.

There she sat, as calm and collected as a flower while

lust pounded through him. It wasn't fair that only he should be so affected.

"Half an hour later, Orrin found me," she continued. "I got the engine working, and we returned to the States."

"You saved his life."

"He has saved mine, as well." She looked forward once more. "Orrin is a good guy. A decent human being. I don't know why he entrusted me with the package. He asked that I mail it. I told him there was no reason he couldn't do it. He didn't say another word about it. I found the package in his seat after I'd dropped off the plane. I had it with me when I discovered the team in the hangar." She paused and took a steadying breath. "I alerted the base, waited for someone to get my statement, and then I rushed to the post office."

Cullen got more information than he expected, and that pleased him. "Coded messages come from Washington to Callie. She deciphers them and gives the message to Orrin, who decides if he'll take a mission."

"This I know," Mia said.

"When you alerted the base, and they discovered Orrin was missing, my brothers and I were immediately sent to Texas. We were ordered to find Dad, but there was no mention of the bioweapon."

"No one considered that he might've killed his men?" she asked with a frown.

"Apparently not." Something that had bothered him.

She shot him a *that's unbelievable* look. "I know Orrin didn't kill his team. Do you?"

"Yes." He dropped his foot to the ground. "For all my father's faults, he'd never betray anyone."

Mia studied him quietly for a moment. "So you returned to Texas and found your aunt and uncle murdered."

"It didn't take long for us to realize it was the Russians,"

Cullen said. "Callie contacted DC to let them know about the attack. Within hours, we were home, and all hell broke loose."

"Who in DC knew about the mission?" she asked.

"From what Callie told us, just one man—Mitch Hewett."

"Men like Hewett don't run their offices alone. There will be several people working for him. It could be him or anyone in his organization."

Cullen drew in a deep breath and slowly released it. "Then we need to know everyone associated with Hewitt."

CHAPTER THREE

Mia could well imagine Cullen's mind attempting to work out if she were part of Orrin's kidnapping or not. Because, despite Callie's assurance that Mia wasn't guilty, Cullen was the type of man to make his own assessment.

If only Callie were there. She wasn't just Orrin's right hand running Whitehorse, she'd also become a good friend to Mia. And right now, she could use a friend.

She'd felt that way ever since she'd walked into the hangar and found the team dead.

"We're ten minutes out from Dover," she told Cullen.

"By now, General Davis will know of your arrest."

As if she needed the reminder. "I'm aware."

"Will that end your arrangement with them?"

"It could. But that's not my concern right now. Orrin is."

Cullen made a sound in the back of his throat. "So much so that you took a job to fly to Panama."

Her head whipped around to glare at him. "Go ahead and waste your energy believing I was part of the kidnapping. I'll continue to focus my efforts on finding Orrin. That's what I was doing in Panama."

"Please explain. I'm dying to hear."

He was just like all the other men, she realized. The fact that he was Orrin's son led her to believe he would be like his father. Then there was the fact that she couldn't stop looking at him—he was so sexy.

But blood relations and sexiness meant nothing in a man's world.

"Camilo runs—*ran*—a cartel that caters to buyers looking for black market items. Many drug cartels, mobs, and even companies have their hands in the profitable business. I'd hoped a connection in Panama might give me some information on the Russians."

"And?"

She blew out a breath. "No one wanted to talk about the Russians. I was told to forget about them. That's not going to happen."

"If the men who took Dad don't already know of you, once they find out, they'll be after you."

"I know." It was why she slept with two guns now instead of one.

She held up a hand when he started to talk and spoke to the tower, getting clearance to land. Mia wasn't looking forward to facing Davis. The General was going to be furious.

But losing the hangar was going to be the least of her problems if her license were revoked or suspended.

It wasn't long before they landed on the base and taxied to the hangar. She looked around, expecting Davis or the Military Police, but there was no one to greet them.

She shut off the engine outside the hangar and unbuckled her seat belt. No sooner had she stepped off the plane than Cullen called her name.

"I want to see where it happened," he said.

She didn't have to ask what he meant. Every time she walked into the hangar, her gaze always went to the area. It was a constant reminder that she'd somehow escaped death. But for how long?

"Follow me," she said.

She led him to the dark spots on the concrete. Those stains were a chilling reminder of how easily friends could be taken.

That's what Orrin was—a friend. Orrin's smile was infectious, as was his deep love of America. He—like his sons—risked his life for the freedom and liberty of every man, woman, and child in the country. Without recognition.

Despite her attempts to keep Orrin from getting close, he was too charismatic, too charming to be denied.

Much like Cullen.

Cullen halted before her and gave a slight bow of his head. "Everything all right?"

"Yeah." She got a close-up view of his very wide, very thick shoulders. Muscles bulged in his biceps, and an image of those arms wrapped around her as they kissed flashed in her mind.

She gave herself a mental shake. Now wasn't the time for her body to suddenly become wanton. Especially not with a man like Cullen. He was the type to love-'em-and-leave-'em.

And she was the opposite. If she gave herself to a man, it was because she saw a future. Cullen was here for Orrin. Once that mission was complete, he would return to his Force Recon unit without a backward glance.

It's what made him a good Marine.

It's also what reinforced that no matter how much she might want to know the feel of his kiss, it would only bring her misery. She didn't know how to have a fling or fool around.

"Callie spoke highly of you."

She pulled herself from thoughts of stripping Cullen naked to let his words sink in. "I talk to her often, though we've only met a few times. She's amazing at coordinating everything. Orrin leans on her a lot, and she's never let him down."

"I didn't realize Callie had gone from being a ranch hand to working for Dad until recently."

Mia didn't miss the undercurrent of animosity. To the casual observer, it would seem like nothing. But she wasn't a casual observer. "You don't approve?"

"This work is dangerous."

"Callie is a grown woman, who can make her own decisions."

Cullen dropped his arms to his sides. "I still remember her as a gangly thirteen-year-old."

"You remember her as you would a sister."

His eyes held hers for a moment. "I do. She needed a family, and my father gave her that."

"Orrin has a way of knowing what people need." Just as he had with her.

"There's more to the story of you and my dad," Cullen said.

She wasn't going to get into that now—or ever if she had her way. "You know Orrin was a planner. He tried to see ten steps ahead and be ready for anything."

"He couldn't be ready for betrayal."

She understood treachery all too well. "No one ever is. Do you have any idea who it might be, besides Hewett?"

"Not yet."

"You want to be sure it's not me before you tell me more."

There was a quick smile before he replied, "Callie said you'd have me figured out."

Figured out? Hardly. That was part of what drew her to him. She knew military men all too well, but there was something much more to Cullen, something that pulled at her like the moon commanded the tides.

And it scared the hell out of her.

As well as intrigued and excited her.

She shrugged her shoulders. "It's common military thinking."

"Perhaps."

She wanted to take a step back, to put some distance between them. The hangar was huge, but with Cullen inside, it felt small and confined.

"Every flight I make is in the log books for FAA regulations, as well as the Air Force since I'm on their base."

"Of course," he said in his sexy Texas accent.

"I make notes of every call, every request, and every person who boards my plane."

He looked at the plane. "I'd like to see those books."

"Of course."

They walked to the office in silence. She stood behind her desk as her mind went blank for a second on what she was supposed to be doing.

She sat and pulled open the bottom right-hand file drawer. After finding Orrin's file, she laid it on the desk. As she kicked the drawer shut and opened the folder, Cullen came to stand beside her.

He leaned a hand on the desk near her and peered at the papers. His nearness jumbled her thoughts. When he glanced at her, he quirked a brow. She cleared her throat and turned her attention to the file.

She briefly closed her eyes and told herself to gain control. Then she motioned to the documents in the folder. "These are my private records."

"Not on the computer?"

"Computers can be hacked."

"And papers can be stolen."

She smiled up at him. "True, but that means they'd have to get into the hangar, which means the culprits would have to get past base security first."

"That's a good point. What about someone on the base?"

"It could happen. It's also why I make three copies. One I scan into my computer and encrypt. The second is in a safe at my home. The third is here, in the files."

"That's a lot of precautions."

She stared at the papers. "It's what happens when someone takes advantage of you once." She quickly changed the subject before he could ask what she meant by that. "The first entry is Callie's email, asking me if the date requested was open. From there, it's a list of our communications—booking the plane, and the destination."

Cullen picked up the file and straightened as he continued reading. She couldn't take her eyes off him as he slowly moved around to the front of her desk where there were two chairs.

By the time he'd finished with the file, she'd undressed him in her mind. Twice. His hazel gaze lifted and met hers. His face was devoid of expression, but that didn't normally stop her from knowing what a person was about to do or say.

Not so with Cullen Loughman, Force Recon captain. He was a blank page, and it left her feeling as if she were falling through the sky without a parachute.

"Callie was young when she came to the ranch," Cullen said. "I've known her for so long, it's like she's always been in our lives. I'm ashamed to admit that I haven't returned home in ages. I doubt I would've gone back to Texas if Dad hadn't been kidnapped. But here I am."

She was silent, wondering what he was getting at.

He tossed the file on her desk. "The thing is, there are some things that never change. Wyatt's abrasive personality or Owen's need to protect that which he cares about. Or Callie's inherent ability to know when someone can be trusted." Cullen folded his hands over his flat stomach. "She trusts you. So, Mia Carter, that means I do, as well."

"Because Callie said so?" she asked, more than a little shocked.

"That, and because I agree with her."

"I could've been working with the Russians." She wasn't sure why she played Devil's advocate, but she wanted to make sure Cullen truly knew she was trustworthy.

His smile was slow and heart-stopping. "You could've, but since Callie checked your correspondence on your cell phone, desk line, and email, you weren't contacted by anyone in DC."

"So you do think it's Hewett?"

"It's looking that way."

This was a hefty pile of manure she was getting herself embedded in, but there was no turning back now. Not that she would.

She held Cullen's gaze as she leaned forward. "Tell me what you know."

CHAPTER FOUR

Cullen couldn't look away from Mia's black gaze. There was no doubt she wanted a piece of the group responsible for the deaths of Orrin's team as much as he and his brothers did.

He had to admit that Mia was more than he'd expected. And he liked it. If his gut were wrong and she turned out to be a person they couldn't trust, he could very well get his father killed.

As he stared at her, he had no idea how big of a team the Russians had. It had to be luck that allowed Mia her life. Otherwise, she'd be as dead as the rest of the team and unable to help him find Orrin.

"Unfortunately, we've not gathered a lot of information. My middle brother, Owen, and Natalie, who used to work for the Russian Embassy in Dallas, are looking into some things."

She raised a black brow. "So we have nothing more than Hewett to go on."

"The Russians put a hit on Natalie when they realized she'd learned about Ragnarok."

"The bioweapon," Mia said with a nod.

Cullen twisted his lips. "In order to help Natalie and

confuse the ones after us, we split up. Natalie and Owen stayed at the ranch. Callie and Wyatt went one way—"

"And you came here," she finished for him.

He grinned. "Yes, ma'am."

She shifted in her chair. "Does our government know you have the bioweapon?"

"No. And we don't intend to tell them."

"That's probably wise," she said. "Until you know who you can trust."

"No one should have that weapon."

"I agree wholeheartedly. But we live in a world where those kinds of weapons are developed again and again. Hiding this one won't stop it from being made once more."

"Nor will it prevent other weapons from being conceived and implemented," he added with a nod. "I know."

She pushed back her chair, the wheels rolling silently on the floor. She rose to her feet and gathered the file he'd perused earlier.

Then she said, "We need to regroup and figure out a plan to find Orrin."

"The men who took him are a good place to start."

"I'd like to have a word with them myself." She rose, half-sat on the desk corner, and folded her arms across her chest. "So, Cullen Loughman. Where should we start?"

"The beginning, of course. It all starts here. On this base."

Her gaze lowered for a moment. "I know this base inside and out. I've looked everywhere to try and find where the men came in and got out. I've found nothing."

"Someone had to help the group."

"This is a military base. They're not just going to let anyone in."

He held her gaze. "Someone did. Just like someone betrayed my father."

The length of her ponytail moved from one shoulder to the other as she shook her head. "Not on this base. I trust everyone here. General Davis is one of the most honorable men I know."

"Why? Because he gave you what you wanted?" Her chin lifted, alerting Cullen that he'd hit a nerve. He shrugged one shoulder. "I think the best advice we can give each other is to not trust anyone."

Her nostrils flared as she drew in a deep breath. "If it's someone on the base, then it's part of my family here."

"It's going to be tough. I'm not going to lie."

"Davis doesn't let us get away with anything."

Cullen looked around. "Then where is he? I'm sure he's already been informed of your arrest and the fact that you flew here when you weren't supposed to."

"I plan to tell him there were extenuating circumstances." A frown formed as she looked out the office windows. "But it is odd that he hasn't arrived. No one has come to talk to us."

"That's not a good sign."

"No. It isn't," she said as she rose to her feet and walked to the windows.

He rose and moved to stand beside her. "Perhaps we should leave."

"And make it look like I'm running? No way." She gave a soft laugh. "You know, Orrin spoke of you often. He told me if I was ever in trouble, that I should turn to his sons."

Cullen felt bad enough that it had been years since he'd spoken with his father. Now to learn that Orrin had urged others to turn to them for help made him feel worse. What a sad state the Loughman men had become that it took his father being kidnapped to bring them together again.

"He said I could trust you," Mia said.

His gaze clashed with hers. "You can."

"You saved my ass back in Florida."

"You were handling yourself very well. The simple fact is that I need your help. You were there for the mission. You took the team to Russian and back. I need to know everything you saw, heard, and said."

"Ever since that night, I've been looking over my shoulder. I don't like this feeling." She looked at her plane. "I'd much rather do the hunting."

"It's why I'm here."

"Since I doubt I'll be flying anywhere anytime soon, I've got plenty of time to help."

He licked his lips, his mind once more on Orrin. "Dad talked about me, huh?"

"A lot," she said with a soft curve of her lips. "He was proud of his sons. Orrin often told tales of each of your exploits. Wyatt with Delta Force, Owen with the SEALs, and you with Force Recon."

Cullen frowned, wondering how Orrin knew of their missions.

"I saw a bit of each of your files," Mia said as she turned away from the windows.

"How did he manage to get our files?"

She laughed as she shook her head. "Your father has many connections and a plethora of friends. He made sure to know what each of you was doing at any given time."

Cullen digested that news. He'd never stopped to think about his dad looking in on them. So many questions arose that he'd love to pose to Orrin about a few missions.

But that was for later.

He got to his feet. "How well do you know the locals?"

"There are many Russians about we could talk to. They run the docks."

"Where I'm guessing there are a lot of warehouses where Orrin could be hidden."

She wrinkled her nose and nodded. "Right you are. It would take days to search them."

"Weeks. And we don't have that kind of time."

"Neither does Orrin."

Cullen wondered what it was that brought his dad and Mia together. Orrin's sons had gone out of their way to all but cut him from their lives, and yet Mia was willing to die for Orrin. So was Callie.

Callie had been a part of their family since she was thirteen and working on the ranch. He understood why Callie loved his father, but Mia was another matter entirely.

"You wanted the story from the beginning," she said as she walked past him. "I left out a few things. I met Orrin my first year in the Air Force. He took an interest in me, urging me to follow my heart when it came to flying."

Cullen watched her walk to the coffee pot, his eyes dropping to her hips as they swayed. She was smart, tough, and sassy. A combination that was a particular favorite of his.

Normally, he could control his reaction if there was an attraction, but she was different. She set him off-kilter in every way possible.

"How did you begin working with him?" Cullen asked.

She poured two cups of coffee and offered him one. "Remember me telling you I have a bit of an issue with taking orders? My time in the Air Force was short-lived, but I'd made good friends here."

"Apparently."

She walked back to her desk. "I'm willing to take missions others won't. I've proven myself multiple times. One such time was when the pilot who was supposed to get Orrin and his team out of Argentina decided it was too dangerous."

"But you didn't think so?" he guessed.

Her smile was wide. "It was exceedingly dangerous, but lives were on the line."

"So you rescued Orrin and the team, and in the process, he became beholden to you."

Her smile faded slowly as a frown took its place. "Do you know your father at all? He's a great man who elicits loyalty and love from anyone who knows him."

He looked away from her penetrating gaze. "I don't know my father like you do."

"What a pity."

"Yes, it is," he admitted.

Her head cocked to the side. "We'll find him."

They'd better. Now that Cullen was in Delaware, he wasn't going to stop until he'd found his father—and the bastards who took him.

"It's late. I think you need to get home."

"This is my home," she argued.

He set down the coffee. He'd had a bad feeling ever since they'd arrived at the base. Something was off, and he suspected it had to do with everything surrounding his father. And Mia had been dragged into it.

But he didn't want to tell her that part yet.

"The sooner we get started, the sooner we can find Orrin," he said.

She gave a reluctant nod. "I'll bring you to Sergei, then."

The night air held a touch of fall as they walked from the office into the hangar. The distinct sound of two F-22 Raptors preparing for takeoff could be heard. The pilots gunned the engines, and in seconds, the most feared stealth aircrafts in the world were airborne.

His gaze immediately went to Mia's plane. The twin-engine, medium-size bomber had been made obsolete nearly as soon as it took its first test flight and was regulated to transport duties. Intrigued by the pilot's choice, he walked to the plane.

He spotted four machine guns placed at the fuselage—the main body of the aircraft—in forward-firing positions. Peering closer, he noted that the weapons weren't those that had originally come with the plane. These new machine guns were modern, mobile, and extremely accurate.

Another four were on the dorsal turret, and another two on the ventral turret. All in all, the plane was armed better than the original—and with advanced weaponry.

But it wasn't the plane's retrofits that impressed him. It was Mia Carter.

She was a strong, capable woman, blazing her own trail in a male-dominated world. And she was doing a hell of a job. No wonder his father had taken such a fancy to her.

Mia's beauty drew people in, but it was her intelligence and cunning that won her the day.

"What?" she asked, glancing his way.

Cullen shook his head, smiling. "I pity anyone who dares to go up against you. I'm not sure I'd have you in the air. I'd have you on ground assault."

She laughed, her black eyes twinkling. It caused a surge of desire so strong, so swift to go through him that he misstepped and nearly lost his balance.

"I like you, Cullen Loughman. But you've not really seen me fly."

"I'd like to." It wasn't just a hasty comment either. He really wanted to see what she could do.

He imagined that she was magnificent. Orrin had gotten to see and experience it several times. Cullen was instantly jealous of his father for being so fortunate.

That drew him up short. He never got jealous over a woman. Ever. He barely knew Mia, and yet the emotion was thick as honey within him.

His expression must have shown what he was feeling because she suddenly stopped and turned to face him. "Forget the estrangement from your father. It'll all be forgotten as soon as the two of you are reunited."

"Yeah," he replied, not wanting to tell her she was completely wrong in her assessment since his head was spinning.

She put her hand on his arm, and something warm and tingling went through him, originating at the skin she touched. Her eyes widened a fraction as she looked at her hand. Then her gaze jerked to him.

Cullen had the urge to slide his hand around to her lower back and slowly draw her to him so he could kiss her long and slow, savoring every breath she took.

Her hand fell away, and she took a step back. "Um. Yes, it's all going to be fine. Your father loves you."

"So you've said. He's been a father to you, as well."

Her tongue peeked out to lick her lips. "I can't deny that. I don't have the best relationship with my father. Orrin always supported me."

There went that surge of jealousy again. Cullen really needed to find a way to stop it. The best way would be to take her to his bed.

A thought he quickly dismissed since he disappeared from a woman's life after sleeping with her. Now that he was working with Mia, that wouldn't work.

There was going to be a lot of cold showers in his future.

As well as hating his father for a whole new reason.

CHAPTER FIVE

Mia continued to her Jeep with Cullen by her side. She was still reeling from whatever had happened when she touched him. It almost felt electric. But it had been warm, and made her long to move closer to him.

Somehow, she'd managed to hold steady and not give in. It'd been close, though.

The night air had a sharp nip to it that cooled her now heated skin. They climbed into the vehicle. She noticed how Cullen took in everything around him with one glance. He was so much like his father, and he didn't even know it.

She started the engine and put the Jeep in drive. They exited the base and drove along the streets toward the docks. She wasn't exactly thrilled that they were headed there.

Her relationship with Sergei was . . . difficult at best. He wasn't a man to be messed with in any form. Sergei was very old school and valued loyalty above everything.

But he also killed without hesitation.

"You don't like going to the docks, do you?" Cullen asked.

She wasn't sure how to answer his question since

there was so much history between her and Sergei. "The docks are a dangerous place, but Sergei might be able to help."

Cullen didn't say more, but she felt his gaze on her several times while she maneuvered through the streets. She didn't take him straight to the dock entrance, but rather to a bridge overlooking the area.

She stopped the Jeep and turned off the engine to look out over the lights that lit up the area. He exited and strode to the railing of the bridge.

Sighing, she followed. As she came to stand beside him, she pointed to the warehouses. "There are a few that aren't being used, but they are all patrolled nonetheless. Businesses pay top dollar to Sergei to make sure their products are kept safe."

"If I were a Russian holding an American captive, I'd turn to my countrymen for help," Cullen said.

"The problem is Sergei."

Cullen's hazel gaze swung to her. "Exactly who is Sergei?"

"Sergei Chzov. As I said earlier, he controls the docks—and a large portion of Dover. Nothing is done without his approval."

"So we need to talk to him."

"He won't give up another Russian."

A small frown furrowed Cullen's forehead. "How do you know so much about the docks and Sergei?"

"My freelance work has put me in contact with Sergei a few times." It wasn't a lie. It wasn't the entire truth either, but for now, it would suffice.

"Perfect. That means you can talk to him. Every man has his price, even a man like Sergei. We need to find what his is."

She shook her head. "He has power and money. There is nothing we have that he wants."

"I highly doubt that. It won't hurt to pay him a visit and learn what we can."

"Are you even listening to me?" she asked in frustration. "It wouldn't be in our best interests to alert the group who took Orrin that we might know where they're holding him."

"That's exactly what we need to do."

She blinked, taken aback. "So they can move your father?"

"So they know we're closing in. They'll make a mistake that way."

She still wasn't convinced. The hit on the team had been done quickly without alerting the base. This "group" didn't seem the type to make such mistakes.

Cullen leaned an arm on the iron railing. "So far, the Russians have had the upper hand. They suspect we have the bioweapon. It's time we let them know we're not going down without a fight."

"It might well kill your father. They're holding him because they think he'll give up the location of the weapon."

"He had you send it to Callie because he knew she'd keep it safe."

Mia slid her gaze to the many warehouses. There was no way around it. He was determined to see Sergei, and she was going to have to talk to the Russian leader. By now, Sergei knew of the fiasco with Camilo.

No doubt there would be an "I told you so" session. She was ready to admit that Sergei had been right about the Colombians, but she'd taken the chance in an effort to find Orrin.

And the money had been good, as well.

At least she didn't have to worry about the Colombians now. With Camilo dead, their attention would turn to finding another leader.

"What if Sergei is part of the Russian group who took Orrin?" she asked.

"Then we'll know that soon enough," Cullen replied. "Information is to our advantage. Unless there's a reason you don't want to talk to Sergei."

He was getting suspicious. She faced Cullen and met his gaze. "He likes to show his power. I'm merely pointing out that we're going to be walking into a place with everyone against us. I'd like to walk out, because if we don't, who is going to help your father?"

"We'll be walking out of there," Cullen promised.

"The same cockiness as your father."

He merely smiled. "You call it cockiness. I call it confidence."

She could only shake her head as he got back in the Jeep. Mia joined him and started the vehicle, but she didn't drive off. "We'll never get to search those warehouses without Sergei's consent."

"We'll have to sneak in."

"He'll double security."

"Then we'll adjust. We're going to search those warehouses with or without Sergei's help."

What Cullen was going to do was get them killed. She would have to keep him in check when they saw Sergei.

She drove across the bridge and turned left toward the docks. There was plenty of activity all around, even in the middle of the night.

When they reached the gates, she rolled down her window and recognized two of the four men standing guard, though she didn't recall their names.

"Can not stay away, huh?" one of the Russians asked with a heavy accent and a smirk.

She flashed them a smile. "I need to talk to Sergei."

"On what business?" another of the Russians asked.

From the corner of her eye, she saw Cullen eyeing the men walking around her Jeep. "That's between Sergei and me."

"He is a busy man."

She wanted to roll her eyes. Why did it always have to be the same dance each time she visited?

"And I'm a busy woman," she replied tightly.

One of the Russians snorted. "We'll see about that," he said and brought his cell phone to his ear.

He turned away so she couldn't hear the conversation. She wasn't at all comfortable with the men circling the Jeep. They didn't usually do that, which meant Sergei was on high alert.

"Relax," Cullen whispered. "It'll be fine."

"You don't know Sergei."

"I know men like him. They're all the same no matter what nationality they are or where they've set up shop."

She hoped Cullen knew what he was talking about. In all her dealings with Sergei, she'd managed to come out on top. How much longer could her luck hold out? Not to mention she was coming to him with a request. Something she didn't like doing and went out of her way to avoid.

"Do you have any weapons?" Cullen asked.

"There's a gun under each seat, one in the glove compartment, and another in the center console. There's a knife tucked in the side of each door."

Cullen reached down between his seat and the door and found the knife that he easily slid into his boot before pulling his pants leg back down.

"They'll search us."

"Which is why I'm not getting a gun," he said with a wink.

So much like his father. She drummed her fingers on the steering wheel and glanced at the man talking on the phone. He didn't look pleased as he hung up and turned to her.

He sent her a glare and motioned to one of the others to open the gate. Mia gave him a big smile and waved with her fingers before driving off.

"He didn't like you," Cullen pointed out.

She shrugged indifferently. "I might've made him look the idiot the last time I had dealings with Sergei."

"Which was when?"

"A week ago."

All too soon, she pulled up to the building that housed the dock offices. The door opened, and two men in black leather jackets walked out.

She shut off the Jeep and blew out a breath. "Let's get this over with."

"You don't have faith I'll get us out of this?"

"I have plenty of faith." That one day, Sergei might be responsible for her death. Then again, she was the one who kept taking his job offers.

Cullen winked at her and unfolded his tall frame from the vehicle. She was slower to follow. She knew better than to bring a weapon to see Sergei. His men always found them, and they were never returned.

She opened the door and exited. Cullen stood at the front of her Jeep, staring at the two men. She walked to the three of them. "Hi, boys. I believe Sergei is waiting for us."

"In a moment," said the one on the left.

She never liked waiting, but it was worse when it was Sergei. He could have someone in there, or he could be getting ready to have a showdown of some sort. One never knew with a man like him.

Each of the men checked Mia and Cullen for weapons, taking the knife from Cullen before returning to their spots against the door.

Cullen leaned back against her Jeep and folded his arms over his chest as he yawned. She was so glad this didn't seem to affect him. Then again, how could it? He had no idea the kind of man Sergei was—or why she was a little scared of the Russian.

For thirty minutes, they waited in the damp before she saw more men exit the side of the office. They wore dark suits. One held a briefcase. They glanced her way before getting into three black Audis.

There were still two Russians guarding them. The one on the left opened the door to the building. "Now you may go in."

She cast another look at the men who were leaving. They were big and had an Eastern European look about them. They could be the men who'd taken Orrin and killed his team.

It was just another reason she didn't want to talk to Sergei. Then again, he knew everything there was to know about Russians in the area. Sergei could impart information—but there would be a price.

She didn't think Cullen was going to like the cost. She knew she never did. And the few times she'd come to Sergei, she hadn't had a choice. It was just how the Russian liked it.

She much preferred it when he came to her. Though, that had been a while. Now, she would be indebted to him. Something that needed to be remedied. And soon.

Mia entered the building, combing her fingers through

her hair. The one thing she'd learned about Sergei was that he liked women.

She intrigued him because she was a female in their world. She didn't take any bullshit, knew how to talk her way out of situations, and didn't hide the fact that she was a woman. It's how she'd won him over the first time.

It was how she kept winning him over.

One of the Russians led the way, while the other remained a few steps behind. She spotted the guns hidden beneath their leather jackets.

They approached another set of doors guarded by two heavily armed men, who watched them warily. As they neared, the two guards stared at her until she was through the double doors and standing inside the plush office of Sergei Chzov.

"Mia!" Sergei said with a big smile and open arms.

The Russian was in his late sixties with a thick swath of snow white hair atop his head. He was tall with wide shoulders, meaty hands she'd seen choke the life out of people, and vivid blue eyes.

"Sergei," she replied, smiling. It was hard not to like him, even if he was a ruthless killer. Every time he saw her, he was grinning, welcoming her as if she were a part of his family.

And in some ways, she was.

What did that say about her? That she was just as ruthless? That she had no problem working with gangsters? Or that she was strong enough to keep her wits about her with such men?

"Sit, sit," he urged, pointing to the burgundy leather couch as he rose from behind his desk and walked toward them.

She stopped by the sofa, but she didn't sit. Sergei's gaze

shifted to Cullen. The Russian's steps slowed, and immediately the men—all seven of them—palmed weapons.

"Who is your guest, Mia?" Sergei asked.

She released a breath. "This is Cullen Michaels."

"Loughman," Cullen corrected her.

She gaped at him, confused as to why he would give his real name. So much for her trying to keep the knowledge of who Cullen was from the men who'd taken Orrin.

Sergei folded his arms over his chest. "Which is it? Michaels or Loughman?"

"Loughman," Cullen replied. "Perhaps you've heard that name before."

"Perhaps. What concern of it is yours?"

She grabbed Cullen's arm and pulled him down onto the couch. As soon as they sat, Sergei's men lowered their weapons, though they didn't put them away.

"Sergei, we need your help," Mia said.

His blue eyes slid to her. "A favor?"

"A favor," she said past the lump in her throat. "I'll owe you."

"Something you swore would never happen again," he replied with a grin. Then he dropped his arms and sank into a chair. "It must be grave for you to break such a promise. Tell me. I am curious to know what could rattle you."

CHAPTER SIX

Being in a room full of killers wasn't a first for Cullen. Nor did he expect it to be the last. It was just another part of his job.

It was how still Mia had become that alerted him she was anything but comfortable. Which was odd, considering the way Sergei had greeted her. Or perhaps that was the very reason.

The longer Cullen was around Mia, the more he was sure she was intentionally keeping something from him. He hadn't yet pieced together what it was, but it definitely had something to do with Sergei Chzov.

And then there was the Russian's reaction to her mention of a favor. Mia didn't so much as bat an eye. She was being entirely too careful in containing her emotions. A tell in itself.

He leaned back on the couch and rested an arm along the top cushions. Though he'd read a lot about the Russian mafia, he'd never seen it firsthand before.

The men who greeted them at the gate were *Shestyorkas*, or the lowest ranking members of the clan. The men who led them inside the building were *Byki*—bodyguards.

The seven inside Sergei's office were *Boyevik*—warriors who made up the main strike force of the clan.

Sergei was the *Pakhan*—boss—but it was the man behind Sergei who caught Cullen's attention. He watched everything, listening intently. He was a killer, and Cullen would bet his favorite rifle that the man was the *Brigadier*—captain and most trusted.

Mia glanced at Cullen but remained quiet while one of Sergei's men carried over a tray of shot glasses and an unopened bottle of vodka.

Russians and their vodka. Cullen had gotten so drunk off vodka once that he'd actually thought he died. When he hadn't, he wished he had. But there was no way he would turn away the *Pakhan's* vodka, not when they needed his help.

Sergei opened the bottle and topped off three shot glasses. He handed one to Mia, who reluctantly accepted it. Cullen leaned forward and took the one Sergei offered him.

"To favors," Sergei said, lifting his glass.

"To favors," Cullen and Mia replied in unison.

Then the three tossed back the clear liquid. Cullen nodded at the smooth taste of the vodka as he set his glass down.

Sergei lifted a white brow and grinned. "You approve?"

"I do," Cullen replied. "It's very good."

"It is my family brand," the Russian said with pride. "The best in Russia." He poured another round. "Now, Mia. Tell me of this favor."

She finished her second shot and set the glass on the coffee table. "We're looking for someone."

"My father," Cullen quickly added.

Sergei didn't drink his second shot. He stared at Cullen for a long time. "Your father?"

"His name is Orrin Loughman, and we suspect he might be held in one of the warehouses here on the docks."

For long minutes, Sergei held his gaze. "My docks?"

"If you know anything, it could really help us," Mia said.

Sergei's blue eyes turned to her. "You believe Russians took him?"

Cullen remained silent as he watched her tuck her long black hair behind her ear.

"Yes, we know Russians took Orrin," she replied.

Sergei's sharp eyes turned chilly. "And you think I'll turn against my own?"

"I was hoping you'd help an old friend."

Out of the corner of Cullen's eye, he saw one of Sergei's men move behind Mia. He wished he had a weapon. No doubt Sergei had one within reaching distance.

Perhaps it was time for Cullen to chime in again, and hopefully, diffuse the situation. "I've not been a good son. I lived my life without any regard for my father."

"Now that he's missing, you remember to be a good son?" Sergei asked, doubt in his gaze.

He lifted a shoulder. "It's a dose of reality. My mother was murdered when I was seven. I blamed my father because I didn't understand. I want the chance to talk to him again."

"My mother was also murdered," Sergei said in a soft voice. His eyes went distant for a moment.

Cullen exchanged a look with Mia. He wasn't sure if he had made headway with Sergei, or made things worse by bringing up something so painful.

"Do you know who killed your mother?" Sergei asked.

He shook his head. "Every lead I investigated led to a dead end."

"I found my mother's killer. It was a rival family trying to gain control of the lands we protected." Sergei tossed back his shot of vodka and softly set the empty glass on the coffee table. "The closure was needed. You did not get that."

"I doubt I ever will," Cullen admitted.

Sergei motioned for his men to leave. They all departed except for the quiet, motionless man who stood in the corner behind Sergei.

"Why was your father taken?" Sergei asked.

Cullen had hoped to omit the reason, but he should've known it would be the old Russian's first question. "My father was sent to find something in Russia."

Sergei sat straighter, his shrewd eyes narrowing slightly. "Sent by your government?"

"Yes."

"Did he find what he was looking for?"

Cullen nodded.

Sergei blew out a breath. "What did he take?"

It was Mia who answered. "A bioweapon."

"I see," Sergei replied and ran a hand over his mouth and down his chin. "How do you know it was Russians who took him?"

"I flew Orrin and the team," Mia said. "I suspected it was Russians the moment I knew what the mission was. It is simply by the grace of God that I wasn't in the hangar when Orrin's team was killed."

Cullen pulled his gaze from Mia to look at Sergei. "I know it was Russians because they came after me and my brothers at our ranch."

Sergei leaned forward, his look intense and focused on Mia. "Explain how you lived."

Mia glanced his way before she answered Sergei. "I had a problem with the plane. I dropped off Orrin and his men at my hangar and took the plane to get checked. Had nothing been wrong, I would've been in the hangar with them."

"And?" Sergei prompted when she paused.

"I returned to find Orrin gone and the team executed."

Sergei turned in his chair and looked at the man behind him. "*Ti znaesh chto nibut ob etom?*"

The man only replied with a single nod of his head.

Cullen leaned over and asked Mia, "What did Sergei ask?"

"If the man knew anything about what I spoke of."

Now they would wait to see if Sergei would impart any information. Cullen thought he might, but it depended on who the men were who'd taken Orrin.

Sergei slowly turned back to face them. He looked at Mia before turning his blue eyes to Cullen.

Cullen waited for Sergei to say something. When he didn't, Cullen asked, "Will you help?"

"I am afraid that is not possible," Sergei stated.

Mia's shocked expression matched his own. "Sergei, please."

"It will do you no good to bat those beautiful eyes at me, *Dochenka Moya*. I cannot help."

"Can't? Or won't?" she asked, angrily.

Sergei swiveled his head to Cullen. "The men you seek are from Russia. They are dangerous. And deadly. If they have not killed your father yet, it is only a matter of time."

"They want the bioweapon," Cullen said. "If they kill my father, they'll never see it again."

Mia's head jerked his way, but he ignored her. He wouldn't willingly turn over the weapon, nor would he allow Orrin to die for something that should have never been developed.

"If these men discover you are here, they will come for you," Sergei cautioned.

"That's what I'm counting on."

"You would put Mia's life in danger?"

Cullen had no such intentions. He opened his mouth to reply, but Mia beat him to it.

"They killed friends and kidnapped another," Mia said, outraged. "I won't sit by while the 'men' do all the work. I'm more than capable of taking care of myself."

Sergei slowly shook his head of white hair. "Not this time, *Dochenka Moya*. You were already spared. Do not tempt fate a second time."

"Orrin is my friend," she said.

Sergei reached over and patted her hand. "Then he is lucky. Did I ever tell you that you remind me of my Nastya? You have her beauty, her courage, and her stubbornness. It got her killed. I fear you are on that same road."

"I have to find Orrin."

Cullen saw the way Mia was physically affected by the idea of being excluded from finding Orrin. There was no way he could stop her. The only thing he could do was keep an eye on her.

"Mia won't be denied," Cullen told Sergei. "But I will protect her with my life."

Sergei nodded, a sad smile in place. "I believe you, Cullen Loughman. But this is much bigger than just finding your father and the men who took him."

"What?" There was something in Sergei's words that made Cullen's spine tingle ominously.

"I warned Mia not to work with the Colombians."

She gave a shrug. "Everything worked out fine. Yes, the cargo was confiscated, and I was arrested. And my pilot's license has been suspended. But Camilo is dead."

"Camilo was not the head of the cartel as he led you to believe. I warned you about him."

Cullen frowned as worry settled in his stomach like a stone. "What is it you know?"

"Camilo once ran the cartel, but another, more powerful group is uniting every criminal faction in South America and Mexico. That is who Camilo answers to." Sergei paused. "They will be coming for you, Mia."

"Who is this group you speak of?" Mia demanded.

But Cullen already knew. They were the ones who'd taken Orrin.

"They are called The Saints," Sergei replied.

Cullen felt his stomach clench with dread. "The same ones who put the hit on Natalie and attacked the ranch."

"And the same people who took your father."

Mia's hand came to rest on Cullen's leg. He turned his head to her, their gazes locking. The Saints would be coming after her now because of Camilo.

How long before they learned that she was the pilot from Orrin's mission?

Or worse, what if they'd known all along? What if Camilo hiring her had been a trap?

Then Sergei's words penetrated his brain. Cullen looked at the Russian. "If The Saints are uniting all the criminal organizations, does that mean you're part of it?"

When Sergei didn't immediately answer, Mia gaped at him. "No."

"They came with an offer," Sergei admitted. "I declined."

Cullen glanced at the man in the corner. "How long until they return?"

"Soon, I suspect." Sergei shrugged. "I will either win or I will not."

Mia was shaking her head. "This isn't right. None of it."

"It is the way," Sergei said and poured himself another shot of vodka. "Money and power run the world, *Dochenka Moya*. I suspect The Saints have worked behind the scenes for more years than we could guess. They are making their move now."

"Then help us," Mia urged.

Sergei gave her a sad smile before he rose and turned toward his desk. "Lev, walk them out."

Cullen rose to his feet and waited for Mia to do the same. She stared at Sergei for a long time before she stood and strode from the office angrily.

"She is a handful," Sergei said from behind his desk. "But worth it."

Cullen wasn't sure why the Russian said such a thing. He nodded at the old man and saw Lev waiting. Cullen followed Mia out with Lev on his heels.

"This way," Lev said in his thick accent, taking them a different route than the one they'd used to enter.

Everyone who saw Lev moved out of his way, getting as far from him as they could. Cullen had seen that kind of respect and fear before. It was always earned.

Which meant that everyone was probably more terrified of Lev than Sergei. Sergei might make the decisions, but it was Lev who carried out those orders.

They turned left, then right, and left again before they came to a door. But Lev didn't open it. He faced them, his short black hair combed away from his face, and his blue eyes as intense as Sergei's.

"Sergei would help if he could," Lev said, his hand upon the door preventing them from leaving.

Mia lifted her face to him. "Who are these men that he's afraid of?"

One of Lev's black brows rose as he glared at Mia. "You misunderstand. Sergei does not fear anything. He is attempting to save you."

"Me?" Mia repeated, surprise in her voice and on her face.

Cullen put his hand on her back. "He did say you reminded him of his daughter."

She briefly closed her eyes. "If it is The Saints who have Orrin, we don't have a choice. We have to find them."

"I know." Cullen lifted his gaze to find Lev staring at him.

"They will know you have been here," Lev warned.

He understood what the *Brigadier* was trying to tell them. He gave a nod of thanks. "We'll be on the lookout."

"Do not return. Sergei will not see you again, Mia, until this has been settled."

She took a step toward Lev. "If Orrin dies because you wouldn't help, I'll be back to exact my revenge on you and Sergei."

Lev's answer was to throw open the heavy metal door. Cullen gave Mia a little push outside. As he walked past Lev, their eyes clashed.

There was something about Lev. Cullen couldn't put his finger on it, but the *Brigadier* seemed to want to help. The people who took Orrin must be powerful indeed to stop Sergei and his men.

Which made Cullen all the more curious. They hadn't gotten any help from Sergei, but they did gain some information. It was too bad they couldn't count on the old Russian. He could've been a good asset.

"We need to get weapons," Cullen said as he caught up with Mia.

"Not a problem," she said as she climbed into her Jeep.

CHAPTER SEVEN

Mia was more shaken from her conversation with Sergei than she let on. In all her dealings with him, he'd never acted so . . . fatherly before.

What was it about the men who had Orrin that caused such a reaction? Sergei instilled terror in all who dealt with him. He gave no quarter, though he was known to be honest and fair.

Just never attempt to betray him.

Sergei had teased her, pushed her, aggravated her, and even angered her. But he'd never given her advice like that before. It gave her cause to worry. Especially when he wouldn't even consider going up against The Saints.

As she drove from the docks, she looked in her rearview mirror at Sergei's offices and wondered if she would ever return again.

There had been a finality to his words that made her sad. Which was ludicrous, since she hated dealing with him.

Didn't she?

Her thoughts turned to the debacle in Florida with Camilo. She should've known it wouldn't end with him. She should've known the moment more men came pouring out of the trees, firing guns, that they wouldn't stop until they had her.

But to know that the Colombians were part of The Saints was like being doused with ice water.

The Russians frightened her because she knew it was only a matter of time before they came for her. Now, it was the Russians and the Colombians.

"How long has Sergei been in the States?" Cullen asked.

"He's controlled the docks for nearly forty years."

Cullen made a sound at the back of his throat. "That means he's been away from Russia that long."

"Meaning?" she prompted.

"The men who took my father and killed his team are from Russia. I knew the ones who were after Owen and Natalie arrived in Texas a few weeks ago, but I thought they were just muscle."

"If it's someone from Russia running things, that could explain Sergei's reaction."

"I believe it *is* Russia controlling The Saints."

The way Cullen said it, with such certainty, had Mia shooting him a glare. "You know who's in charge."

"Just a gut feeling."

"I wish we knew for sure. A name and a face would make things seem less scary."

Cullen kept his gaze dead ahead, as if he were the one driving, not her. "Information gathering takes time, especially when we're doing it ourselves."

"Because we can't trust anyone." She made a right on the way to her apartment.

"It does make things difficult."

She came to a stoplight. "It could be anyone running things."

"I suspect it's someone with power already."

"That would make sense."

"Any Russian in the States comes under suspicion, then."

She pulled into the lot of her apartment and drove into a parking space. She turned off the ignition. "We could start looking into them, but without clearance, it's going to be more than tricky."

"You're right."

She climbed out of the Jeep and made her way to the building. Cullen was on her heels as she punched in the code that allowed her inside.

"How often is your cargo checked?" he asked as they bypassed the elevator and took the stairs to the third floor.

It was a curious question, and a change of subject, but she didn't mention it. "I never know when it's going to be checked. Sometimes it's on every trip. Sometimes, it's a long time before they stop me."

"But the Air Force knows everywhere you go?"

She gave a nod, stopping at her apartment door and unlocking it. "Everywhere."

"So the base knew you were headed to Russia."

"General Davis did. He won't give approval for me to fly out if I don't let him know."

She walked into her place and began pulling guns from her various—and many—hiding places throughout the two-bedroom apartment.

"You had to tell Davis despite it being a Black Ops mission?" Cullen asked in surprise.

She lay on her back on the floor and pulled out a rifle and two clips of ammunition that were taped beneath her sofa. "That's an affirmative."

"Does Davis have dealings with Sergei?"

She pulled another two clips and a knife that were taped beneath the coffee table free before she rolled to her knees and grabbed one of the pillows from the couch. She unzipped it and took out a handgun. "Anything the military needs is brought directly to the base, not through the docks and Sergei. But yes, Davis knows Sergei. You can't live in Dover and not know who Sergei is."

Mia went to her bedroom and gathered more weapons. Then she returned to the kitchen, laying everything on the table before turning to the cabinets.

She took out a gun from a pot, another from the oven, and one more from the pantry. She returned to the table and looked up at Cullen. "Will this do?"

"I think I'm in love," he replied with a wink.

She shook her head and picked up a Glock, checking the clip even though she knew it was full. "Why do you think there's a connection between General Davis and Sergei?"

"We know for a fact that someone betrayed Dad. Our first thought was that it was Hewett in DC. Once you told me Davis knows every flight you take, he became a suspect, as well. We're not just looking for The Saints, Mia. We've got to stay ahead of them because they'll be coming for both of us."

"You because you're Orrin's son," she said.

He gave a nod. "And you because you flew Dad and lost cargo for Camilo."

"Well, shit."

A grin lifted the corners of his lips. "Exactly."

She let Cullen choose the weapons he wanted. "The General might have known where I was taking Orrin and the team, but he didn't know what for."

"It wouldn't take a lot to put it together. Dad was Black Ops. I gather that wasn't a secret to Davis?"

"Orrin is friends with him. Most people think Orrin retired. Only a few know that he put together his own team."

Cullen's lips twisted. "Another mark against Davis. He knew you were headed to Russia, and he was aware Dad was Black Ops. It would only take a few calls to find out what the mission was."

"Orrin was careful about who he trusted."

"In this business, betrayal eventually finds you—no matter how careful you are."

That didn't make her feel any better. She felt as if a timer had been put above her, counting down to when The Saints would find her. She'd lost considerable time after her run-in with Camilo.

How long did she have before someone betrayed her? It made her stomach pitch and roll.

"It could be anyone," she said.

"Yes."

She gathered the remaining weapons and put them on her person. "What now?"

"Food. I'm hungry. Since I saw your bare pantry, we'd better go out."

She shot him a look. "So I don't like to cook. It's not a big deal."

"Of course, it isn't," he said with a knowing smile.

"I suppose you can cook?"

"I'm damn good at it, if I do say so myself."

Was there anything he *wasn't* good at? She was beginning to think not.

Now fully armed, they left her apartment and returned to the Jeep. Since it was well after midnight, there were few places open.

She took him to one of her favorite spots. The diner had been around since the fifties but had some of the best food and coffee around.

They quickly settled in a booth, both on high alert. She tried to take the bench where she could see the door, but Cullen beat her to it. Instead, she slid into the opposite side of the booth and smiled as the waitress, a woman in her sixties with blonde hair turning gray and kind brown eyes, walked up.

"Hello, sugar," she said to Mia. "You're in late today. Or should I say early?"

Mia couldn't help but smile. "Hey, Molly. I'll have my usual."

Molly's eyes shifted to Cullen. "Well, hello, handsome. It's about time Mia came in here with someone around her age."

"Molly," she warned.

The waitress's eyes widened. "What? Can't I look out for you, sugar?"

"I'll have a three egg omelet with tomatoes, bell peppers, and ham. Add a side of hash browns, extra crispy. Oh, and your largest mug of coffee," Cullen said.

"Got it," Molly said and walked away with a smile.

Mia moved the sugar shaker to line up with the ketchup and salt and pepper. She could feel Cullen's gaze on her. He stared as if he could see into her mind, and she was beginning to think that he just might be able to.

"What is it about you that makes people want to protect you?" he asked.

She shrugged. "I don't know. My charming personality, I guess."

He raised a brow in question. "You do dangerous work. You willingly put your life on the line. Why?"

"Why do you do it?"

"I do it because it's what men in my family do. It's been that way since the American Revolution, and I suspect it'll continue on long after I've turned to dust."

"Because I'm female, I can't have that same ambition?"

He gave a nod of thanks as Molly delivered two coffees before walking away again. Cullen poured in sugar and stirred the liquid. When he looked up at Mia, he said,

"Your sex has nothing to do with it. You got out of the military. You still work for the Air Force as well as men like my father and Sergei. But why? Why do it without the protection of the government?"

"I like to do things my way. If I saw someone in trouble, I wasn't going to have a commanding officer tell me I couldn't save them simply because of some order."

Cullen took a sip of coffee before he leaned back, putting his arm along the back of the booth. "You're like most pilots, then. You live for danger."

"You can't climb into a plane or helicopter and not love danger. Each time we go up in the air, we face a multitude of things that could go wrong and send us plummeting to the ground. Does it feel amazing to have such a large machine to control? To make it do things the creators said it couldn't do? Yes. There's no greater joy than taking my plane up in the clouds and seeing how tiny the world really is."

His hazel gaze simply watched her.

She wasn't finished, though. "Everyone makes comments about pilots and our cockiness. Yet everyone in the military—especially the Special Forces branches—is the same. You're just as cocky when you pick up your gun and head out on a mission. You appreciate and grasp the same danger when you engage the enemy."

"Yes, I do."

"Then why question me?" she demanded.

"Because I want to know what makes you tick, Mia Carter. You fascinate me."

CHAPTER EIGHT

Sklad

Orrin jerked at the chains holding his wrists. His broken left wrist twinged in pain, but he disregarded it.

The only way he knew what time of day it was came from one of the machines he was hooked to that flashed the time. It had been nearly twenty-four hours since Yuri taunted him with the news that someone had died at the ranch. Every time he wondered if it was one of his sons or Callie, he wanted to bellow his fury.

His beloved Melanie had died because of him. Now, someone else he loved had been taken. And why? Because of some fucking bioweapon the US government had to have because they weren't smart enough to develop it themselves first?

They'd used the excuse that it was to keep the Russians from using it. But Orrin knew the truth. His government wanted it in their arsenal.

How many injections had he been given throughout the years to combat various—and numerous—weapons that could be released through the air or in water?

He fought to keep his country safe, but the truth was that no one was safe. Ever. First, it was nuclear weapons. Now, it was bioweapons. What would be next?

He closed his eyes and blew out a breath. The duty he

felt to serve his country had cost him everything. His wife, his sons, and his happiness.

No matter what, he pushed on with the knowledge that he was keeping the world secure for his sons and their wives and children. It struck him hard that it had all been in vain.

Everything he'd done had been for nothing. He'd been betrayed by someone he trusted. Of that, he was certain. Only a handful of people knew of his mission to Russia to steal the bioweapon.

One of those individuals was responsible for his team's assassinations, the killing of his brother and sister-in-law, the destruction of his home, and now, the death of one of his sons or Callie.

Orrin wasn't as young as he used to be. Age slowed him down more than he liked. The hits hurt more, and his body took too long to heal.

None of that was going to stop him from getting free of his old friend, Yuri, killing him, and then tracking down those responsible for coating his family with more blood.

He wouldn't rest until everyone responsible had paid.

The door to Orrin's room creaked. His eyes opened, and his gaze fell upon the familiar red hair and beautiful face. The doctor was being blackmailed by Yuri. She had to treat Orrin if she didn't want her son to die.

He wanted to ask her name, but to do so would alert Yuri and his men that he worried for her. If it was the last thing he did, Orrin was going to do everything in his power to get her back to her son.

"How are you feeling today?" she asked as she came to check the monitors.

He didn't answer. The less communication they had, the better. Already, she risked much by having given him something to help him heal faster.

There was nothing she could do about his broken wrist or ribs, though she had put his dislocated shoulder back in place. It was going to be a hell of an escape, injured as he was, but when it came to family, he would walk through the fires of Hell itself.

She checked his IV, her head bent so that a lock of her thick hair brushed his arm. Orrin's gaze was drawn to her hair. It was such a vibrant red that he itched to touch it, to let the silky strands run through his fingers.

"He's in a meeting," she whispered.

She meant Yuri. Orrin couldn't look away when her head lifted and her gray eyes met his. She was a stunning woman. Despite the fear, he saw courage in her gaze.

"I'm not worth it," he told her. "Do the minimum you must and protect your son."

In response, she took out another syringe from her pocket and stuck it in his IV before slowly pushing it in the saline. When she'd finished, she tucked the syringe back in the pocket of her white lab coat and picked up his file.

She then turned her back to him but stayed beside his bed. "I won't allow you to remain here and be hurt. You're an American."

"These men will kill your son and you in the blink of an eye. Don't test them," he warned.

But he knew his words were falling on deaf ears. He'd wanted her help at first, had been ready to say or do anything to get it.

The death of one of his sons had brought everything into crystal clear focus. Too many people had already died because of him. He wasn't worth any of it.

There was too much blood on his hands. He couldn't have any more.

"He lied," she said.

Orrin closed his eyes again. He didn't want to hear any more. He needed to concentrate on taking the names of all those he would kill when he got out.

A warm, gentle hand briefly touched his. "It was his men that were killed. Not your family. I overheard them talking."

The words were said in a quick whisper. Orrin's eyes flashed open. His heart thumped with renewed hope. Could everyone still be alive?

He knew just how good his sons were, and Callie could match them any day. It had come as a shock that the Russians had managed to surprise them.

Now Orrin knew the truth. He wanted to smile, but he kept it hidden—as with all of his emotions. Yuri wanted him broken. Orrin could give him that.

It would feel so good to kill Yuri. Would he choke the life from him? Or would he sink a blade into his heart through his ribs? Perhaps a bullet through the brain.

They all sounded justifiably perfect. Because there was no way Orrin would allow Yuri to get free. The US government would readily take him in and offer Yuri protection. Then Orrin would never get his revenge.

No, Yuri would die. Slowly. Painfully. But the life would be extinguished from his body.

Every man and woman who worked under Yuri, who'd attacked his family and destroyed his ranch, would die. It didn't matter how long it took, Orrin would see it done.

"Thank you," he whispered to the doctor.

He hated that there were no windows for him to catch a glimpse of the sky. Then again, it was meant to disorient him.

The door suddenly opened again. His gaze landed on the tall form of a soldier with blond hair and hard, brown eyes. The rifle he carried was pointed at the floor, but he held it as if he wanted to turn it on Orrin.

Orrin watched him, wondering what he was up to. The soldier ordered someone to "come" in Russian. He moved farther into the room, followed by two more men.

"Doctor," the blond said in a thick Russian accent as he handed her a syringe.

Her face was grim as she stared at the needle. "What is that?"

"Something to make the patient sleep."

Orrin put the faces of the men to memory. The doc had no choice but to do as they asked. She turned to him with the syringe in hand, her gaze full of remorse.

He didn't look at her. Instead, Orrin kept eye contact with the tall Russian. Almost instantly, from the time the liquid hit the IV, Orrin felt the medicine pull him under.

Sleep weighted his eyelids, and even though he knew there was no use fighting it, he did. Within seconds, the blackness took him.

"He's out," Kate said and took a step back. She wasn't at all comfortable being around so many armed Russians.

The blond soldier in charge gave a nod to the men. A ladder was brought in along with equipment. She tried to see what they were doing, but the blond's large hand wrapped around her upper arm.

"Time to leave," he said.

She was unceremoniously ushered out of the room. Kate walked slowly as the Russians began to speak. She didn't understand their language, which was of no help to her or Orrin.

Ever since she'd discovered he was an American, Kate had done whatever she could to discover who he was. It took her far longer than she cared to admit before she learned his name.

With the way Yuri and his men monitored her electronics, there had been no time to look Orrin up or find someone to contact to let them know he was alive.

Her "vacation" to Bermuda kept her from having to go into work. Thankfully, that was coming to an end soon. Not that returning to the hospital was going to solve anything. In fact, it would most likely put more people in harm's way.

Then there was her son. He had no idea what was going on, and she wanted it kept that way. While he stayed with her ex-husband, enjoying some "guy time," she was fighting for all of their lives—his, hers, and Orrin's.

At first, all she thought about was her son. But that had quickly changed after talking to Orrin that first time and overhearing his conversation with Yuri.

Yuri was one of the most evil people she had ever encountered, and she couldn't get away from him fast enough. Though she had no idea why Yuri was holding Orrin and torturing him, the fact that he was doing it on American soil was enough to feed her anger.

There were a few things she'd overheard while being held at the warehouse. *Sklad*, she'd heard them call it. It must be the Russian word for warehouse.

Orrin was in the US military. She didn't know what branch, and it didn't matter. He was an American citizen being held against his will by a foreigner.

For the most part, Kate kept to herself except when she needed to check on Orrin. She was given free access to the room full of various medicines.

It's how she had gotten ahold of the calcium, magnesium, Vitamin D3, and Omega-3 to boost Orrin's bone healing. She wasn't sure how much longer she would be able to secretly give it to him, though. The blond soldier Yuri had put in charge watched her like a hawk.

She'd begun to suspect that the blond knew she was giving Orrin something extra. He hadn't seen her, but that didn't mean he wasn't keeping track of the doses.

Kate slowed her steps on her way back to her room when another three soldiers passed her in the hall. She spotted a small camera in one of their hands, and her heart skipped a beat.

More troubling was that there were more men now that weren't in uniform. She wasn't sure if they were Russian or American, and it really didn't matter. Whoever was involved was an enemy.

Why was Yuri installing a camera in Orrin's room? That had to be why they wanted Orrin knocked out, so he wouldn't know. And neither would she.

Kate was horrible at hiding things, especially her emotions. She was the world's worst mom at Easter and attempting to hide the eggs. And this was a hundred times more dangerous.

It would be best if she stopped giving Orrin the dose of vitamins for a while. And somehow, she'd have to let him know about the camera. Though she didn't know if it would have audio or not. That was something else to take into consideration.

This was giving her a headache. How in the world was she going to continue her ruse? The face of her son flashed in her mind. His wide smile with his braces. His long hair that fell into his eyes all the time. His tall, lanky form and voice that pitched low every now and again as his body changed.

He was her world. He was the only thing she had to live for. Her maternal instinct told her to protect him at all costs. But she also felt the need to safeguard Orrin.

Kate stopped and watched the soldiers pass her. It was then that she realized the blond was following her, his dark eyes watching every move.

The yellow, fluorescent lights overhead were harsh, casting shadows onto his face. She hurriedly turned away, kicking a flake of paint that had fallen to the floor as she did.

She walked into her room and immediately went to her bed. She sat, her hands gripping the mattress in a bid to keep her fear locked inside.

The blond halted within her doorway. For long minutes, he stared silently at her. She wanted to shout at him to say something or go away, but her throat locked around the lump of terror.

"Remember your son," he said.

Kate jerked her gaze to him. "Always."

"Good. It would be stupid to do something foolish and jeopardize him."

With that, the blond closed the door and walked away.

She buried her face in her hands and cried.

CHAPTER NINE

The longer Cullen was with Mia, the more certain he was of two things.

1. She was doing everything she could to prevent him from discovering what it was that she hid. The Marine in him suspected it might have something to do with his father, and that kept him from fully trusting her.
2. Mia was one of the most fascinating, alluring, aggravating women he knew. And he wanted her with every fiber of his being.

He'd never been in such a situation before, and it left him more than a little off-kilter. To want someone as desperately as he wanted Mia but to wonder if she was somehow embroiled in his father's kidnapping . . .

Yet, he couldn't believe she was involved in the deaths of the team. Her reaction was too visceral to be anything but the truth.

"So, I fascinate you?" she asked.

Cullen smiled and took a drink of coffee, both his forearms resting on the booth table. He wasn't sure why he'd told her that, but he didn't want to take it back. "Is that so shocking?"

"I'm like anyone else, so, yes."

"You're far from being like anyone else." Was it his imagination, or had that been a pleased look that flashed in her black eyes?

She took a drink of coffee. "You say you joined the military because it's what your family does, but you're good at it."

"Good" didn't mean he liked it. In fact, he hated being in the military. It was a secret he'd kept to himself all these years, and one he would continue to keep.

"Nothing to say?" she asked. "I read about some of your missions. You always get the job done."

"I'm good at killing," he said with a shrug. "Not exactly something I'm proud of."

Her grin vanished then. She took a bite, chewed, and swallowed before she said, "You have a gift. One that you don't want."

"I didn't say that." He'd already said too much. There was something about her that made it easy for him to talk—not something he did a lot with women. Not meaningful conversations anyway.

She set down her fork. "You did. Not in words, but in the way you stiffened and your eyes grew distant and hard."

"You kill enough, whether for pleasure or because of an order, and it eventually empties your soul." And he was running low on the soul part.

He'd endured these past years, but it was coming to an end. As soon as he found Orrin, he was leaving the military. All he wanted to do was return to the ranch and raise cattle and ride horses all day.

It's all he'd ever wanted.

Her hand rested atop his. That same shock went through him, and he moved his thumb so that he was holding her hand as much as she was his.

Big, black eyes watched him. "You're a good man, who has saved countless people. Yes, it involved killing, but that doesn't diminish who you are. Be proud of what you've accomplished."

He'd never thought of it that way. As he looked into her eyes, he saw himself as she did. And somehow, it absolved him of some of his sins.

She pushed aside her half-drunk cup of coffee. "You've finished your meal, so what now?"

"I'd like to talk to General Davis."

She glanced at her watch. It's after two in the morning."

"We can head back to the base so I can look around more before I see Davis."

Without question, she scooted out of the booth and looked around for Molly. He missed having her touch—and touching her. He tossed money for the bill on the table, along with a large tip, and put his hand on Mia's back as they walked from the diner.

They got back in the Jeep and pulled out onto the road toward the base. Ever since he'd asked about a connection between General Davis and Sergei, he'd wanted to talk to the general. There was a piece missing. He was sure of it. All he had to do was look under a few more rocks and talk to some more people, and he might figure it out.

Mia said there was no reason for Davis to have dealings with Sergei, but Cullen wasn't so sure. The fact that Davis knew of Orrin's assignment was something else that bothered him.

Mainly because it was another person who could've betrayed his father. There were too many variables, too many things up in the air, too many people who could've turned on his dad. It all left him with a bad taste in his mouth.

Then there were The Saints. How long did he and Mia have at the base before the group showed up? The sooner they uncovered all they could and moved on, the better.

He glanced over at Mia, who seemed as lost in her thoughts as he was. Who was she really? Callie couldn't say enough good things about her.

His firsts instinct was to have Callie dig into Mia's background. Callie might get defensive and argue against it, mainly because all he had was his gut instinct and no hard facts.

Since Callie and Mia had worked together several times, Callie wouldn't understand. Then again, the love she held for Orrin might change that.

He wasn't sure who wanted to find Orrin more, him or Callie. Looking back, Cullen should've seen how important Callie had become to his father.

He and his brothers had left the ranch and Texas as soon as they could. All Orrin had was Callie. It was no wonder he doted on her and loved her like a daughter.

Mia drove them through the security checkpoint into the base without a problem. It wasn't until she'd parked outside the hangar and turned off the ignition that she turned to him.

He raised a brow. "What is it?"

"What's your plan? So far, you've just told me where you wanted to go. I'm part of finding Orrin, so I'd like you to clue me in on your thinking."

"I don't have a plan." It wasn't exactly a lie. What little part of a plan he had was to track down any lead that might take him to those responsible for Orrin's betrayal and kidnapping.

She rolled her eyes. "That's a load of shit. No way would

Orrin raise any of his sons to go into a situation and not have a strategy in place."

"I want to talk to General Davis first."

She roughly opened the Jeep door and got out, slamming it behind her. He grinned at her show of outrage before he followed her inside the hangar.

He watched as she walked inside the office to her desk and began looking through papers. He used that time to move through the hangar alone. Skirting the bloodstains, he walked the circumference of the building.

Nothing was out of place. She kept the hangar neat and orderly. The tools were clean and each had a specific spot. Even the concrete floor was clean—aside from where the murders happened.

He turned to the plane. The Valkyrie. His gaze took in the red lettering. A man might've added an image of a scantily clad woman with a sword and a Viking helmet. But Mia had no such adornment.

She'd named the plane, but he thought the name was more about Mia. She didn't seem to realize that a strong female putting her life on the line was rare and amazing.

He walked around the aircraft once more, though this time, his thoughts were on the flight to Russia and back. She'd mentioned that Orrin and his team had seemed on edge after the heist.

Did his father know they'd been betrayed? That was highly likely. Why then, had Orrin gone through with the mission? Unless his father hadn't discovered the treachery until the bioweapon was stolen. Or possibly during the job.

That was going to make things even more difficult for Cullen. If only he could talk to his father. Then again, if Orrin were there, the government never would have called him and his brothers in.

He turned to the bloodstains. They were nearly black

in color now, though there was no denying what it was. He knelt in front of the six spots. Not a single drag mark. No one had tried to crawl away, or even turn over.

They had been executed, just as Mia said.

He stood and moved behind the stains with his back to the large hangar door. It would've been open that day since Mia was supposed to pull the plane in.

Cullen looked over his shoulder. The doors were massive. Open, anyone could've seen in. The Russians hadn't cared. It was as if they had known they could get away without being seen.

Or that it wouldn't matter since someone on the base knew they were there.

He raised his arm, using his fingers as a gun, he pointed it at where Orrin's team would have knelt with their hands behind their backs. One by one, he pretended to shoot all of them before dropping his arm to his side.

In that situation, no man as highly skilled as those on Orrin's team would've waited around to be shot. After the first shot, they would've jumped up and tried to attack or run.

They would never have remained kneeling, waiting to die.

"There was a shooter for each of the six team members," he surmised aloud.

He'd thought there was a small team of Russians who had somehow gotten the drop on Orrin and his men. Now, he was beginning to think that there had been eight to ten men.

That would be quite a feat to get that many men past the gate and into the base. There was no denying the men hadn't just slipped in. They'd had help.

Someone let them in.

Someone who knew what they were after.

Someone who had the kind of power and pull where no questions would be asked.

More than ever, he wanted to speak with General Davis. Old friend of his father's or not, he now suspected that Davis was helping The Saints.

It wouldn't be the first time a general had been part of a murder or kidnapping. And Cullen doubted it would be the last.

That kind of power went to people's heads. It was worse sometimes in the military because of the weighty decisions such men had to make. It was life or death.

And so easy for those men to get a God complex.

He sighed, not liking the feeling his findings caused him. The further he dug into everything, the more he realized he was neck deep in shit.

Cullen looked at Mia. She had her chin resting in her hand and was blinking her eyes rapidly. Her exhaustion was evident, but he couldn't stop. Not yet. This time alone to look over everything was crucial to his investigation and might help save his father's life.

But more importantly, it would keep Mia safe.

Walking back outside the hangar, he closed his eyes and listened. Even at night, the base buzzed with activity—the fighter jets landing from their night flights, the hum of vehicles driving around, the laughter of men as they worked.

His eyes opened. Everywhere he looked, he saw personnel. Mia's hangar was one of the farthest away, but there was no hiding. Too many people either patrolled the area or had the hangar in their line of sight as they went about their business.

During the day, the number would more than double. All of this confirmed what he'd discovered earlier. The Saints had help.

He didn't believe it was Sergei. The old Russian couldn't

hide his affection for Mia. Or the thread of concern when he'd learned that the Saints might be coming for her.

Cullen wouldn't remove him from the list entirely. Sergei was just moved farther down. Though the Russian's warning of what might come helped to clear him somewhat.

It was General Davis who interested Cullen the most right now. He would have to be careful with the general. Even if Davis wasn't the one pulling the strings, his outrage at being called a conspirator could have him talking to his staff—one of which might very well be the culprit.

This wasn't Cullen's first encounter with such a muddle. There had been another mission in Iraq several years ago. The mistakes he'd made then wouldn't be repeated now.

He turned on his heel and walked to Mia's office. For long minutes after he entered, he stared at Mia, who had her head down on the desk, asleep.

Unable to help himself, he moved a lock of her long, black hair away from her cheek. She tempted him beyond reason. Maybe it was because he knew he couldn't have her that made him ache for her so, but the longer he was with her, the more it grew.

At least, now he was sure she wasn't part of the group responsible for kidnapping his father and murdering his aunt and uncle.

To learn that a member of your team, someone you trusted with your life, had betrayed you in such a way changed something vital within you. It altered you, shaped you into something hard and angry.

Cullen should know.

He dropped his arm and moved to the couch. Lowering himself, he rubbed his scratchy eyes with his thumb and forefinger.

Tomorrow was going to be another long day. He should rest while he could, because, at any moment, all of this could blow up in his face.

He dropped his head back and closed his eyes. Before sleep claimed him, he pulled up a mental image of the map of Dover in his mind, remembering what he'd seen when he'd looked it over on the flight from Texas. There were several ways he could get out of the city. It wouldn't take him long to get to New Jersey, Maryland, or Pennsylvania.

There was a cabin in the Blue Ridge Mountains of Maryland where he could lay low if needed. If it came to that . . . things weren't looking good for the Loughmans.

CHAPTER TEN

Mia woke with an awful crick in her neck. She rubbed the spot, grimacing as she pulled open a desk drawer and found the large bottle of Tylenol.

This wasn't the first time she'd fallen asleep at her desk. In fact, she hadn't slept at her apartment since Orrin had been taken.

There was just too much fear and worry for her to feel safe enough to crawl into her bed. Ah, but she missed her soft mattress and fluffy pillows. The nights were getting colder, and she longed to curl up and snuggle beneath her plush blanket and flannel sheets.

But that wasn't going to happen anytime soon.

She opened the bottle and dumped two pills into her hand. Then she swiveled her chair around to the small fridge she kept stocked with drinks and the occasional sandwich.

Inside the refrigerator were two bottles of water, a Coke, half of her sandwich from two days ago, some raspberries, and a slice of cheesecake.

Mia grabbed the carton of raspberries and a water and kicked the door closed before turning back to her desk. Her gaze landed on the sofa and the very awake, very male specimen who watched her.

"Hungry?" she asked.

He gave a shake of his head. "I'm fine."

Good. More for her. She hadn't eaten anything since . . . Mia frowned. When was the last time she'd eaten? She'd tried to put a few bites of the fried egg and toast in her mouth at the diner, but she'd been too wound up. Now, she was regretting not eating more.

Her stomach rumbled at the thought of the rich, greasy food. Oh, how she wanted to sink her teeth into that fried egg now.

She opened the carton of berries and popped one in her mouth. The wonderful flavor rejuvenated her. She ate another handful before she opened the water and took a long swallow. Then she took the pills and went back to eating the rest of the berries.

A look at her watch showed it was just after six. Those few hours of sleep had done wonders. To save her neck and back, she was going to have to learn to make it to the couch and stretch out.

An image of her curled against Cullen there made her breath catch. If only she weren't so aware of him and everything he did. It was unnerving.

"What time does Davis get in?" Cullen asked.

She shrugged, grateful to have something to think about other than him. "Early, but not this early."

Cullen rose and went to the coffee pot. He set about brewing some without uttering a word. She used that time to study him more. What had he done while she slept?

He looked as if he'd gotten a full eight hours of sleep. And though she had no need to find a mirror, she was positive she had large bags under her eyes and was in need of a shower.

It wasn't until after the coffee was brewed and he had

a cup in hand that he turned toward her. "You've been sleeping here."

"Sometimes, yes."

"I'd say from the bag of clothes behind me that it's been a lot more than sometimes."

She put the last of the raspberries in her mouth and chewed. It gave her time to think of an answer. The truth was that she was scared. But she didn't want Cullen to know just how much.

"I don't know who to trust," she confessed.

That was the God's honest truth. Everywhere she looked there was a potential enemy. She was doing everything she could just to keep her head above water, but she was sinking fast.

Was it luck that brought Cullen to her? Or was it fate finally telling her that her time was up?

"Is there a place to shower?"

Now *that* she hadn't been expecting. She pushed back her chair and stood. "It's not far. I noticed you didn't bring a bag. There will be clothes you can use."

"Good. Let's go." He set his coffee down and bent to retrieve her bag.

She didn't bother to take it from him. If he wanted to lug it around, then she'd happily let him. She shut her office door behind them, the automatic lock clicking into place.

Then she led the way to another hangar where the back portion had showers. That's when she reached for her bag and took it, turning to the right for the women's. Cullen had a smile on his face as he strode into the men's shower.

She took out all her weapons, hiding them in her bag. Next, she removed her clothes and folded them to set on the bench next to the bag. When she stepped beneath the spray of water, she closed her eyes and sighed. She remained beneath the hot water longer than usual as she tried to work out the pain in her neck.

It was another twenty minutes before she walked from the showers with her hair still damp but in clean clothes. She stopped short when she spotted Cullen in a sand colored tee that made his sun-kissed skin appear even darker. He hadn't tucked the shirt into his jeans, instead letting it hang about his trim hips. His jeans encased those long legs of his.

When her gaze rose back to his face, his hazel eyes were trained on her. He gave a nod to a group he'd been talking to and met her as they walked toward each other.

"How's your neck?" he asked.

"The Tylenol has kicked in, and the shower helped. I'll be fine."

"Of course, you will."

He said it without a smile, as if he believed it. She wasn't sure what to think of him. Every time she thought she had him figured out, he'd do or say something to make her rethink everything.

The talk last night at the diner had shown a side of him she hadn't realized he had. He really didn't like doing his job. She couldn't understand why he didn't just leave the military. He'd served his time.

It made her long to ask him what he really wanted to do with his life. All she wanted to do was fly. It had led her to make some very questionable decisions along the way. That then put her in this position.

After a quick detour back to her hangar to put away her bag, she led him toward the dining facility. The closer they got, the more her stomach churned with anxiety. Mainly because she wasn't exactly sure of what Cullen was thinking. And that frightened her.

This was her livelihood. The situation she had with

General Davis and Dover AFB was a fluid one. It was a give and take. For the last three years, it had worked. And frankly, she wasn't ready for it to end.

Though she had probably already done that herself by being arrested.

She halted before they reached the building and turned to Cullen. "I need to know what you plan."

"I already told you," he replied.

"Tell me again."

He held her gaze for a long moment. "How many men do you think came into your hangar, killed the team, and took Orrin?"

She blinked, trying to recall the scene she'd walked up to. "I don't know. Four. Maybe five."

"There had to be at least eight."

"Eight? That's not possible."

He crossed his arms over his chest and widened his stance. "Really? All six of my father's highly trained men were on their knees. Would they fight after the first one was shot, or remain still, waiting for their turn?"

"They'd fight," she answered immediately. Then it dawned on her. "There had to be at least one Russian for each of the six team members."

"Exactly. Another two or four to stand guard and grab Orrin."

She glanced around to make sure no one was listening as she took a step closer to Cullen. "Two or three of them might have been able to slip through and get onto the base. But eight or ten? Someone helped them."

"That's what I concluded last night. Someone with the authority and power not to have an order questioned."

"Davis." She turned her head toward the dining hall.

"The truth is that it could be a number of people on this base."

She shot him a glare. "That doesn't make me feel any better."

"Good. Because this is the biggest pile of shit, and it's growing. You were right to believe that you couldn't trust anyone."

Though he didn't say it, the only one she could trust was Cullen. He was looking for his father, and willing to do whatever it took to uncover all the ugly truths of what had happened.

It was simply a matter of time before he discovered hers.

"Davis's wife makes him eat egg whites every morning with no coffee allowed. As soon as he arrives on base, he comes to the dining hall and grabs a donut and coffee," she told Cullen.

He smiled, dropping his arms to his sides. "Are there a lot of people inside."

"More than I'd like listening."

"Perhaps we'll get his attention enough to either answer us where no one can overhear and find out the truth, or he'll bring us to his office."

She snorted. "You obviously don't know Davis if you really believe you'll get anything out of him easily. He's tighter than Fort Knox."

"We'll see," Cullen said as he started toward the doors.

She caught up with him and entered the dining facility first. She scanned the tables and spotted the General's salt-and-pepper hair off to the left in a corner.

She didn't look to see if Cullen was with her as she walked toward Davis. Halfway to the table, the general looked up and saw her. There was a small frown that deepened when he looked over her shoulder.

Mia had no idea if Davis knew Cullen. Anyone who was close to Orrin knew about his sons. Though she knew there had been a rift between Orrin and his three sons that had to do with his wife's death, she didn't know specifics.

Did Davis? Was that why he was scowling as he looked at Cullen? She'd get her answers soon enough because they reached his table.

"Good morning, General," she said, forcing a smile she didn't feel.

He gave a nod toward her. "Carter. I'm dying to hear your explanation of what happened in Florida."

"I'll be happy to tell you."

"I see you brought a friend."

"Cullen Loughman, sir," he said as he stepped around her.

Davis set down his half-eaten donut and blew out a breath. Then he motioned to the chairs. "Sit. Both of you."

She took one side of Davis while Cullen sat on the other. Cullen kept his face devoid of emotion. It was a trait she really needed to learn. There hadn't ever been cause for her to want to hide anything.

Until now.

The general pushed away his donut and leaned his elbows on the table. "You're Orrin's youngest."

Cullen nodded. "I am."

"And you're here to find him," Davis said.

"Yes, sir."

Mia watched the exchange with interest. The men were feeling each other out. Though she knew the kind of power Davis wielded, she put her money on Cullen coming out the victor.

Davis glanced at her. "I'm sure she's told you everything we know."

"She's told me what she knows," Cullen said. "I'd like to know your thoughts on a few things."

The general leaned back in his chair. "All right."

She hurried to speak before Cullen did. She knew Davis from her years in the Air Force, and as a civilian contractor working on the base. He was an exceptional liar, but she knew he had a tell. As he lied, his right eye narrowed.

"General," she said. "We were looking at the scene where Orrin's men were murdered. Cullen pointed out the fact that those men would've been killed together, not one at a time. The number of men that got onto the base would have to be double what we initially thought."

Davis's lips thinned as he looked between the two of them.

"That many Russians couldn't have snuck in," she continued. "Someone had to give the order to allow them onto the base."

"And you believe it was me? You're wrong."

Mia laughed because she was nearly frozen in terror. Davis's right eye had narrowed. He was lying. "I told Cullen it couldn't be you. You're a good man who would never betray a friend like that."

"Damn right," Davis said. He leaned forward again. "Is that all? Or was there something else you wanted to accuse me of?"

"That's all," she said, keeping her smile as she stood. Thankfully, Cullen followed suit. "We're very sorry to interrupt your breakfast."

Davis grabbed her wrist as she tried to walk away. She jerked around to him. Out of the corner of her eye, she saw that Cullen was slowly moving toward the general.

"I expect you in my office for an explanation about your arrest and suspended license," Davis said.

She licked her lips. "Yes, sir."

"I'll see you in an hour."

"She'll be there, sir," Cullen said.

CHAPTER ELEVEN

"Don't say another word," Cullen cautioned Mia as they walked from the dining hall.

If it hadn't been for her slight stiffening, he would have never known the general lied. Because he'd been watching her and not Davis. The need to get as far from the base as possible pushed at him, hard.

"Loughman."

His steps halted at the sound of General Davis's voice. He slowly turned around. "Sir?"

Davis rose from his table and walked toward them. Mia shifted to the side so she could watch, but she leaned toward the door as if she were already mentally outside.

There were at least thirty officers in the dining area. If Davis wanted to detain them, fighting their way out would be pointless. Even if they made it outside, there would be airmen waiting for them.

He gave a slight shake of his head to Mia to keep her still. She wasn't happy about it, but she also recognized the situation for what it was.

Davis reached them. He put a hand on Cullen's shoulder and released a loud sigh. "Orrin is a good friend. It kills me to know that he's being held against his will. I'm offering my services if you need them."

"I appreciate that, sir."

"Orrin and I have been friends for over three decades. He would do anything to find me if our places were reversed. I'm not as free to do the same with my position. However, I'm more than willing and able to use what power I do have."

Cullen looked into the General's brown eyes and saw the truth in them. Davis wanted to help find Orrin. Why then had he lied earlier?

Davis turned Cullen and put an arm around his shoulders as they walked to the door. The general then lowered his voice as he said, "I'm going to look into who might have let the group in. Both of you were right. It would take someone higher up in rank to get it done."

"Thank you," he replied.

Davis smiled and dropped his hand. "Orrin has had my back more times than I can count. We'll find these bastards."

Cullen recognized their dismissal. He turned and walked out with Mia beside him. They didn't say a word until they were in her hangar.

Only then did she run to her office door, punch in the code, and hurry inside. He waited at the doorway, watching as she opened her laptop and began pressing keys.

"What are you doing?" he asked.

"Erasing any correspondence Callie and I had about Orrin."

He frowned. "All of it?"

"Of course, not. The initial email and everything following regarding the mission to Russia is still there. Just anything private about Orrin and the team after the murders." She finished and closed the laptop as she straightened. "Davis was lying."

"I know. I saw your reaction."

She swallowed, nodding. "Did he notice?"

"Hard to tell. The fact he stopped us could mean that he suspects we believe he lied. Or it could be that he wanted to make himself look better, so he offered to help."

"What do we do?"

Cullen leaned his shoulder against the doorjamb and crossed his arms over his chest. "We have a few options. We could remain and continue our investigation until you have your meeting with him."

"On the base?" she asked wide-eyed. "You want to remain here?"

"It'll be dangerous. If Davis didn't authorize the group's access to the base, then someone else did. Are they working for the Saints? Hard to tell at this point. If Davis starts asking questions, whoever it is will immediately look our way. Which means, we'll be at risk."

"The other options?" she urged.

"We leave and hide. Our investigation will take twice as long because we'll be on the run. We won't have the same access or be able to move as freely."

She walked around her desk and leaned back against it, her hands on either side of her hips. "If we leave, we'll be safer but hindered. We won't be able to check out the warehouses at the docks."

"That'll be problematic either way. Sergei told us not to return."

"He knows I will."

"He also knows how dangerous it'll be for you," Cullen pointed out.

She raised a black brow. "That hasn't stopped me before."

"This group of rogue men isn't just some of those who've made their home in America. Callie discovered there were some who came from Russia. This faction kills without regard, slaughters without hesitation. You saw it firsthand. The Saints have the power right now until we can get the upper hand."

"Are you trying to talk me out of helping you?"

Was he? Cullen wasn't sure. He didn't like the idea of being put in such situations, but then again, his father hadn't thought twice about it. That meant Mia had proven herself to Orrin multiple times.

Why should he question her?

"No, I'm not," he answered. "I'm merely laying out what's ahead."

She tucked a strand of hair behind her ear. "How much time do we have?"

"As long as Orrin stays alive through the torture, and as long as my brothers and I keep out of the Saints' hands."

"It was a good thing the three of you split up, then."

He gave a nod. It was. Though, he missed his siblings.

"What is it?" she asked.

"I went years without seeing or speaking to my brothers. Not even a text. I thought it would be odd, or even challenging to work with them."

She smiled then. "But it wasn't."

"It felt . . . good."

"Then you three went separate ways."

And he was back to being alone. It was how he preferred things. It was easier.

"You each have your strengths," Mia said. "The three of you are using those strengths to find your father. That's still working together, even if you aren't side by side."

He held her black gaze and realized she was right. That didn't make him miss his brothers—or Callie—any less. In fact, he wished he were back on the ranch under the wide-open Texas sky.

"We have to stay," Mia said into the silence.

He pushed away from the door and dropped his arms. "We have some time before you have to see Davis. We use that time to dig deeper."

"Into?"

"The general."

She looked at him as if he'd lost his mind. "I'm not a hacker like Callie. How are we going to find out anything?"

"We talk to his aides."

A bark of laughter followed his words. "They won't talk."

"Not to me," he said with a grin.

There was confusion on her face. "You want to use me?"

"Have you looked in the mirror lately?" Or noticed how the men watched her wherever she went? He didn't mention the last part, but he'd definitely noticed.

"I'll try, but I doubt we'll learn anything."

He walked to her and touched a strand of hair. He immediately regretted it when she became suddenly still. That's when he realized how close he was to her.

She smelled like honeysuckle and vanilla. He found it impossible to breathe as his blood pounded through his veins—and went straight to his cock.

He became lost in her eyes, falling into them without a care. The cool strand of her hair slid through his fingers like satin.

The urge to sink his hands into her lustrous midnight locks was overwhelming. He couldn't let her hair loose so he wound it around his finger and held steady.

There wasn't an ounce of makeup marring her flawless skin. And he liked it. What you saw was what you got with her. There was no denying her femininity from the curves showcased by her jeans and shirt to her delicate features and long hair.

The fingers of his other hand brushed against hers. Another shock went through him. The slight hitch in her breathing said she'd felt it, too.

It was in his nature to seduce. He'd had numerous women in his bed, but none were there for more than a night. He wanted no entanglements, no strings of any kind. The fact that he would be with Mia for several more days kept him from leaning down and taking her lips right then. Because he craved her, lusted for her.

Hungered for her.

His body demanded that he satisfy himself, but he held back. They had a mission. This wasn't the time to give in to desires that would only cause more problems between them. There were already enough issues to deal with as it was. It would be stupid and pointless to add another.

She stood, causing their bodies to touch. He fought against the need to claim her lips. But his eyes drifted to her mouth anyway.

Her lips were parted, her pulse beating wildly in her throat. He wondered how she would taste. Sweet? Sexy? Wild?

Fuck. It killed him not to know.

"Did you have something to say?" she whispered in a deep, husky voice.

His knees almost gave out. She'd hidden her vixen side. And it made him yearn for her even more.

She lifted her face so their lips were millimeters apart. "Are you saying you think I should use my wiles on the men to get information?"

He tried to answer, but nothing came out. He ended up nodding instead.

"All right."

What did she agree to? He blinked, searching his mind for their conversation. He'd been too embroiled in gazing at her and picturing her as he removed each piece of clothing she wore that he hadn't heard anything.

Her eyes lowered as she tilted her head to the side, exposing the slim column of her neck. He drew in a steadying breath even as he clenched his hands to keep from grabbing her.

Cullen couldn't remember the last time he'd felt such need. What was it about Mia that drew him? He found it harder and harder to ignore the desire that continued to grow despite his attempts to disregard it.

Long lashes rose as her lids lifted. She placed a hand on his chest, searing him through the cotton of his shirt. No longer could he deny what he felt.

Nothing mattered but tasting her, holding her.

The moment his lips touched hers, the world fell away. He began kissing her, slowly, sensuously—savoring every detail. He wanted the next few hours to be spent holding her as he continued to kiss her.

Then he realized that wasn't possible. They were too mired in deception and secret organizations at the moment. Yet he still couldn't pull away. Not when he wanted this so badly.

Mia was the one who ended the kiss. She cleared her throat and looked up at him. "Let's get this done."

The next thing he knew, she was in the doorway. He had to pull himself out of the fog of desire and shake it off quickly.

She stopped at the door and looked back at him. "What if Davis finds me?"

"Lie."

She nodded, considering his words. "Right. I can do that. Where will you be?"

"I'm going to walk the perimeter of the base."

"To see if there was a way they could've gotten in? 'Explore all options,' Orrin always says."

He nodded, wanting to adjust his aching arousal. Had his father said such words? It made him comprehend just what he'd missed with Orrin.

But all that was going to change.

CHAPTER TWELVE

Mia walked away from Cullen with her blood drumming in her ears. And desire so intense her legs threatened to give way. Her breathing had yet to return to normal, and it was everything she could do to walk away from him.

The kiss had been . . . amazing. The kind of kiss that she would remember fifty years from now. The kind of kiss that left a person breathless and aching.

The kind of kiss that crushed resolve.

That's exactly what was happing. She'd known better than to get that close to him. No matter how much she wanted him, they were partners in this mission. Everything needed to remain platonic.

Though that was now out the window.

She pressed her lips together. They still tingled from the kiss. She lengthened her strides and exited the hangar, furious at herself. It didn't matter if she and Cullen worked together for the next ten years or ten seconds. He was her partner. Becoming involved with a colleague never turned out well.

Mentally, she gave herself a shake and then swallowed and turned her mind away from Cullen. Her focus needed to be on the seduction of someone other than him. And, obviously, she needed to work on her skills, because she'd had no effect on him whatsoever.

That fact didn't bother her. Or she wasn't going to allow it to. It couldn't bother her.

It *wouldn't* bother her.

Why did he have to move her so? Why couldn't he be uninteresting or ugly? Why couldn't he have something—anything—that kept her from craving his touch?

Perhaps she was just lonely. It had been . . . well, a while since she'd put herself in the dating scene. It had been easier to concentrate on her work.

She wasn't looking for a relationship. Far from it, actually. Why then couldn't she stop thinking about him?

There was also the small manner of what she kept from him. She was thankful she was near a building as she put a hand on the side to help hold her. It wasn't as if she could come out and tell him that she'd had dealings with other Russians besides Sergei.

Or that she suspected she'd taken jobs from the Saints before Camilo. She blew out a frustrated breath. It was all theory, but the more she thought about it, the more it made sense.

What a fucking brilliant mess she'd gotten herself into. Never in her wildest dreams had she thought the faction she'd dealt with and the decisions she'd made would come back to haunt her.

"Oh, Dad would love to say 'I told you so,'" she murmured to herself.

Not that her father would ever learn of this. She did whatever she had to in order to keep her life private. Still, she knew he paid others to keep him informed of her movements. That's what money could do.

And he had plenty of it.

Not that she was above using it to get what she wanted. She'd managed to buy a cabin in the mountains, hadn't she? But that was the last time she'd used family money for anything.

Everything else she had—her job, the hangar, her apartment, the Valkyrie, and weapons—she'd gotten with her own money.

It felt amazing to break away from family ties and be her own person. That dream had alienated her from her father, however.

All communication had been cut off from her stepmother until and unless she talked to her father first. She missed the long calls with Cindy. Her stepmom was the closest thing she'd ever had to a best friend.

For her father to take that away had solidified her decision to walk away from the Carter family wealth and connections.

How simple it would be to call her father and be sheltered by his power. It would be the easy thing to do. He would make everything go away.

How could she live with herself, though? Orrin wouldn't run and hide. He'd look for her. He'd done it once already.

She owed Orrin that and so much more.

"Mia?"

She looked up into the face of Airman Schenck. His eyes were bright, curious, and held a hint of concern as he gazed at her. He had a long, thin face with thick eyebrows and wide-set blue eyes. With his tall, lanky form, he could be picked out anywhere.

"Schenck," she said and pushed away from the wall. "I didn't see you."

"Are you all right?"

She put a smile on her face. "Right as rain."

"You were leaning against the building. And you looked like you were in pain."

He wasn't going to let it go. She had to give him some

sort of explanation. "I've a bit of a headache. Nothing that some coffee and an aspirin won't cure."

"You sure?" His frown had deepened.

She'd always liked Schenck. His German roots were strong, and everyone knew it by the food he always brought to share. He was proud of his heritage. Young and ambitious, Schenck was honest and loyal.

That would change. It made her sad to think of it happening to him, though. He was a good kid. But the military chewed up and spit out good kids like him.

"I'm sure," she told him. "I was hoping you might know what General Davis planned to do to me?"

He shot her a lopsided smile. "What?"

"I saw the general at the dining hall earlier. I've got a meeting with him."

"I've not seen anything come across my desk about you. Perhaps Bailey hasn't sent it to me yet."

She let him mull that over for a moment. "Odd that you don't know about any kind of punishment or anything, isn't it?"

"Very." He scrubbed a hand over his chin. "This doesn't happen. I always know where you're sent."

Well, that was something she hadn't known before, and definitely a tidbit that would help. Since she had to work with Schenck and Bailey, she didn't want to make anything awkward by flirting with him and not doing anything about it.

It just seemed wrong. Especially with Schenck. Maybe because she'd been just as wide-eyed and innocent when she'd entered the Air Force. More so because her father had sheltered her from anything that might harm her.

She'd had to learn fast. A few times, she hadn't been sure if she would survive, but she never gave up. Never. She wasn't going to start now.

"How long have you been Davis's aide?" she asked.

His chest puffed out. "Two years. I'm being promoted to Airman First Class next week."

"Congratulations. That's great news."

He ducked his head, a slight blush staining his cheeks. "Thank you. You've always been nice to me."

"Why wouldn't I be?" She threw him a bright smile. "This world is a cruel place. It's good to have people like you in it."

He stared at her as if she were a gift, something to be worshipped. And it made her uncomfortable. All she wanted to do was give him encouragement that might help him in the years to come.

She looked away and started around him. She'd taken two steps when he said her name. She turned back to him.

"Did you need something from General Davis?" Schenck asked.

"I was curious if you knew anything about the night of those murders in my hangar."

He took a step toward her, lines of worry bracketing his mouth. "I was very grateful to learn you weren't there during that mess."

"Thanks. I was, as well." She tried not to think of the bodies and blood she'd found.

"If you're curious about what the general was doing, he was at a dinner with the governor."

That gave him an alibi for that night, but that didn't mean he hadn't sent out the order to allow the Russian group inside the base.

"I see," she mumbled.

Schenck's dark eyes widened. "Do you think General Davis had something to do with it?"

"Of course, not. I'm just trying to figure out how the men got onto the base and off again without being seen or questioned."

His head of sandy blond hair nodded. "For that to happen, the order would have to come from very high up."

"Indeed."

He covertly looked around, then leaned down and whispered. "Come with me."

Mia followed him into the building all the way to Davis's office. The general's door was cracked, showing he wasn't there.

Schenck sat at his desk and began searching on his computer. She looked around at the plaques that lined the walls, stating some award or achievement the general had gotten during his years in the military.

"Mia," Schenck whispered.

She spun around and hurried to his side. There, pulled up on the computer, was none other than the order signed by Davis himself to allow a team of ten Russian military men onto the base for specialized extraction training.

So that was how they'd gotten Orrin off the base without being stopped.

The order was vague. But it clearly stated ten men from the Russian military. Cullen had suspected it could be a group of ten. This was the piece they'd been looking for.

"Can I get a copy of that?" she asked.

Schenck hit a key. The paper popped out of the printer a few seconds later. She took it and folded it several times, stuffing it in her bra.

"How could he do this?"

She saw the look of desolation and bewilderment on Schenck's face. "We don't know that Davis was in on this. Perhaps it's as innocent as it seems."

For everyone's sake, she prayed that it was. Not just for Schenck, but for herself, as well. Orrin counted Davis as a close, personal friend.

If the general did know about the plan to kill the team

and take Orrin, his betrayal ran so deep that it would affect numerous people.

It hurt her heart to see Schenck so stricken by what they'd uncovered. Unfortunately, this would be the first of many times the world would prove how vicious it could be.

The sound of voices approaching stopped her from saying more. She turned as General Davis, followed by none other than Major General Yuri Markovic, walked into the office.

"Carter," Davis said when he spotted her. "It's not time for our meeting."

She tried not to look at Yuri, keeping her attention directly on Davis. "Of course, sir."

"Come back at your scheduled time," Davis stated, dismissing her as he continued into his office.

Yuri stepped so close, she could smell his aftershave. It nearly made her gag. He could be the one who'd taken Orrin. Yet she couldn't confront him. Not now. Not when she didn't have Cullen.

Cullen. Shit. If she told him about Yuri, she would have to tell him the rest.

"Thanks, Schenck," she said over her shoulder and hurried out of the office.

She had to find Cullen. First, she needed to figure out what to do. They could follow Yuri back to whatever hole he'd crawled out of, which might lead them directly to Orrin.

If Cullen would allow her to come once he discovered that she hadn't just worked with Yuri before, but she had helped him. It had been a side job, something to make enough money to put aside for the future.

Never in her wildest dreams had she ever imagined such choices would begin to chip away at the world she'd created for herself.

CHAPTER THIRTEEN

Cullen hadn't gotten very far walking the perimeter of the base when a Jeep pulled up, and two Military Police got out.

"Looking for something," the short redhead asked.

"Several nights ago, a group got on this base, murdered a team of Black Ops, and kidnapped my father. I'm trying to figure out how they got in," Cullen stated.

The second MP took a step closer. He was taller with hawkish features. "Most of us knew the Admiral. I'm sorry about your father."

It had been a long time since Cullen heard anyone call his father "Admiral." Orrin's rank while he was still a SEAL had been Vice Admiral. The nickname had stuck.

"I'm Wallace."

Cullen shook Wallace's hand and noted his rank. "Thanks, Lieutenant. I'm Cullen Loughman."

Wallace jabbed his finger at his partner. "That's O'Mara, but we all call him Red."

Red moved closer. "The first thing Wallace and I did was check the perimeter."

"You were both on patrol?" Cullen asked.

Wallace shook his head. "They called us to duty when the bodies were discovered. We were only supposed to inspect one side, but Red thought we should drive the entire base."

"We didn't find a single place where they could've gotten in," Red said.

This wasn't good news. He'd hoped that Davis didn't have anything to do with Orrin's kidnapping, but it was looking more and more like he was involved.

"This makes us appear like we're not doing our jobs," Red continued. "I didn't have a mark against me until this."

Cullen ran a hand over the top of his hair. "As you said, you weren't on duty until after the murders."

"It doesn't matter." Wallace shared a look with Red. "It goes against every MP on base."

"There would've been eight to ten men. Someone should've seen them. If they didn't sneak in, someone let them in."

Red's face mottled with anger as he said, "I knew the fucking bastard lied."

"Who?" Cullen pressed.

Wallace held up a hand to stop Cullen from talking any more. He turned to his partner. "He said he didn't see anything."

"How did that crew get inside, then, Wallace? They didn't fly over. They would've been seen parachuting in. Besides, they left with the Admiral."

Wallace's chin dropped to his chest. "Which means, they drove. He did lie. Fuck! And we believed him."

"We all did," Red said, his hands fisted by his sides.

Cullen was fast losing patience listening to the two talk. "Who?"

"Second Lieutenant Ernie Mendoza," Wallace replied.

"I'd like to talk to him." Because Cullen knew Mendoza would be able to answer most of the questions he had.

Red turned and motioned to the vehicle. "He's not on duty. Hop in."

In no time, they were at the barracks. Cullen followed the two men into the building to Mendoza's room. Wallace knocked on the door, but there was no response.

Red then pounded on it. "Mendoza! Open the damn door."

By this time, the noise had caught the attention of others. Cullen looked at every face, catalogued expressions, and took mental notes of who spoke with who. And who left.

"He's not going to come out," Red said crossly.

Wallace shrugged. "Then we make him come out."

"What's this about?" someone asked.

The two MPs ignored the others and prepared to kick down the door. Just before they did, there was a commotion as someone pushed through the crowd.

A major, followed by the man Cullen had seen depart, stalked toward Wallace and Red. "What's going on?"

It was Wallace who stepped forward. "We need to question Mendoza about the night the Admiral was taken, and his team was executed."

"Why?" the major asked, brows knitting.

"Because someone let the men responsible inside," Cullen said.

The major's attention swung to him. "And you are?"

"He's the Admiral's son," Red said.

At this, the major's shoulders dropped. "I could've saved you a visit. We're doing our own investigation."

"I'm glad to hear it," Cullen said. "However, our government pulled me and my two brothers off missions around the world specifically to find our father. Continue your investigation, but I'm going to do my own."

"I'll need to talk to General Davis," the major began.

Cullen stopped him by saying, "I already saw Davis this morning. He knows I'm here and what I'm doing."

With no other recourse, the major pulled out a set of keys and moved to Mendoza's door. He unlocked it and pushed it wide. Cullen was behind him, with Wallace and Red right on his heels.

All four came to a halt when they saw Mendoza hanging from the ceiling with a noose around his neck. There would be no getting information out of him now.

"He killed himself," Wallace said from beside Mendoza's desk.

Cullen glanced around for a suicide note. When he didn't find one, he turned on his heel and made his way out of the room. There would only be one reason for Mendoza to kill himself. He'd had an order and executed it. Only after, did he learn what had come out of that order.

When questions began, Mendoza most likely tried to answer as best he could without alerting anyone to the truth. But that truth had weighed too heavily. The deaths of fellow military brothers were too much for Mendoza to bear.

Cullen walked from the barracks. While others rushed to see what was going on, the sound of a fighter jet taking off drowned out everything else for a moment.

The one person who could've given them answers was dead. Whether by suicide or murder, Mendoza wouldn't be talking to anyone.

Cullen started back toward the hangar. At every turn, the search for his father was being blocked. Who were the Saints? And how did they have such connections?

Connections that seemed to reach everywhere. Including targeting Mia on a seemingly unrelated job. She'd thought she was safe on the base, but that wasn't true.

If the Saints could kill six men and kidnap another, they

could get to Mia anywhere. So what had they been waiting on?

Then it dawned on him. They'd known that one of the Loughmans would visit Mia. The Saints could then take out both him and Mia at once.

He pulled out his phone to call Owen and Wyatt to fill them in on everything when he caught sight of Mia. Except she wasn't alone. She was talking to an older man in uniform. A guy in a Russian uniform.

Stuffing his phone back in his pocket, Cullen hid so he could watch them. Mia didn't say anything. In fact, she refused to even look at the man.

The major general spoke using stiff hand gestures. She then turned and walked away. The Russian didn't stop her.

Cullen wanted to get closer, but if he moved from his spot, they'd see him. If he hadn't stopped to call his brothers, he'd never have seen her and the general.

A few seconds later, the Russian pivoted and strode away in the opposite direction. Then Cullen lost sight of him. His gaze swung back to Mia to find that she'd ducked behind a building and was taking in deep breaths.

Another two minutes ticked by before she pushed away from the structure and headed toward the hangar. He remained where he was as his mind raced with possibilities.

He'd known Mia was keeping something from him. Was it coincidence that it involved the Russian military? That was doubtful.

For now, he wouldn't let her know he'd seen her with the Russian. It was another piece to the ever-growing puzzle, but this one annoyed and worried him.

When he entered the hangar, she was looking over her plane. The way she whispered to it and stroked it as if it were a lover turned him on.

He watched her hands glide softly over the metal and

wished her hands were on his body. His gaze moved to her mouth, his balls tightening as he recalled their searing kiss.

It wasn't his nature to not go after a woman he wanted, and yet that was exactly what he was doing with Mia. Suddenly, her dark gaze turned to him, causing him to rein in his desires.

Her hair was in a ponytail, the long, black strands falling in a cascade down her back. "Hey. I was hoping you'd get back soon. I found something."

"Me, too," he replied.

"Want to go first?"

He watched as she closed a hatch and wiped her hands on her jeans before facing him. "You go first," he said.

She smiled and reached into the neck of her shirt to pull a piece of paper from her bra. There was a smile in place as she waved the paper. "Here is the order from Davis allowing the Russian crew inside."

He eagerly took it from her and opened it to reveal a copy of the order. It was signed by Davis, which meant he'd lied to them earlier, just as they'd known.

"I have a feeling that he's going to send me away so I can't help you," she said.

Cullen could investigate alone, but he did find it curious that Davis wanted Mia gone. "That won't stop me from looking."

"It'll make you easier to kill."

He raised a brow. "Then Davis obviously doesn't know who I am."

"I think that's the point."

He folded up the paper and put it in his back pocket. "Why not kill you, as well? Wouldn't it be easier to take us both out together?"

"That's a good question." Her forehead furrowed.

"Where did you get the copy of the order?"

"From Schenck. He's one of the general's aides."

Cullen jerked his chin to the plane. "Are you headed out soon?"

"I like to be prepared just in case. Oh," she said, eyes wide. "Davis arrived at his office while I was there, but he wasn't alone. There was a Russian major general with him."

He had to give her credit for adding that bit into the story. But he doubted she'd tell him about the confrontation she and the Russian had. "I've not seen any other Russian military on the base."

"About a year ago, five arrived and trained with our pilots. We weren't the only base that had such a training exercise. Something about our two countries working together."

"Did you talk to any of them?"

She hesitated for just a second, but it was enough that Cullen noticed.

"I did."

"The Major General that was with Davis?"

She nodded woodenly. "Him a few times. I was more interested in speaking with the three pilots. You said you had news?"

"I did." He walked around the wing of the plane, noticing how she'd swiftly changed the direction of their conversation. "I found two MPs who said they'd done a perimeter check the night Orrin's team was killed."

"You believe them?"

"I do. Especially when they said they knew the man who was on duty that night."

She followed him around the wing. "Did you talk to this man?"

"Mendoza. And we tried. He hung himself."

"What?" She halted, her face going slack with shock. "He's dead?"

"There wasn't a suicide note."

"So you think he might've been killed?"

He raised a brow. "I do."

"I can't believe this," she said. "What now?"

He walked to her, stopping a foot away. He smoothed away a lock of hair that had caught in her lashes and saw her pulse at the base of her throat jump.

The hunger to pull her into his arms was strong. Almost stronger than the need to find answers.

"I want to know all your secrets, Mia Carter."

CHAPTER FOURTEEN

Mia's heart clutched painfully in her chest. Did Cullen know? Had he seen her with Yuri? Her mind halted, words lodging in her throat. She couldn't formulate an explanation.

"Who are you?" he asked.

She licked her lips, wishing he weren't so close. It was impossible to not think of kissing him again, even when she should be keeping her head clear to answer his questions.

His nearness wreaked all kinds of havoc with her body. That, combined with the fact that her brain seemed to have stopped working, made her panic.

"Who am I?" she repeated since she couldn't think of anything else to say.

His hazel eyes held hers as his voiced dipped lower. "What are you hiding?"

Oh, shit. *He knows.* That looped in her head on repeat for what felt like an eternity. All the excuses that came to mind sounded lame as she went through each one.

"We all have secrets," she replied, lifting her head. It was better that she turn the conversation away from her.

The truth would come out, but not now. She was prepared to tell him everything once they had Orrin. But if

Cullen were anything like his father, he wouldn't stop until he learned what he wanted.

That's what she feared. That he would be relentless in his quest for the truth. The truth was never as black and white as everyone wanted it to be. There were always other factors involved.

Cullen grinned at her statement. "Turning the attention away from you. Well done."

"It's true. We all have secrets. There isn't a single person out there who can honestly say they aren't hiding something."

"I suppose."

She heard the slight pause and knew that he did carry a secret. She could've jumped on it, but decided it was better to leave things alone. "I'm not prying into your life."

He leaned a hand on the wing of the plane and tilted his head to the side. "Because you already know everything about me."

"I only know what Orrin chose to share with me. I saw only a few files with reports on your missions. I don't know you personally."

"But I'm the only one you trust," he deduced, the cocky grin still in place. "You don't press me for answers because you don't want me doing the same to you."

She wasn't going to get out of this. He was merciless in his endeavor to discover the truth. So much for thinking he was patient. "Fine. What do you want to know?"

"What are you hiding?"

There was so much she hid from the world. None of it she liked to talk about, but perhaps it would buy her enough time.

"My father is Stockton Carter."

The smile vanished as surprise filled Cullen's gaze. "The shipping magnate?"

Her father had taken over the family business that dated back a century. There weren't many living on the east coast who didn't know his name.

Or his reputation.

But shipping wasn't the only thing her father dipped his fingers into. It didn't matter how much wealth he accumulated, it was never enough.

"Money comes and goes, Mia. You should always have a backup for when one plan goes awry so the money will continue to come in."

He'd drilled those words into her from the time she was a toddler. The Carter family had lost many fortunes but always managed to pull themselves out of it again and again. Stockton Carter wanted to make sure the family didn't suffer such a fate again.

She watched as Cullen's gaze changed as he stared at her. It was always the same once people discovered who she was. Except, Cullen was different.

His gaze didn't sharpen with monetary interest, as with most. Instead, there was a hint of understanding in his eyes. That surprised her. Then again, perhaps it shouldn't.

She knew Orrin as a leader and former SEAL with skills that boggled her mind. But in Texas, because of the size of their ranch, the Loughman name was probably just as well known.

"You actually believed who your father is would make a difference to me?" Cullen asked with a quirk of his brow.

Now that he said it like that, it made her sound . . . spoiled, and stupid. She lifted her chin and gave him a scathing look. "To most it does. I like to make my own way in the world, without my father's money to open doors for me."

He gazed around the hangar before his eyes turned to the plane. After a moment, he looked back at her. "Did you do all of this?"

"I bought the plane." It was her pride and joy, the thing she was most proud of in her life. "I saved money and haggled the previous owner until we could come to terms."

"Without using any family money?"

She laughed as she shook her head. "I didn't touch a single penny in my trust, if that's what you're asking. This plane is all mine with money earned while I served in the Air Force."

"And your deal with Davis?"

"I'd like to say I did that on my own, but my father stepped in behind my back while I was negotiating things. It's one of the many reasons I no longer speak to him."

"Because he gave you what you wanted?"

"He thought by helping me, I'd be grateful. My father has a horrible habit of hearing only what he wants. Me telling him I wanted to make it in the world without using family money fell on deaf ears."

Cullen drew in a deep breath and dropped his arm to his side. He was silent for so long that she grew uncomfortable. It was obvious that while she had shared something about her life, it wasn't what he'd hoped to hear.

Well, that was too damn bad. Some secrets were best left hidden.

"What about you?" she asked. "What are you hiding?"

A small frown furrowed his brow, as if the question had caught him off guard. Or he didn't like the response that sprang to mind. Either way, he didn't look happy.

"We probably don't have time to find out if Mendoza killed himself. If he didn't, then his murderer is our link."

She almost smiled at how hastily he'd changed the subject. Just like her, he didn't want to delve too deeply into things better left alone.

She was going to have to remember that because she had a feeling this same scene would arise in the not too distant future. With a man like Cullen, it was always better to be prepared.

"The timing of Mendoza's death is what causes me to pause. Why now?" she asked.

"I didn't search the room, but I didn't see a suicide note sitting about."

"People usually always leave a note."

"Could it be on his computer?"

She crossed her arms over her chest. "I suppose. Was there one with him?"

"A laptop. It was closed."

"Why do I get the feeling that there is something much larger at play than a simple group of men looking for a bioweapon?"

He gave her a shrug, his lips twisting. "Probably because there is. My brothers are looking into different things."

"While you came here." Was it by chance that Cullen was in Delaware? She didn't believe in coincidence. But the idea that fate had brought him to her made her extremely uneasy.

Her life was complicated enough without someone like Cullen Loughman. Not that he would stay long enough for it to be a problem. She knew his type.

Normally, she kept her distance from such men, and yet, she felt drawn to him. Almost as if destiny had set their paths to intersect. Thereby leaving her no alternative but to continue.

Because she would. For Orrin.

And for herself.

Cullen cocked his head to the side. "With Natalie back in Owen's life, I was going to make damn sure my older brother stopped being an idiot and rekindled their love."

She waited, unsure what his brother's love life had to do with anything.

"Then there's Wyatt," he continued. "I think there's something between him and Callie."

At this, her eyes widened in shock. "Callie? Are you serious? The few times she and I spoke of you Loughmans, she never had anything nice to say about Wyatt."

"Because I believe he hurt her terribly. You should've seen them together at the ranch. Two people with such animosity toward each other but who covertly stare at one another must have something going on."

She nodded in agreement. "I think you're right. I would've never guessed by the way she talks about Wyatt."

Which meant Cullen was here simply because he was the odd man out. Why that upset her so much, she didn't know. Why should she care which of the brothers came to Delaware?

She took in Cullen's thick shoulders that narrowed to his trim waist, making her mouth water. It would've been better if another of the brothers had come. Yet, she was glad it was Cullen.

"Given time, my brothers and I will gather the information needed," he stated with a firm nod.

"But how much time does Orrin have? How much time do any of us have against the Saints?"

Some of his swagger diminished. "We're all doing the best we can."

"And we can't call anyone in DC because they might be the ones who betrayed him."

"Not to mention, they put a big target on you."

At the comment, she wrinkled her nose. "Don't remind me. I feel like they set it all up, including having the cargo seized."

"To keep you grounded and in one spot."

"I really hate these people." She dropped her arms and

licked her lips in an attempt to hold back her anxiety. "We still have Davis."

"He won't give us anything unless we can blackmail him into doing it."

Stifling a yawn, she lost the battle, turning her head and covering her mouth. She was bone tired, and it would be many hours before she could find the rest she needed.

She began to reply when the door to the hangar opened. Their heads turned to see General Davis's second aide, Airman Bailey.

"Carter," he said when he spotted her. "The general will see you now."

A look at her watch showed that she still had another thirty minutes. She glanced at Cullen to find a tinge of worry showing in his gaze.

She started toward Bailey when Cullen leaned close and whispered, "Be ready for anything. And be careful."

He didn't need to remind her. She was trapped in the spider's web. The only way out was with Cullen. If they could get away before everything closed in around them.

Even then, she knew the chances of surviving were slim at best. As she walked from the hangar and her plane—the only thing she'd loved for the past few years—she was reminded of how close to the edge of danger she walked. Or rather, flew.

It had always given her a thrill. Testing herself to see if she could get the plane to do what she needed. Challenging her mental capacity under pressure. Assessing her weaknesses to fortify them.

And yet, not a single thing had ever prepared her for Cullen Loughman.

Odd how her thoughts were on him as she walked to the office of the man she believed worked with the Saints and could try to kill her.

CHAPTER FIFTEEN

Sklad . . .

Orrin came to slowly, as if stepping from a dense fog. It was difficult to think. He tried to shake his head to clear it, but it did nothing.

"It will not help."

Yuri. Orrin's gaze snapped to the foot of the bed where there were shadows. A shape emerged from the darkness to reveal his nemesis.

"What did you do to me?" Orrin demanded.

Yuri lifted a shoulder and brought a cigar to his lips. His cheeks hallowed as he drew in a deep breath. After blowing out the smoke, Yuri flicked the ashes to the floor. "You have no idea what you have walked into."

"It's quite obvious, actually. A man I thought was a friend betrayed me."

Yuri stared hard at him with blue eyes. "Are things really that simple, *stariy droog,* old friend?"

"Yes."

"Never."

That set Orrin's teeth on edge. "You killed my men."

"And you've killed plenty of mine in the past."

"I didn't line them up and put bullets in their heads."

Yuri blew out a breath. "Where is Ragnarok?"

So they were back to that again. Orrin would never tell

Yuri anything. It didn't matter how much torture he was put through. It didn't matter how tired his soul got, how he might long for death.

The words would never pass his lips.

"Do you even know what you stole?"

He frowned at Yuri's question. There was a note of something peculiar in the Russian's voice that caught Orrin's attention. And put him on edge. "A bioweapon."

"That does what?"

Growing apprehension made his blood turn to ice. "It kills. Like all such weapons."

Yuri drew in a deep breath, his chest puffing out before he released it slowly. He then looked down at the cigar in his hand. "Oh, it kills, *stariy droog*. But not in the way you think."

The beeping of the monitor matched the thumping of his heart. In all his years serving his country, Orrin had seen weapons progress at an astonishing rate. Then came the next generation of weapon—biological agents.

The idea had sickened him. But nothing so much as seeing how such weapons could disfigure and kill from within seconds to years later. But all weapons had one thing in common—slaughter.

Yuri was suggesting yet another way to come to such an end. What could be worse than death? He searched his mind, recalling reports from scientists about varying ways a bio-agent could kill.

"You have not figured it out," Yuri said in a tired voice. "You will not."

"Then tell me."

Yuri lifted his gaze. "Do you know what Ragnarok means?"

"It's the end of the world."

"The developer of this particular weapon, Konrad

Jankovic, named it thus because it is just that. A destroyer that strikes without anyone even realizing it."

The more Yuri talked, the more troubled Orrin became. "A weapon like that would have immediate effects."

"Normally. Not this one." Yuri sighed loudly and snuffed out the cigar on the wall. He tossed it into the corner before looking back to Orrin. "Dr. Jankovic led us to believe it would kill as soon as it was inhaled. It was my country's defense against continuing threats coming our way."

"But . . ." he pressed when Yuri halted.

"Another scientist discovered what Jankovic really developed. We were immediately notified, but by then, he was in the wind."

"You lost him?" Not something Yuri would be happy about. Orrin was beginning to see what drove his old friend.

Yuri shrugged indifferently. "That was someone else's concern. I was brought in after. During the hunt, the scientist who told us what Jankovic had been doing was murdered."

"Jankovic killed him."

"*Da.* Then we were told you were coming to steal Ragnarok."

Orrin simply stared at Yuri. Knowing he'd been betrayed didn't get easier to hear no matter how many times it was said.

"That angers you," Yuri said with a smirk. "I have that same rage within me. You see, I had Ragnarok moved to another location. Yet, somehow, it wound up back in the lab for you to steal."

"Who betrayed you?"

"It could not have been a single person." Yuri shook his head, his eyes lowering once again. "I brought men with me who I can trust to find Ragnarok."

At least Orrin's mind was clear now, but it didn't seem

to help him sort through the tangle of lies and deceit. Orrin wasn't sure what to believe.

"Tell me what the weapon does."

For several minutes, Yuri remained silent. When he faced Orrin, his face was lined with regret and exhaustion. "Ragnarok was named so because it can be released in anything—food, water, air—and no one would know. It would take generations for anyone to realize there was something wrong."

"Yuri. What does it do?"

"They would blame many things first. The point is that it could be done without any blame coming to any country or person."

"Yuri, dammit," he said, anger lacing his words as his voice rose. "What the fuck does it do?"

"It prevents women from becoming pregnant."

The words hit Orrin with all the force of a 50mm bullet. He couldn't wrap his head around something so heinous.

"I think I had that same expression," Yuri said wearily. "Disbelief. Outrage. Horror. Confusion. Last, but not least . . . fear."

"Dear God." He thought of Callie, Mia, and Natalie. Women who he had brought into his family or were connected somehow. He thought of his sons never having children of their own, and it left him sickened to the depths of his soul. "Why? Why would Jankovic create this?"

"Because he could. And he was offered millions."

He snapped his gaze to Yuri. "Who asked this fucking slime to create such a weapon?"

"You should know, *stariy droog*. It's your country."

Orrin recoiled at the venom in Yuri's voice. "That makes no sense. Why pay Jankovic to craft such a thing only to have me go in and steal it?"

"It divided our attention. Ragnarok and Jankovic. We

could not focus on a single thing. That allowed the scientist to slip out of the country."

"You know that for sure?"

"We found coded messages in pictures on a social media site. Though we are looking, we do not know for certain where Jankovic will arrive on American soil."

Orrin shrugged. "It doesn't matter. As soon as he asks for asylum, my government will give it. You've explained what the weapon does, told me about the designer, and your role. You've then tried to implicate my country. You've still not told me why you killed my team."

"You do not get it, do you?" Yuri looked up at the ceiling and laughed, the sound hollow. His head lowered, and he leveled Orrin with an intense stare. "*Stariy droog*, we were both used. There is a shadow organization that infiltrates everywhere, but they originated in America. They're called the Saints."

"I've heard of them." He wouldn't bother to mention that he suspected Yuri was part of the group.

"Your entire team was Saints."

It was his turn to laugh. "That's not possible. I knew those men personally. I vetted them myself."

"The Saints are smart. They surround us from the highest authority to the beggar on the street, always listening and watching. And waiting."

"For what?"

"Anything. Everything. What do groups like that want? Power. Absolute control."

And they would have it with Ragnarok in their possession. He was never happier that he'd had Mia mail the vial to Callie than at that moment.

Except it put his sons, Callie, Natalie, and Mia in imminent danger.

"Do you understand why I must find Ragnarok?" Yuri asked.

Orrin shifted on the bed, wishing he were on his feet. "What I know is that I can't trust anything. You could be telling me the truth. Or you could be part of the Saints."

"I am trying to save the world!" Yuri roared.

Orrin raised a brow and calmly said, "Then know that Ragnarok is safe, and in a place that no one can get it."

If Yuri truly weren't part of the Saints, then he would accept what Orrin said. If not . . . well, then he would know the truth about his old friend Yuri.

"One of us has to trust first," Yuri said with a narrowed gaze. "I think of my four daughters. I already have one grandchild. I cannot imagine telling my girls that I had the chance to stop this but did not. That it is my fault they are unable to have any more children." Yuri ran a hand down his face. "Are you sure it is safe?"

"I know it is."

"You sent it to your sons?"

He smiled and shook his head. "I didn't, actually."

Yuri let loose a string of curse words. "All this time, I had men going after them when your sons did not even have it."

Whatever smile began, soon faded as he recalled Yuri's earlier visit. "Who died at my ranch?"

"Your sons are safe and unhurt."

That made him feel a little better. He wouldn't be content until he saw his sons and Callie for himself.

It was then that he noticed Yuri had moved closer to the side of the bed, his voice lowering as if he didn't want to be overheard.

"What aren't you telling me, Yuri?" Orrin demanded.

"I'm pretending to work for the Saints. I'm going to

keep Ragnarok from them. In order to do that, I had to agree to help Egor Dvorak."

"You're telling me Dvorak is a Saint?"

"I am."

"And your proof?"

"None that I can show you."

So he was to take Yuri's word. Could he? As Yuri had said, someone had to trust first. If Yuri relented in his search for Ragnarok, then he would trust him—to a point.

The fact was, Orrin couldn't put his faith in anyone.

"Dvorak does not trust me," Yuri said, bringing his attention back to the present. "I have not proven myself to the Saints. There are more than just my men here."

"Dvorak's?"

"He has had Russians coming to the States for weeks now. They are prepared. You caused disorder by not having the bioweapon with you."

"And if I had?" he asked.

"I would have had to kill you."

Orrin grunted. "Now what?"

"I do not know."

"We need to get out of here."

Yuri crossed his arms over his thick chest. "The last time I followed you, I got shot."

"In the arm. It was a minor wound."

The grin that formed died on Yuri's face quickly. "Did you ever discover who killed Melanie?"

"No."

Yuri made a sound at the back of his throat before he turned on his heel and walked from the room.

The question had Orrin thinking about his wife's murder from a different angle—and he didn't like the direction of his thoughts.

CHAPTER SIXTEEN

The wind gusted just as Mia opened the door to walk into the building containing General Davis's office. She briefly wondered if it was fate warning her not to go inside.

Behind her, Bailey waited patiently to follow her. She yanked at the door and stepped over the threshold. Bailey was silent as they made their way to Davis.

As they entered the small room where the aides worked, she noticed Schenck was gone. It was too bad. He always had a friendly smile.

She forced down her rising fear and panic. Davis couldn't do anything in the middle of the day in his office. There would be too many questions. Besides, Cullen knew where she was.

Cullen would come looking for her. She was sure of it.

She drew in a steadying breath and opened Davis's door, stepping into his office. He looked up from his desk, the phone to his ear, and motioned her inside.

After she was sure the door was closed behind her, she made her way to the set of chairs before the desk. She took one and waited for Davis to finish with his call.

She tried to pretend she wasn't listening, which wasn't too difficult since Davis had yet to say anything.

Finally, he said, "Let me know what comes of it." Then

he hung up the phone. Davis stared at his desk for a moment before he lifted his gaze to her. "I've had the charges against you in Florida dropped since you were working undercover for me."

She blinked, unsure if she'd heard him correctly. Because she hadn't been working undercover. Why was Davis trying to help her?

"That means your license is no longer suspended."

"Thank you," she said into the silence.

Davis drew in a breath and slowly released it, as if mentally preparing for something. "I know your suspicions about me."

Deciding it was in her best interest to remain silent for the time being, she held her tongue.

"It would be easier if I could tell you everything." The general sat back in his big chair with a long sigh. "But I can't. I brought you in ahead of our meeting because it's imperative that you leave this base. Immediately."

That certainly got her attention. She gripped the arms of the chair, her mind racing with the implications of what Davis had said—and what he hadn't.

"Your life is in danger, Mia. For piloting Orrin, for losing the cargo in Florida, and because you're a threat to them."

For the first time, she noticed the lines of strain around the general's mouth, and the stress that was making his face gaunt.

Her heart hammered wildly in her chest. "General, what aren't you telling me?"

"I've made up a mission to get you away," he replied, ignoring her question. "When we're done, get in the Valkyrie and leave. Don't trust anyone."

She scooted to the edge of the chair and put a hand on his desk. "General Davis, tell me what's going on."

"Things are out of my control. I did all I could, but they're closing in on me."

"Who?"

"The Saints."

Oh, God. "I can't leave. I'm helping Cullen."

"You won't survive this if you remain. You're our only chance," he said, eyes bulging as he leaned forward. He slammed his hand on his desk. "Do you understand?"

Now she was completely freaked. She could only gape at Davis, wondering if he was having a panic attack. It was the fear she saw reflected in his brown eyes that told her it was the truth he spoke.

"How much time do I have?"

"Not nearly enough," Davis said in a hushed whisper. He pushed back his chair and rose before coming around the desk.

She got to her feet. "Come with me."

"That's not possible. You're one of the best pilots I've ever seen. All the skills you learned are going to come in handy. Trust your instincts. They'll get you through this."

"You make it sound like I'm surrounded by enemies."

"Because you are. I know Cullen found Mendoza. Tell him that he's right. Mendoza was killed."

She swallowed hard. The thudding of her heart reminded her of the terror and foreboding that had assaulted her after finding the team dead.

Davis turned her toward the door and slowly walked with her. He leaned close, his voice a thready whisper. "I know it's my signature on the paperwork to allow the Russians onto the base, but I never signed such an order."

Her mouth opened in shock, but he continued, "Follow the trail left by the Saints. That's how you'll uncover the truth."

There was no time to reply because he opened the door

and gave her a nod. Mia's legs felt wobbly as she turned and found both Schenck and Bailey at their desks.

"Good luck," Davis said and promptly closed the door behind her.

She jumped at the sound. It sounded so final. Her life was in danger. That flashed in her mind like a lighted marquee. Instead of getting in gear and moving faster, she was stuck.

"Carter?" Bailey asked.

Schenck hurried to her. "Is everything all right?"

She forced a smile. "Yes. Sorry. Lack of sleep is taking its toll," she said with a forced laugh.

"Where is the general sending you?" Bailey asked.

Don't trust anyone. "I'll see you boys soon," she said, ignoring the question and waving at them as she strode from the office.

On the way back to the hangar, everyone she saw made her feel as if they were watching and following her. It put her on edge, making her feel as if she were under a microscope.

As soon as she was inside the hangar, she slammed the door behind her, wishing there was a lock.

"Mia."

She spun around, her hand instinctively drawing her gun. Then she found herself looking at Cullen down the barrel of her pistol. If she didn't get control of herself soon, she was going to do something stupid.

Blowing out a breath, she lowered the gun. "You scared me."

"It's more than that." His gaze narrowed as he closed the distance between them. "What happened?"

She walked past him to her office where she grabbed the bag she always kept for just such emergencies and hurried to the plane.

Opening the door to the Valkyrie, she tossed the bag

inside and began her preflight inspection. "Davis is scared. He confirmed Mendoza was killed."

"Damn."

"He also said that though his signature is on the orders letting the Russians in, that he didn't sign it."

Cullen nodded slowly. "What else?"

"He said I couldn't trust anyone. He's using a false mission as a ruse so I can get off the base, because apparently, my life is in danger."

A hand on her arm stopped her from walking away. She turned her head to Cullen. She saw the determination in his hazel eyes. He wasn't going to let her move until she told him everything.

She faced him then, pulling her arm from his grasp. "He said they were after me because I flew Orrin, lost the cargo in Florida, and because I'm a threat."

"The Saints," Cullen said tightly.

"Yes," she replied briefly, squeezing her eyes closed. "Davis said things were out of his control now, that he'd done all he could."

"Did he say anything else?"

She slowly nodded her head. "He said the Saints were closing in on him."

Cullen's entire body tensed. "Son of a bitch," he ground out.

Mia was scared. Truly scared. And she was beginning to realize that there wasn't anywhere she could go where she would be safe.

"There's nothing else we can do here," Cullen said, running a hand down his face. "Do as Davis ordered. Get away."

"And go where?"

"Is there somewhere you can stash the plane? Somewhere no one would think to look for you?"

She gave a nod of her head, thinking of the small cabin in the Allegheny Mountains. "In Maryland. Backbone Mountain."

"I know it," he said with a nod. "The fastest route would be for me to take US-48, but that would make it easy for anyone to track me."

She was glad that he was going to meet her. As much as it pained her to admit it, they were better as a team. Especially when he was the only one she could trust.

"There are back roads," she suggested.

"It'll take me longer, but it'll be better."

She pulled out her keys to the Jeep from her pocket and tossed them to him. "Leave now. It'll take me another thirty minutes to get the plane checked before I can get it on the runway."

"I'm not leaving until you're in the air."

His tone told her his decision was made. She licked her lips. "Davis told me to follow the trail left by the Saints. That I would find the truth."

"Then that's what we'll do. As long as I'm breathing, they won't touch you. I've always been the hunter, and that's what we'll do now."

Hunting. Yes. She liked the sound of that. Cullen gave her a wink.

She turned away and began her inspection of the Valkyrie. Each minute that passed and she wasn't in the air left her feeling exposed. It wasn't an emotion she liked. In fact, she was beginning to hate it.

Finally, the inspection was done. While she climbed into the plane, Cullen opened the hangar doors. She started the engines and put on her headset.

She gave him a wave as she drove the Valkyrie forward from the hangar. Only then did she contact the tower. "Tower this is N3874X, ready for departure."

"N3874X, we have your clearance," came the male voice through her headset.

Just as she'd expected. She turned the plane onto the runway. She gave the tower a false heading when asked. Every second she waited for them to clear her felt like a lifetime.

There was a crackle through the headset before the tower said, "N3874X, you're clear for takeoff."

She gunned the engines. The plane moved forward, accelerating rapidly. She glanced at the base as she zoomed past. When she reached the desired speed, she pulled up on the throttle. The Valkyrie's nose lifted, and within seconds, she was airborne.

It was out of his hands now. Relief speared through Davis as he stood at his window, his hands clasped behind his back while he watched Mia Carter fly out of sight.

By sending her away, he'd signed his own death warrant. No longer did he fear the inevitable. For more than thirty years, he'd served his country to the best of his ability.

In all his training, no one had taught him how to handle a secret organization that threatened the very way of life he'd risked everything for—that every man and woman who served risked.

The listening device he'd accidentally found in his office three days ago had prevented him from telling Mia everything. His paranoia extended to everyone and everything now. He felt sure that there were others who watched him. Still others who made sure to overhear things.

He doubted there was even time to notify Yuri of the new development. Then again, word would reach Yuri of his death soon enough. That was really all the Russian needed to know to figure things out.

It was too bad he wouldn't get to talk to Cullen. Orrin's youngest son had a tough road ahead of him. Then again, so did Orrin.

At least he wouldn't be around to see what would come of it all. Would the Saints win? Would they find Ragnarok and unleash it on those the organization deemed unworthy to produce children?

How many civilizations and countries would be wiped away by the evil bioweapon? How quickly would the great powers of the world crumble when they realized what the Saints were capable of?

There wouldn't be a war. How could you fight something like the Saints? Their reach was far and wide. They were untouchable, their influence and authority staggering.

Davis heard the door to his office open. He turned around to face his would-be killer. Ever since Orrin had left for Russia, Davis had suspected that one of his aides was with the Saints.

And now he had confirmation.

"You'll never get her now," Davis stated.

The young face he'd once trusted smiled. "Of course, we will, General. All you've done is make it a little interesting. As well as seal your death."

Davis opened his mouth to speak, but the aide lifted his hand and blew a powder into the general's face. His throat immediately closed up, blocking any air.

He reached out his hand to grab at his aide as he slowly suffocated. Davis crashed into his desk, scattering papers and knocking over the phone.

His aide smiled in enjoyment. "Call the medic! The general has fallen!"

Davis clawed at his throat, desperately trying to take in air. Pain wracked his body.

And then there was nothing.

CHAPTER SEVENTEEN

As soon as Mia was airborne and away from the base, Cullen walked to the Jeep and drove to the main gate. Instead of letting him through, the sergeant stopped him.

He was prepared to ram his way through until he saw the two MPs from earlier. Nothing was going to keep him at the base, but he was curious to see what the two men might want.

Red reached him first. "You're not remaining for the investigation, Captain?"

He looked between Wallace and Red. "I'm following a lead regarding my father. Did you find anything else out about Mendoza?"

"Other than the absence of a suicide letter?" Wallace asked.

Cullen decided not to tell them what Davis had shared with Mia. "You checked everywhere?"

"Even his emails," Red confirmed. "We found bruising on the knuckles of Mendoza's right hand."

Wallace gave a nod of confirmation. "There was a struggle. Mendoza didn't kill himself. A formal investigation has been opened."

"I'm curious about the findings. I'll catch up with you two when I get back."

"Be careful, sir," Wallace said.

Cullen looked at him a long time, wondering if the lieutenant knew more than he let on. With a nod to the MPs, he turned toward the sergeant, who opened the gate for him to pass.

With the base fading in his rearview mirror, he knew he hadn't left it behind for good. That would be too easy. How long he had before someone came looking for him was anyone's guess. But he was going to make the most of his time.

He tried to call Owen, but the phone wouldn't connect. Cullen then tried Wyatt. The phone rang once, and then disconnected. As convenient as technology was, it was also frustrating at times.

A thought popped into his mind that the Saints might be preventing him from making calls. But how could they? They didn't know where he was.

Dropping the cell in the cup holder, he concentrated on the road. There was a minimum of a five-hour drive ahead of him. He wasn't sure what he would find, but by the location, it was deep in the mountains. That would be a good place for them to hide the plane and give them a day to make a plan.

And start the hunt for the Saints. Davis had urged Mia to follow the trail. No doubt the Saints had left a lot for them to find. Most likely, it would lead back to Dover.

After two hours on the road, Cullen pulled over at a convenience store for gas, food, and an energy drink. While the gas pumped, he examined the Jeep for a tracking device. He was happy to find nothing.

Just to be sure, he checked his phone. As a precaution, any time he had his cell phone with him, he turned off the GPS locator.

To his shock, it was on. He quickly switched it off. His

mind raced with possibilities of how it could've gotten turned on. It hadn't been out of his hands since before he returned to Texas.

And he'd checked while at the ranch. The GPS had been off.

His gaze lowered to the phone. Yet it had been on. Someone must've hacked his phone and made sure the GPS was activated. That wouldn't have been Callie. She knew better.

The Saints.

At that moment, his phone rang, Owen's name appearing on the screen. Cullen wanted to answer it, but he couldn't take the chance. He declined the call and made his way into the store.

A beat-up pickup truck revved to life. A moment later, the driver put it in reverse to back out. Cullen walked close to the truck and tossed his phone into the back.

He paused before entering the store to see the truck heading back the direction Cullen had come. He was still smiling when he returned to the Jeep with an armload of food and drinks—as well as a map—a few minutes later.

He wouldn't be able to contact anyone, but neither could he be tracked. It was his only option at this point. Even if General Davis had had a mental break and everything he'd told Mia was false, there were still the Saints coming after her.

What Cullen wished he could tell his brothers was that this mess with Ragnarok extended past the Russians. It even stretched farther than whoever had betrayed Orrin.

The threat was much closer to home than any of them realized.

Cullen opened the energy drink and gulped it down. Tossing the empty can in the trash, he climbed into the Jeep and spread out the map.

He studied and memorized the different back roads to Backbone Mountain from various directions. Folding the map, he looked around as he started the vehicle.

Cullen drove away, watching to see if any cars followed. When he saw nothing, he breathed a sigh of relief. His next stop was going to be finding a burner phone so he could contact his brothers and Mia.

All of them needed to be prepared for what was coming.

It was an hour later when he spotted an electronics store. He hastily pulled in and bought two phones. As soon as he'd paid, he opened one of them and sent Mia a text–

IT'S CULLEN. TRACKING BEING USED. GET RID OF YOUR PHONE.

Soon, he was on the road again. Hopefully, Mia would lose her cell phone quickly. It wouldn't do them any good to hide the plane if they were being tracked.

His drive time greatly decreased once he exited the main highway and began zigzagging through the back roads. But it made it easier to see if he was being followed. So far, so good.

As he drove, he thought of his brothers. He grinned because he knew Owen wasn't going to allow his second chance with Natalie to go by without a fight. Those two belonged together. It was time they were finally together.

Cullen chuckled when his thoughts turned to Wyatt and Callie. He well imagined that Callie was giving Wyatt hell at every turn—and he hoped she was. No one deserved to be knocked on their ass more than his eldest brother.

The odds of all of them coming out of this alive were diminishing with every day. That thought caused his smile to disappear. Without contact with his brothers, Cullen couldn't exchange information with them.

As his thoughts swung to the daredevil pilot, he wasn't

sure what to make of her. Her beauty and courage were undeniable. She valued honor and friendship. Yet, whatever she was hiding caused him to hesitate in giving her all of his trust.

There was no doubt she'd been involved in some shady dealings, but he didn't think that was what she kept hidden. Nor did it have anything to do with her family.

He recalled seeing her with the Russian at Dover. No matter how he tried to pin Orrin's disappearance and the team's execution on her, he couldn't seem to do it.

There was genuine distress about what she'd found after the murders, too much for her to be faking. Nor did he believe that she'd made up the engine problem so she wouldn't be in the hangar.

How that connected back to the Russian and her secret, Cullen had yet to work out. All he needed was time and information to put it all together.

His travel slowed on the winding paths of the Allegheny Mountains. It had been several years since he'd been to this part of the Appalachian Mountain Range.

The Alleghenies encompassed the western-central part of the Appalachians. The dense forests were perfect hiding places—as he'd learned in specialized training.

By the time he pulled over for gas and more food, night was fast approaching. He used the time out of the vehicle to stretch his back, neck, and legs. Then he cleaned out the Jeep, getting rid of the wrappers and empty cans.

He restocked his stash of food and drinks, taking another look at the map before setting off again. If his timing were right, he should arrive at Mia's in a couple of hours.

Just as he was about to start the Jeep, something in his side mirror caught his attention. He spotted a black

Suburban parked to the side, and even though the light was fading and the windows were tinted, he still managed to see someone staring at him while talking on a phone.

He wasn't going to take the chance of someone following him. He got out of the vehicle and returned to the store.

The owner, an elderly woman with steely, watchful eyes, looked up. "Forget something, son?" she asked with a grin.

"Can you point me to the back exit?"

She slid off her stool and came to stand at the counter. Then she looked at the set of four small monitors to where the SUV was parked. Her gaze swung back to him.

Cullen laid his hands on the counter. "Ma'am, I'm a captain in the US Marine Corps, Force Recon. I'm on my way to help a friend, and I've got some . . . unfriendlies who would like to stop me."

"You have an honest look about you," she stated. "And I always did have a soft spot for a Texas drawl."

He shot her a grin. "As soon as I take care of this little problem, I'll be out of your hair."

"Well, I didn't say you had to leave," she teased, winking. Then she lifted a wrinkled hand and pointed to the back left. "It's right there."

"Thank you, ma'am."

"You be careful!"

He winked at her over his shoulder and walked to the door she'd pointed to. Cullen made his way quietly out of the store.

With his back pressed against the building, he peered around the corner to see the driver open the door and step out of the SUV.

The light inside the vehicle came on to show that there was no one else within. He watched the man adjust the jacket to his black suit, cussing beneath his breath. Not once did the man take his eyes off the Jeep.

Cullen soundlessly came up behind the man. "Looking for me?"

The man whirled around, reaching for his gun. Cullen caught the man's wrist with his left hand and punched him in the kidney with his right.

There was a loud grunt from the man. Cullen knocked the gun out of his hand and slammed him back against the SUV. He then sent two more jabs into that same kidney.

"I take that to mean you are looking for me," Cullen said.

The man bent over, gasping for breath, his face turning purple as he glanced up. Cullen slammed his elbow down on the back of the man's neck, knocking him out cold.

Cullen stepped over him and looked inside the vehicle for the cell phone to check for last calls in and out. After committing them to memory, he dropped the phone on the ground and stomped on it, breaking it to bits.

"Leave him to me."

Cullen spun around at the sound of the old woman's voice. "It's better if you don't get involved."

"No one will ever know."

He began to argue, but he noticed how she stayed out of the line of sight of the camera, and she'd turned him so that his face wouldn't be seen clearly. Nobody watching the tape would have any idea he was talking to anyone.

Her smile was wide as she held up a cell phone. "Get going, Captain."

With a nod her way, he turned and walked to the Jeep. He wasn't sure what made the old woman help him, but he was glad for it.

As Cullen drove off, he took one more look at the

convenience store. Was it just a fluke that someone had spotted him?

He wasn't sure. General Davis had told Mia that the Saints were everywhere. If that were the case, anyone could be a part of the group.

Cullen hated not having information. Whatever steps he and Mia made next would have to be done thoughtfully and carefully if they wanted to stay under the radar on their hunt.

His hands gripped the steering wheel harder as his foot pressed the accelerator. He sped down the road, a sudden need to get to Mia immediately riding him.

CHAPTER EIGHTEEN

Mia stood on the porch, surrounded by darkness, her arms wrapped around her to ward off the cool breeze. Whenever she escaped to the cabin, it was because she wanted to hide from the world, but she'd always been able to go back to her life when ready.

Not only was that option not readily available now, but she also felt disconnected from everything without her cell phone. As soon as she'd gotten the message from Cullen, she'd tossed her phone out of the plane.

She'd taken a chance because the text might not have come from him. Then again, few knew they traveled together.

She was already hyper-aware, but it had kicked into overdrive after that text. Now, every sound out in the night was an enemy approaching. She kept her gun and knife close, but that would only be good if someone attacked her. It wouldn't do anything if there were a sniper.

As a precaution, she'd flown low to keep off the radar. No one had come after her, so she assumed it worked. Her weapons gave her a feeling of control, but it was an illusion.

She knew better than most how a team of highly skilled

individuals could come in quietly and take out their target within seconds. All without alerting anyone.

The cabin was isolated and situated deep in the mountains, surrounded by thick forest. Total seclusion was what she'd wanted when she bought it. Now, the difficult location could be the very thing that saved their lives.

She rolled her head from side to side, stretching her neck to help relieve the stress. It was a two-mile hike to her plane, which she'd landed on a short runway and covered with camouflage.

Normally, the walk helped to clear her head. This time, trepidation and fear of what might be following—or what awaited—her had her moving quickly.

Her stomach rumbled with hunger. She hadn't bothered to eat. With her nerves stretched so thin, she knew food wouldn't sit well.

And where the hell was Cullen?

She kept watch down the mountain for approaching headlights. So far, no one had come up the drive. With each passing hour, she grew more and more worried.

Had the Saints caught him?

Was he even now in their grasp?

It wasn't as if she could remain at the cabin indefinitely. It was only a matter of time before someone figured out she owned it. She'd paid cash and used her mother's maiden name, but that would only buy her a little time.

If Cullen didn't arrive by morning, she was going to have to decide what her next move was. She didn't have a vehicle, which would make traveling more difficult. Yet she couldn't stop what she and Cullen had begun.

Follow the trail the Saints left.

That was her final order from General Davis, and she was going to follow through with it. For Orrin. For the team. For Cullen and his brothers.

For herself.

She wasn't going to spend the rest of her life looking over her shoulder, worried that a Saint was watching and waiting to kill her.

Either she would find a way to end the Saints, or she'd die.

There were many obstacles before her. In the cockpit of a plane, she could do anything. She didn't have that same confidence on the ground amid a group that caused fear in a man such as General Davis.

She shivered at the thought of hunting the Saints alone. Against . . . shit. She didn't even know who she was up against. And that terrified her.

First, she believed it was the Russians. After her conversation with Davis, she was sure it extended to the Colombians, and probably far beyond that.

The Saints.

It was a holy name, but she suspected their agenda was far from divine. Especially now, when they wanted Ragnarok. She frowned, thinking of the bioweapon. What was so special about it?

Something caught her attention out of the corner of her eye. She turned her head and saw an outline of a man in the moonlight. It was heartbeat later that she realized it was Cullen who stood on the edge of the porch.

She was so relieved that she rushed to him, throwing her arms around his neck. He caught her, holding her tightly.

For several seconds, neither said anything as they held each other. His warmth enveloped her as his strong arms held her firmly. She closed her eyes, saying a quick prayer of thanks that Cullen was with her again.

Then she realized what she'd done. But his hard body felt heavenly against her. She drank in the feel of him, savoring it and putting it to memory, before stepping back.

Instantly, she missed him. Moonlight streamed around them, giving the scene an otherworldly feel. When she lifted her gaze, chills raced over her skin as she saw the blatant desire reflected in his eyes.

It became difficult to breathe under such flagrant need. With her body heating and her heart thumping, she couldn't move. Longing unfurled low in her belly.

Dangerous!

Yes, Cullen was dangerous. To her body and her heart. But she still craved his touch.

But now wasn't the time.

If she were smart, there would never be a good time to give in to the need to take Cullen as her lover. No matter how much she hungered to feel his hands run over her body or to have him fill her.

It had been such a long time since she'd tasted desire as exquisite and powerful as what assaulted her now. It made it nearly impossible not to act on it.

She swallowed and looked away. "I was getting worried."

Silence stretched between them as he scrutinized her. What did he see? What did he think?

"I parked the Jeep below," he replied in a deep voice laced with hunger.

She turned and walked into the cabin. It was imperative to put some distance between them before she did something stupid.

"Did you get rid of your phone?" he asked as he followed her.

The one-bedroom cabin was small. With Cullen inside, the building felt as tiny as a thimble, his presence was so large. Though there was electricity, she'd opted to keep the lights off and had lit candles instead.

"I did." She walked to the fireplace and stoked the fire. "How did you know someone was tracking us?"

He lowered himself onto the couch directly behind her. "I always keep the GPS service off on my phone. Someone hacked my phone and turned it on."

"Who are these people?" she asked in frustration.

"They're very well connected. Over two hours east of here, I stopped for gas. I noticed a Suburban and a man inside with a particular interest in me. He was American."

She turned to the side to see him, fear spiking through her. "What happened?"

"I knocked him out so he couldn't follow me."

She felt a little better at the news. "Did he know you would be there?"

"These people knew where I was before I ditched my phone. Most likely, they had others spread out, searching for me."

She put down the poker and sat on the opposite end of the couch since it was the only furniture besides the bed and kitchen table and chairs in the cabin. Being so near to him was making it impossible for her not to want to be closer.

"I flew low to avoid the radar, but anyone could've tracked me," she said.

"Meaning, anyone could've seen you land?"

"Yes. The plane is two miles away, and I paid cash for the cabin and used my mother's maiden name."

"But they'll still find it," Cullen said with a nod. "It gives us two days, max. We should leave tomorrow morning."

She turned her head to the fire, staring at the flames. "Where do we go next?"

"I don't know." He sat forward and ran a hand down his face.

It was then that she saw his fatigue. Neither of them had gotten much sleep the night before. If they didn't get proper rest, they wouldn't last long.

She rose and walked to the kitchen. The candlelight had been a precaution so no one would think she was there. Now, it set a romantic mood, reminding her of the attraction that continued to grow the longer she was alone with Cullen.

In an effort to forget such thoughts, she began to fix them something to eat. The pantry was stocked, but the fridge only had a few items. That left little with which to cook.

"I got you a burner phone," Cullen said.

She filled a pot with water and put it on the stove to boil. "Good. I feel weird not having one."

"There isn't service up here."

"Part of the appeal of buying this place," she said as she found him holding up his phone, looking for a signal.

He sighed. "I'd hoped to talk to my brothers. We're flying blind here. We can't go back to the base, and even returning to Dover is chancy."

"I've been going over what Sergei told us. He was quick to send us away, but I don't think it was because Orrin is there."

Cullen's brow furrowed. "Why do you think that?"

"I think he knows where Orrin is. He sent us away to try and point us in another direction."

Cullen scrunched up his face and shifted on the sofa to better see her. "I suppose that could be one option. The docks seem like a good location to hold my father, though. It's close to the base, and in the hands of a Russian."

The water began to boil. She dumped the pasta into the pot and began cutting up cubes of cheese. "I thought that same thing when we thought it was the Russians controlling everything. Davis and Sergei told me about the Colombians' involvement. Now you say Americans might also be a part of the Saints."

"We know nothing of this group."

"I don't think they took Orrin far from Dover. Sergei sent us away, and Davis said to follow the Saints' trail."

Cullen nodded as he listened.

"Sergei knows these people, this secret group who works from the shadows. I've never seen him or General Davis fear anything, and yet, in the space of one day, I saw it on both of their faces."

Cullen grunted. "The Saints seems to have a long reach. That means unlimited money. If they span two continents and three countries, who's to say it's not even larger than that?"

"Why did they name themselves the Saints?"

"I'm more interested in why they want Ragnarok."

She finished with the cheese and rinsed off the knife in the sink. "Orrin knew something was off. He couldn't figure out what it was."

"He knew enough to send the bio-agent away. That's the only thing that saved his life."

"But how did he know?"

"Instinct," Cullen said with a shrug. "Both you and Callie mentioned that Dad wasn't completely comfortable with the mission. It went so deep that he traveled to Dallas and spoke to Owen's high school sweetheart, Natalie. Dad didn't ignore his gut, but he couldn't find anything concrete to go on."

"If only Davis would've told me something, given us something to go on regarding this organization," she said with a sigh.

He scratched his forehead. "You said yourself that Davis wanted you gone immediately. He told you what he could, knowing you would figure it out. His motive was to save your life. Which he did."

"I'm a pilot, Cullen. I can fly anything. I do no one any good on the ground," she told him before dumping the cooked noodles into a colander to drain the water. "We're walking blind in unknown territory surrounded by enemies."

Then she mixed the noodles and various cheeses together. Only then did she pull out a package of smoked salmon from the pantry and add it.

Once mixed together with salt and pepper, she dished them two bowls and brought it to the sofa.

He grabbed her arm when she handed him his food. "First, this is nothing new for me. Second, you're more than capable. I saw you with Sergei."

"Because I know him."

"It was more than that. Trust yourself."

The current that passed between her and Cullen was thick and strong. It was becoming more and more difficult to ignore the need pulsing within her.

"This place will give us the time we need to sort things out," he said and released her.

She sank onto the couch. Slowly, she began to eat.

"This is really good," he said around a mouthful of food.

She smiled and sat back, cradling her bowl. In the hours before his arrival, she'd gone over what Davis had told her. Then she'd tried to piece together the information Sergei had given. There were too many holes to make any sort of sense of it.

But there was one connection—Yuri.

If she told Cullen about Yuri, then the secret she wanted to keep hidden would be revealed. Yet what choice did she have? The Saints needed to be stopped.

"There is someone we can ask about Orrin."

Cullen's gaze lifted to her. "Who?"

"His name is Yuri Markovic. He's a major general in the Russian army. I saw him with Davis earlier."

"You think this Yuri will help. Why?"

"Because he and your father used to be friends."

CHAPTER NINETEEN

Mia waited for Cullen to do something, say something after her revelation. Instead, he simply lifted his fork to his mouth and took another bite.

He was taking it better than she'd expected. Then again, she hadn't told him much.

"Markovic and Orrin worked several missions together as the US and Russia sought to continue strengthening relations. It began during the Cold War," she said.

Cullen shrugged and continued eating.

She blinked and placed a bite in her mouth. Once she'd swallowed, she said, "Don't you find it curious that Yuri was in Dover? The very place your father was kidnapped?"

"I do. I'm waiting for you to tell me how you know him."

The food lodged in her throat before it slid down. Her gaze locked with his. She thought he might've seen her with Yuri when they'd talked at her hangar. Now, she knew for certain.

"Why didn't you ask me while we were at the base?" she demanded.

He lifted one shoulder nonchalantly. "I'd hoped you would freely give the information."

It wasn't like she had a choice now. "I didn't lie before. Some secrets are better left alone."

"Secrets become heavier the longer they're carried," he replied smoothly.

Damn him. She looked down at her food and ate, no longer tasting the pasta as it hit her tongue. Her stomach churned with emotions—anger, fear, remorse, embarrassment.

Shame.

When she'd had all her stomach could handle, she set her bowl on the floor and tucked her legs against her on the couch. She focused on the flames as they flickered wildly in the fireplace.

"I flew my first plane at eight," she said into the silence. "It was one of my father's. I begged for lessons, and he made sure I had the best instructors. As soon as I sat in the pilot's seat, I felt . . . like I was home. Like I'd found what I was destined to do."

She smiled at the memory of being so joyful each time she stepped into a plane. "I went from flying Cessnas to executive jets. It was never enough. I wanted more. So I made sure I knew how to fly helicopters as well, and as wonderful as it was to be in the air, I still preferred planes.

"I spent every minute that I could flying. I racked up hours at an amazing rate. By the time I was sixteen, I was going to airshows and flying biplanes in aerobatics demonstrations. It was thrilling. For a while. At one of the shows, a colonel from the Air Force approached me. I barely listened to anything he said. I took his card and didn't think about it again.

"A maid found the card while she was doing laundry and gave it to my father. Dad lost his shit. His face turned several shades of red as he ranted about me never serving in the military. He didn't relent even when I reminded him some of his closest friends were military. My father had plans for me, you see."

Mia took in a deep breath and slowly released it when the anger began to build up again each time she thought of that day.

The fire was mesmerizing, giving her the illusion that it beckoned her to continue her story, even though Cullen hadn't made a sound. "I knew better than to argue with my father. If he knew what I really planned, I would've been sent off to some boarding school with my every move watched. So I kept silent and never brought up the subject, but I kept flying."

It didn't bother her that Cullen had yet to reply. In some ways—a lot of ways, actually—it was easier. Not looking at him, not seeing his expressions.

"The day of my high school graduation, I called up the colonel. We spoke for an hour, and he sent me to the nearest recruiter's office where I filled out all the paperwork. Then I returned home for the huge celebration my father had planned. As his only child, he tended to go overboard with things.

"He didn't learn what I'd done until three months later, when I told him I was leaving for boot camp. That was the second time I saw him go batshit crazy. He threatened all kinds of things. In the end, it was my stepmother who intervened and prevented either of us from saying something we might later regret. She drove me the next day. He was so angry, he didn't come down to see me off."

Mia hated that memory. His rejection of what she'd decided for her future had hurt her deeply. The wound went deep, affecting her over a decade later.

She rose from the sofa and put another log on the fire.

The warmth of the flames beckoned her to remain, so she sat cross-legged on the floor.

"My problem with authority stems from my father. I hated the day-to-day crap in the Air Force. The only time I was truly happy was when I was flying, but my insubordination kept me out of the skies more times than not. Some people called my confidence cockiness and took offense that I was better than they were. I came to hate everything about the Air Force, except the access to such magnificent aircraft. My father sat back, expecting me to return home with my tail between my legs. I didn't. I came up with my own plan.

"It was a good one. I'd made a lot of friends and contacts during my time in the military. I knew a good pilot would always be in demand. So I began reaching out to some of those people. The first to respond was Sergei.

"I knew getting involved with him would be dangerous. I'd only met him once through a friend, and even then, I could tell that I might be in over my head. But Sergei offered me a lot of money. I took the job—a legitimate one, I might add—flying one of his planes to Florida to drop off a shipment and return. I earned more money on that Saturday than I did in an entire year with the Air Force.

"I resigned my commission six months later. By then, I'd already lined up several jobs. It didn't matter what I was flying, as long as I was in the air. I found the Valkyrie during one of those trips. Once I had my own plane, the money doubled. During that time, I rented a place at a private airstrip for the Valkyrie.

"Davis didn't accept my resignation well. It was like he'd been planning for it, though, because when I broached the subject about my willingness to work as a private contractor for the military, he agreed on the spot. And when I mentioned the hangar, he consented quickly."

She shook her head, remembering that day. "I thought I'd won a big battle. I discovered later that my father had a hand in it. But I had what I wanted, so I let it go. There was more work offered to me than I had time to take on. I was able to pick and choose what jobs I wanted. I took the most dangerous ones the military offered. Sometimes using my plane. Sometimes theirs.

"For my other jobs, Sergei was becoming a regular. He warned me about getting involved with the wrong kinds of people. I foolishly believed I could distinguish between them myself. I was wrong. I got mixed up with a bad group in the sex trade."

She almost looked at Cullen to see his reaction. Then she thought better of it. "I believed them when they gave me a manifest of what was in the crates. It wasn't until my third trip to South America that I heard crying after I'd landed. I opened the crate and found the girl. She was no older than twelve. Dirty, starved, and riddled with needle marks on her arm.

"One by one, I opened the other crates to find more girls. I was disgusted. At the men who'd hired me. At myself. I wasn't about to hand the girls over. But I didn't know where to take them. I knew my best chance was in the States. So, I got back in my seat and intended to take off. The men had other ideas. They shot one of my engines. I managed to kill several with the guns from the Valkyrie, but in the end, they captured me and took the girls."

She had to pause in her retelling of the story. Those five days locked in that room, bound and gagged as the men stripped and touched her had been the worst of her life.

There was movement behind her, but she didn't turn around. She kept her face averted from Cullen.

"The men informed me that I was going to be sold as a sex slave. The entire time I was locked in that room, naked and bound, all I heard were the cries and screams of the other women. It was the most horrid place I'd ever been in. And I knew I wouldn't get out.

"I was drugged, bathed, and dressed to be displayed and bid upon. Whatever they gave me wore off quickly. I recalled all of my training, and I wasn't going down without a fight. I attacked one of the men holding me, killing him. Then I shot two more before they had me on my knees with a gun to my head.

"Suddenly, a door opened, and a man walked in. It was Orrin. He gave me a smile, but when he looked at the men, the vengeance I saw was palpable. He lifted his arm, gun in hand, and killed them all. He saved me and all of those girls that night."

If only it had ended then. If only she had listened to Sergei. If only . . .

There were so many "if only's." But she'd chosen her road, and she was walking it.

"What happened then?"

She jumped because his whispered question came from directly behind her. When had he moved? Mia blew out a deep breath. "I tried to get past it all. Your father was there, helping me through it. He even managed to get my plane back to me. When I thought I was able, I began flying again. On my second flight, I had a job in Bulgaria. Another part of the sex trade group was there, waiting for me. They tried to capture me again.

"I got away after killing several of them. But something inside me had changed. I ignored Sergei's warning and began working for others of . . . questionable ilk. I transported drugs and weapons for anyone willing to pay my rate. I don't know why. I knew it was wrong, and a part of me wanted to get caught. I even flew paths that would ensure my cargo was checked. It never was.

"That's how I came in contact with Yuri. He had me smuggle his men into the States. I never asked questions. I accepted the money and flew. After a couple of those trips, I realized I'd begun to hate flying. I returned to the base after a journey to find Orrin in the hangar. He didn't say anything, just put his arms around me."

Mia had cried for what felt like days. It had been cleansing, healing. "I spent two months in this cabin. When I returned to the base, I felt like my old self again. But I always knew my past decisions would come back to haunt me."

Cullen moved to sit beside her. "You learned a lesson and came out stronger for it."

"I think I worked for the Saints."

He shrugged, glancing at her. "You worked with and for a lot of people."

"Yes, but it isn't the same."

"It is. Look how long you worked with Sergei. You didn't betray anyone just because one of your clients was the Saints."

She closed her eyes, wanting to believe him. But in her heart, she knew the truth.

"This is what you didn't want me to know?"

"Yes."

"You thought I wouldn't trust you because of this?"

She frowned, turning to face him. "I certainly wouldn't."

"It was your secretiveness that made me hesitate to trust."

"Do you? Trust me?"

"At this point, we only have each other. We have to trust one another," he said.

It wasn't what she'd hoped to hear, but it was good enough. Her thoughts returned to the prison Orrin had saved her from. "I know what it's like to be held against your will. I wasn't beaten, but I was fondled and groped. I thought I would die that way. I found out later that it was Sergei who'd told Orrin where I was. I want to return the favor and rescue Orrin."

"We will. He's trained for this. He can withstand a lot. He's tough."

"You're lucky to have him as a father."

He looked down, shamefaced. "I wouldn't know. I've not spoken to Dad in five years. He's the only parent I have left, and I've ignored him."

"Sometimes it's easier to push parents away rather than deal with them or the past."

"The past. It always comes back to that."

She studied his profile while he stared into the fire. There was something about his expression that caught her right in the chest. It was a mixture of regret and hope. "This is about your mom, isn't it?"

He gave a snort. "Most people don't bring her up. They're afraid to. Where I grew up, her name is whispered for fear of upsetting one of us. No one knew how much I wanted to talk about her or what happened."

"Then talk to me," Mia offered.

CHAPTER TWENTY

Cullen swallowed as he considered Mia's suggestion. His mother's murder had followed him from the small town of Hillsboro into the Marines and beyond.

He was treated like everyone else—until it came to his mother. Then most handled him with kid gloves. Others avoided the issue altogether.

Yet here Mia was, facing it head-on.

And daring him to, as well.

How could he pass up such a chance? He'd thought after so many years, being reunited with his brothers to search for Orrin might have dulled the pain enough for them to talk about the murder. Not so in this case.

It made the ache inside him grow. The same hurt that had begun the day of his mother's death had only expanded, swelling within him until he felt he might burst because of it.

"Orrin never spoke of it," Mia said into the silence. "I didn't know about your mother until after working with him for a few years. Even then, I didn't bring it up. I figured that he had all that time to tell me, and he chose not to for a reason."

"No one in my family likes to talk about it," he admitted. "I was seven when she died, and Dad only sat me down once to speak of it. He told me that someone had come into our house and hurt Mom. He tried to soften the blow of what had happened, but you can't live on the ranch and not know about death. Then he swore to me that he wouldn't rest until he'd found the person responsible."

Her brows shot up. "That's it? He didn't ask if you needed to talk?"

"That was it. I didn't think much of it at the time. I didn't want to talk about it. But Dad's grief was tremendous. After we buried Mom, he disappeared for weeks. When he returned, he was different, harder. As if whatever tenderness had been inside him withered with her death."

"He loved her deeply."

Cullen slowly nodded and swung his gaze to Mia. "I never saw her. The day she died. I know why Wyatt and Owen kept me away, but it pissed me off. It still angers me. She was my mother. I had a right to see her."

"They were protecting their younger brother."

"I know." It didn't make it any easier. "I read the police report years later. That comes from living in a small town and knowing everyone."

She tucked her hair behind her ear. "What did it say?"

"There was a storm that day. We hurried to the house because we thought there might be a tornado. I'll never forget that because there were some gusts that swept me off my feet. And the lightning. It was beautiful and terrifying. When we reached the house, something caught my brothers' attention. Wyatt refused to let me in the house. He ran to the barn, and Owen took my hand and led me to a hiding spot at the side of the house.

"The rain was so heavy, we were soaked in seconds. I spotted Wyatt coming from the barn with two guns. He gave one to Owen, and they disappeared inside the house. Then the strangest thing happened."

She leaned toward him. "What? What happened?"

"The rain and wind stopped. It was like someone had pressed pause. I sat huddled and shaking, waiting for my brothers. It felt like hours before they came running out. The next thing I knew, they'd saddled one of the stallions. It was the fastest horse we had, but he was as wild as they came." Cullen gave a shake of his head. "He stood still as stone after they'd saddled him, waiting for me to get on his back. It was like he knew something was wrong."

"He must have," Mia said.

"I raced the stallion over several miles to our nearest neighbor, Wyatt's words ringing in my head. When I got to the Decker's, all I could say was what my brother had told me. 'Send the police. Mom has been murdered.' The Deckers flew into action. Mrs. Decker pulled me off the horse while Mr. Decker called the authorities. I tried to return to the ranch, but they wouldn't let me. I was at their house for two days before Dad came for me."

A soft hand touched his arm. "They wanted to protect you from seeing anything."

"I know. But it's the unknown that's the worst." Cullen liked the feel of her hand on him. It comforted him, soothed him. "I imagined all sorts of scenarios about what happened. When no one would tell me anything, I eventually lashed out. My brothers ignored me. Dad, however, understood. He was the one who explained with that one discussion."

To his irritation, Mia let her hand fall away as she asked, "Was your mother's killer caught?"

"No." Not yet anyway. "We all suspect it had something to do with Dad and his work as a SEAL."

He leaned back, bracing his hands on the floor and stretching his legs out so that his feet came close to the heat of the flames. "There were no fingerprints found, no DNA of any kind."

"That means it wasn't your Average Joe who committed this crime."

"Exactly. It was an expert. Just one more clue that directed everything back to whatever Dad was working on."

"Did you never talk to him about it?" she asked with a troubled frown.

To his shame, he hadn't. Pride had been the culprit. He'd wanted to show his father he could be the best. That meant Melanie Loughman's murder had been pushed to the side as Cullen lived his life.

"As I said, it's not discussed."

Her gaze hardened. "It's rather difficult to solve anything when you allow five years to pass without talking to your family."

"What about you?" he fired back.

She lifted her chin. "I might allow months to pass, but I speak to Dad on Father's Day. I try to see him on his birthday, my stepmom's birthday, and even mine. But I make damn sure I'm there for Christmas and Thanksgiving."

He winced, the truth of the situation slapping him in the face. "Things changed after Mom's death. Dad did the best he could, but then he left for another mission. My aunt and uncle moved to the ranch to raise us. It became a habit for us not to talk to Dad because he was never there. That continued when I went off to college and then the Marines."

Mia wrapped her arms around her legs that she'd pulled up against her chest. "He checked in on all of you every month. You might not have thought about him, but you three were never out of his mind."

Now he felt like a first-rate ass. Then again, that's exactly what she wanted. She'd seen another side of his father. She'd been the recipient of Orrin's advice and laughter. He only had snippets of memories from throughout the years of his father returning home for a few weeks before leaving again.

He jerked at the realization that he was jealous of Mia. Envious of the time she'd had with Orrin, time that should've been Cullen's. Resentful that his father had so willingly taken in others when he had three successful sons of his own.

Who hadn't needed him.

Cullen met her dark gaze. She'd needed his father. So had Callie. How could he be anything but happy that Orrin had been there to aid both of them?

"What?" Mia asked at his look.

He shook his head. "Nothing."

"What did the police report state about your mother's murder?"

"It wasn't just the local police. The FBI, CIA, the Navy, and even the State Department all had investigations going. Over the years, I've managed to get my hands on each of the reports."

"Anything that could help?"

"The facts were all the same. Melanie Loughman let her attacker inside the house. There was a half-drunk cup of coffee on the kitchen table that belonged to my mother. Because of that, it's suspected she was strangled there."

She recoiled. "Strangled? Dear Lord."

"An up close and personal kill," he replied with a nod. "I know. That's what stands out for me, as well. She could've been taken out by a sniper at any time while Dad was away and we were at school. There were only four workers on the ranch, and all were out herding cattle that day."

"Leaving her completely alone."

"With no evidence, none of the investigators learned exactly where she was murdered. But the killer made sure to place her on my parents' bed."

Mia's face scrunched up in revulsion. "This was definitely about Orrin. The killer wanted to leave him a message."

"I believe so, yes."

"You should ask him about it."

Cullen's lips turned up in a grin. "As soon as we find him and deal with the Saints, I'm going to. It's time my mother's killer was brought to justice."

"Even if it is Loughman justice," she stated with a smile.

He had to admit, it would be difficult not to exact revenge on the son of a bitch as soon as he was caught. Suddenly, Cullen frowned. "Was it a coincidence that Orrin was asked to steal Ragnarok?"

"He's good at what he does, but there are younger men who could've done it, as well."

"So why my father? Why not send in a SEAL team? Why not send in Delta Force? Why a Black Ops? Why Dad?"

Shock made her face pale in the orange light of the fire. "You think this all goes back to your mother's murder."

"Dad was supposed to have the bioweapon when y'all landed at Dover. It was his instinct that made him give it to you to mail off."

"If he'd had it, he would be dead along with the others," she said with disgust.

He nodded, a sick feeling roiling in his gut. "They wanted him dead, removed."

"Orrin outsmarted them."

"Do you think it was Yuri who took him?"

She shrugged helplessly. "Who else? We saw the order from General Davis granting those ten Russian soldiers admittance onto the base that night."

"This morning, I was convinced Davis was a part of this. You seeing him with Markovic doesn't help. However, the things he said to you about the Saints, as well as Davis getting you off the base lends to his innocence."

"It could be that the general regretted joining the Saints and had a change of heart."

Cullen bent one leg and leaned forward. "Or he was forced into helping them."

"There is that, as well. We won't know until we talk to him again."

Cullen suddenly recalled something the general had told Mia. "Didn't he tell you they were everywhere?"

"Yes," she said, nodding. "He looked up at the ceiling when he said it."

"There was a listening device in his office, and one probably watching him, too."

Her face fell in remorse. "He did say there wasn't much time. No wonder he didn't say more."

"And what he did tell you may get him killed."

She dropped her forehead to her arms. He understood how she felt. It was difficult to take it all in. Conspiracy, deception, and lies combined with deceitful individuals was enough to make a person's head spin.

"The general helped me," she said, lifting her head.

"And I'm thankful for that."

She pressed her lips together. "I should've helped him."

"We don't know anything for sure."

"That's the problem. We're guessing."

"They're educated guesses," he reminded her.

She threw out her arms. "That has gotten us nowhere with no idea of what to do next?"

"I know what to do next. We find Yuri Markovic."

CHAPTER TWENTY-ONE

The forest was still but buzzing with sounds, making the night seem alive. It was electric, stimulating.

Stirring.

Mia searched for an excuse—*any* excuse—to stop thinking about Cullen. And found nothing.

It was disheartening to be sure. Especially when she wanted him so acutely.

That need swirled through her, slowly at first, but increasing steadily. The kernel of desire that had begun when she'd first seen him had turned into an inferno.

She used the time alone while he did a sweep of the area to try and get herself under control. When he'd spoken of his mother's murder and the years after, she'd been unable to keep her hands from him. And that touch had only inflamed her need for more.

In order not to throw herself at him, she'd had no choice but to release him. Which had been harder to do than she'd expected. What was it about Cullen that enticed and captivated her?

What about him persuaded her to let down her guard and invite him in?

Was it his arousing, sexy voice that cajoled and seduced? Was it his charming words that tempted and lured?

Or was it those hypnotic hazel eyes with their mysterious mix of green and gold that coaxed her?

Her stomach fluttered at the thought of giving in to desire. The attraction was there, hovering over them like a cloud. She wasn't sure how much longer she could resist. So far, her mind had remained strong, but her body was turning the tide swiftly.

Not even a mundane chore like cleaning the dishes could ease the rising desire. It burned. Blazed hot and relentless. Cullen was the type of man she couldn't outrun or ignore.

He demanded her attention with a simple look. The promise of pleasure in his gaze was there whenever she sought to see it. And that terrified her.

But it also exhilarated her.

With her hands braced on the sink, she closed her eyes and imagined what it would be like to give herself to Cullen. Her head rolled to the side as her nipples puckered, tingling with the need to be touched.

Chills raced over her body, as her breaths came faster. With his name on her lips, she reached down and touched herself, trying to ease the need rising rapidly.

Her eyes opened. In the reflection of the window, she saw him standing behind her. Their gazes clashed as the fire popped. Desire smoldered within his hazel depths.

There was no turning back now. Mia didn't even try. The path was laid bare before her, and it was too good to let it pass her by.

She turned around. For long moments, they simply stared. She was afraid to move—and afraid not to.

The desire was so tangible that the air was thick with it. She was shaking when she took that first, tentative step toward him.

He met her halfway, but even then, they didn't touch.

Mia was scared that once she did, the primal, savage longing for him would take over.

It was Cullen who reached out first, putting a hand on her waist and slowly drawing her closer. Instinctively, her arms bent, grasping his forearms.

Candlelight and firelight bathed them in a soft glow. She was spellbound, caught in the web of longing and need reflected in his eyes.

His head bent forward gradually, giving her time to push him away. Except she was long past that. Her face lifted, anticipating his kiss.

The first touch of his lips against hers made her breath catch. His mouth was firm as he moved against her, teasing and coaxing.

She willingly opened for him. When his tongue swept in and touched hers, she sighed and ran her hands up his arms, over his shoulders, and around his neck.

He held her tightly, his arms like bands of steel as he deepened the kiss. Molten desire poured through her. If there were any last reservations about giving in to her longing, they faded away.

Sparks of pleasure skidded along her skin as he kissed her vigorously. She melted against him, wanting—*needing*—more.

A moan rolled through her when he slid a hand into her hair. Then he turned her, backing her around the sofa and moving closer to the fire.

She was the one who reached for the hem of his shirt and yanked it upward. The kiss ended long enough for him to pull the tee off and toss it away.

Mia's lips parted as she stared at the specimen before her. She splayed her hands over his chest, then kissed the bullet wound on his right shoulder and the other closer to his waist. On the left side, she ran her lips and tongue across the three-inch scar along his abdomen that had come from a knife.

She met his gaze and smiled. The thick sinew beneath her palms strained as he fought not to touch her. He jerked when she reached between them and unbuttoned his jeans.

The sound of the zipper was smothered by his moan. With her heart hammering in her chest, she placed her hand over his thick arousal through his jeans.

The slim thread of control Cullen had clung to shattered when she touched his cock. He yanked her against him, plundering her mouth with a brutal kiss.

Her fingers slid into his hair, her nails gently scraping his scalp. He couldn't get her close enough. She'd been tempting him since he'd first laid eyes on her.

But walking into the cabin and finding her touching herself had surprised and excited him. Now that she was in his arms, he wasn't about to let her go.

Tomorrow and the day after meant nothing as they gave in to the longing, the craving for one another.

He struggled to get her shirt off. Finally, she was the one who removed it. Her bra quickly followed. Then he had a handful of shapely breast.

When he ran a thumb over a taut nipple, she groaned, her nails sinking into him. As if in mutual understanding, they parted long enough to shed the rest of their clothes.

And then they were together, flesh to flesh.

Cullen gloried in the woman in his arms. He ran his hand down her side to the indent of her waist, and then over the flare of her hip before grabbing a handful of her ass and pulling her against his cock.

He smiled when she gave him a wicked grin right before she jumped, wrapping her long legs around his waist. Kissing her again, he held her while he lowered himself to his knees.

With one hand on her back, he leaned forward until his hand touched the floor. Slowly, he lowered her to the ground. She kept her legs locked around him, her hands all over his body.

He didn't stop her when she rolled them over and straddled his hips. She flipped her hair over her shoulder with a flick of her head. Her hands were braced on his chest as he held her waist.

Desire pounded through him, thick and demanding. His cock jumped, eager to be inside her. Unable to help himself, he cupped both her breasts and squeezed her nipples.

Her head dropped back while her hips rocked against him. He'd never seen anyone so sensual, so wickedly sexy in his life. She was such a rare creature, one that he wasn't sure he could ever let go of.

That thought startled him since he'd made a point to never find himself in a relationship.

Then he stopped thinking altogether when her long, slim fingers wrapped around his cock. He watched as she held him and lowered herself.

He moaned at the feel of her slick folds enveloping him. His head dropped back, his eyes falling closed as she took him deeper, her tight walls gripping him.

The sensation was exquisite and poignant.

Once she had taken all of him, she rotated her hips. His lids snapped open because the passion was too great now. As they stared into each other's eyes, there was no denying the tangible need.

His breath left him in a rush as she leaned forward and began to move. He lifted his head and took a hard nipple into his mouth.

Her startled cry of pleasure urged him onward even as she increased her tempo. He licked and teased her nipple until she was jerking against him.

Then he moved to the other breast.

She trembled beneath his hands, her cries coming louder and faster. Suddenly, she sat up, dropping her head back as she rode him hard.

He gloried in the sight of her breasts swaying as the fire-light covered her. Her eyes were closed, her lips parted. A look of pleasure so intense, so pure shone on her face.

His chest clenched as he realized he had such a woman in his arms. How fucking lucky was he?

Powerless to keep his hands off her, he splayed his hand on her stomach and used his thumb to find her clit. Then he slowly circled the swollen nub.

Within moments, she shuddered and quaked as a climax tore through her, her walls clamping around his cock. He ground his teeth together, holding off his own orgasm.

He flipped her onto her back, and with her climax still pulsing, he braced a hand on either side of her head, pulled out of her, and thrust.

"Cullen!"

The sound of her screaming his name sent him over the edge. He moved his hips faster, plunging deep. He felt her jerk as another orgasm took her.

He looked down at her with her dark hair spread around her, her swollen lips parted, and her body flushed from pleasure. It was a sight he would never forget. It was branded into his memory forever.

She reached up and touched his face, something in her gaze that he didn't recognize—or didn't *want* to recognize. But the moment couldn't be forgotten.

Then her devilish grin appeared right before she locked her ankles around him and lifted her hips to meet his thrusts. That was all it took to send him over the edge.

He gave a final plunge, burying himself deep as the orgasm swept him away.

When he came to, he was lying on Mia's chest with her arms around him, gently caressing his back. Normally, this kind of affection sent him running away fast. This time, however, he didn't want to move.

It had nothing to do with the fact that there wasn't anywhere for him to go, or that he felt like he needed to protect her.

He didn't want to look too closely at the reasons he preferred to remain locked in her embrace. It was enough that he was content for the first time in his life.

It was a strange, astonishing feeling. He'd be lying if he said that Mia didn't perplex him on all levels. Yet he'd been unable to ignore the attraction or his need to have her.

Though he wasn't one to turn away a lover for the night, she was different.

And he felt different after being with her.

He couldn't explain what had changed, but it touched him all the way to his soul. It echoed through him, silencing the demons that had been with him for as long as he could remember.

When she kissed his forehead, he closed his eyes. It was time to stop thinking and wondering. It was time to enjoy the bliss that followed such amazing lovemaking.

Though he couldn't help but wonder what she might be thinking. Did she regret what had happened? Because he certainly didn't.

In fact, he was glad he had no choice but to stay near her. Another first for him.

Odd how that didn't bother him in the least.

CHAPTER TWENTY-TWO

Sklad . . .

The seconds ticked by in Orrin's head as he thought over everything Yuri had told him—and what he hadn't.

What did he believe? Did he dare to trust his old friend? Yuri's explanation sounded good, but that could be all it was. Then again, it might very well be the truth.

That was a sobering thought. A terrifying one, as well.

What he did know was that Yuri was scared. A bone-chilling, soul-deep fear that kept a man awake at night. It was that alone that prevented Orrin from dismissing Yuri's statements out of hand.

Orrin's thoughts shifted to Ragnarok. He rubbed his chest as he imagined the potential outcome if such a weapon were released. It didn't matter if it was a small village or an entire country—the results would be staggering.

The door opened to his room, and the doctor walked in. She kept her gaze averted from him as she moved her hair from behind her ear.

His mind was too occupied with everything to worry about why she wouldn't meet his gaze. He closed his eyes while she began her routine.

"There's a camera," she whispered. "In the left corner facing you."

He opened his eyes into slits to glance at her. She kept

her back toward where she'd said the camera was. Orrin thought back to when the soldiers had come in, and he was given something to knock him unconscious.

"They're watching everything."

Obviously. Was it Yuri, though? Or the Saints? He couldn't ask Yuri about it in case it was his doing. Then Yuri would know that she was talking to him.

Shit. He hated situations like this.

What to believe? Who to trust? One wrong move, and it could mean his life or his sons'. Too many people had died already, but he knew things weren't finished by far. More would die.

It was inevitable. A truth every man and woman in uniform understood. But people like the doctor didn't comprehend such things. Neither did Natalie.

He'd gotten Natalie involved, and Orrin would have to live with that. There were too many factors at work for him to feel confident about an outcome now.

"Orrin?"

The sound of her whisper dragged him from his thoughts. He grunted, letting her know he'd heard her words. There was a need swelling inside him to shield her and her son, but how could he when he couldn't help himself or his own family?

The helplessness that assaulted him was horrendous. He'd never felt anything like it before, and he loathed it. He couldn't wait until he could shake off the feeling and get back to doing what he was meant to do.

He wasn't surprised to find Yuri strolling into the room with two of his armed men beside him. Orrin opened his eyes and watched his old friend.

"How is he, Doc?" Yuri asked.

She closed the chart. "He has improved at a remarkable rate."

"Improved enough to return to his cell?" Yuri asked with a raised brow.

There was a bit of hesitation from her before she said, "I wouldn't recommend it. Not yet."

"It is . . . how do you say? Out of your hands," Yuri replied with a cold smile.

Orrin watched the exchange with interest. The doctor was trying to protect him the only way she could, but that time was over now. And in some ways, that was a good thing.

"You're right, Yuri." He waved his hand at the monitor and IV. "I no longer need any of this."

Which meant, Yuri could let the doc return to her life and her son.

Yuri nodded to the IV. "Unhook him."

Once more, he made sure not to look at the doctor, even as her hands shook while she removed the IV.

When he was freed from everything, Orrin threw off the covers and swung his legs over the side of the bed. His body twinged, but the pain wasn't as severe as he'd expected. Even his ribs didn't hurt as badly as they should. Then he looked at Yuri, waiting to see what would happen.

Yuri swung his gaze to the soldier on his left, the tall blond who always seemed to be about. The soldier left the room, only to return a second later with clothes and boots.

They were placed at the foot of the bed. Orrin stared at them. The only thing better than clean clothes would be a shower.

"Get dressed," Yuri ordered. "Come, Doctor."

Once everyone had departed, Orrin gingerly stood, testing his legs and the rest of his injuries. Whatever the doc had given him had rapidly helped him heal. And he was more than thankful.

He pulled on the olive green tee first. Then he removed

his dirty, bloody pants and reached for the tactical trousers. It wasn't easy fastening them with his broken wrist. Then came the boots. It wasn't until he'd grabbed them that he saw the fresh pair of socks.

Wiggling his toes against the cold tile, Orrin sat back on the bed and put on the socks and shoes. By the time he'd finished, his wrist throbbed, his broken ribs made it impossible to breathe deeply, and any movement caused pain.

But it wasn't the first time he'd had broken ribs in a combat situation.

He was still sitting on the bed, attempting to push the pain down when the door swung open, and Yuri filled the doorway. Yuri looked him over before he motioned for Orrin to follow with a tilt of his head.

Orrin rose and trailed Yuri, expecting that he would return to the small, damp prison he'd originally been in. He wasn't wrong.

The door slammed shut behind him. He turned but found himself alone. Just what was Yuri up to?

It was several hours later before Yuri returned. To Orrin's surprise, there were no soldiers with him. While Yuri leaned back against the door, Orrin got to his feet.

They stared at each other for a long while. Then Yuri said, "Your youngest is in Delaware."

He'd anticipated that at least one of them would return to the last place he'd been seen. A smile threatened as he imagined Cullen and Mia together. Both could be reckless, but they would work well together.

"I'm sure you predicted that."

Yuri shrugged. "A decision needs to be made. My loyalty to the Saints has come into question."

"Is that why I was drugged? What did they do in that room I was in?"

"Installed a camera."

So maybe it wasn't Yuri. Orrin still wasn't completely sure yet. It could all be a trick. "To watch me?"

"To make sure I am doing my job."

"There could be a camera in here."

Yuri gave a single shake of his head. "There is not. I checked."

"So what now?"

"Now, we decide what to do. You say Ragnarok is somewhere no one can get it. That is good to know, but it does not stop everything else. The scientist who made Ragnarok, Jankovic, can make more."

Orrin moved slowly, so as not to aggravate his injuries. "He needs to be found."

"And the Saints stopped."

"Agreed. How do we do that?"

Yuri smiled slowly. "We leave here, of course."

"Of course." It wouldn't be nearly that easy. "And your men?"

"Are still mine. There are several of the Saints' men here, though."

"Watching and listening," he said with a nod.

Yuri pushed away from the door and walked to Orrin. "We leave in the night."

"If you leave your men behind, they'll be killed."

"There is an exit strategy I put into place before we left Moscow. They will split up, depart separately."

Orrin leaned against the wall. "How will they return to Russia?"

"A man named Sergei Chzov."

Orrin didn't bother to tell Yuri that he knew Sergei. Though that was only because of Mia. Whenever someone told Mia it was impossible, she made sure that it wasn't. Many had told her it was impossible to get involved with

Chzov if you didn't have Russian roots. And yet Mia had developed a bond with Sergei.

Orrin said, "You need to let the doctor go."

"Already done. I no longer need her services."

He felt better knowing she was away from Yuri. Still, he was going to miss those gray eyes of hers and that amazing red hair.

"She demanded to know what I had done with you. Can you believe that?" Yuri asked with a snort.

He smiled because he could. "What did you tell her?"

"To leave well enough alone."

If they left, he was going to have to get her a message not to contact the government. Not yet anyway. There was too much he and Yuri had to do before anyone discovered what they were up to.

"Can you do what is needed?"

He shot Yuri a hard look. "What the hell is that supposed to mean?"

"You are hurt."

"I've had worse." A lot worse, actually.

Yuri's grin held a note of misery. "We are not as young as we used to be."

That was for sure. Even ten years ago, Orrin would've bounced back quickly from such a beating. But he wouldn't be feeling as good as he was if it weren't for whatever the doc had given him.

"I'll do what I have to do. It's what I've always done."

"*Da*. You and me both," Yuri said. He pulled a gun from the back of the waist of his pants and held it out, butt first, to Orrin. "We will have to leave quickly."

Orrin grasped the warm metal of the Glock, the weight familiar—and welcome. "I'll be ready."

After Yuri had left, Orrin put his back to the wall and

slowly lowered himself to the floor. There were so many things that could go wrong.

He had no idea of their exact location or the layout of the building. That meant Orrin had to trust Yuri. There was no other choice. If he wanted out, he had to follow his old friend.

Just because he was willing to work with Yuri now didn't mean he trusted him. In fact, Orrin didn't. There was some truth to what Yuri had told him, but there were other parts that he wasn't so sure about.

From the very beginning, nearly thirty years ago, when he and Yuri had first met, they'd had a contentious relationship. Their friendship would begin to strengthen, and then something would make one of them mistrust the other, destroying whatever had begun.

It was a bitter circle they had never been able to halt. The current situation changed things a little, but not nearly enough.

Yet Orrin knew there would come a point in the very near future when he would have to decide whether to trust everything Yuri said—or walk away.

In this cat and mouse game, he would have to keep his wits about him at all times and trust his instincts. They had gotten him out of bad situations before.

He'd be calling on them soon because Orrin was determined to see his sons again. He wanted to see Callie, Natalie, and Mia, as well.

There was so much he hadn't told his sons. He'd always thought there would be time. However, time was running out.

And he still hadn't caught Melanie's killer. He'd vowed to find the bastard, and if it was the last thing Orrin did, he would do that for his beloved wife.

CHAPTER TWENTY-THREE

Mia stretched, missing Cullen's warmth. She yawned and opened her eyes to find him putting more wood on the fire. He turned his head to her and grinned.

That crooked smile made her stomach flutter. She held out her hand for him, which he took. Then she pulled him back toward her.

A long breath left him as he lay on his back and brought her against him. They hadn't spoken since making love, and in truth, she wasn't so sure she wanted any words to shatter whatever was happening between them.

It was an illusion, she knew. One that would be broken shortly when they left the cabin. But for every heartbeat they had, she held to it tightly.

"The sun will be up soon," he said, putting his other arm behind his head.

She tried not to be disappointed, but couldn't quite manage it. "I know."

"I don't want to leave either."

Her eyes closed. If only she could make the world stand still. But it wasn't fair for her and Cullen to find any sort of pleasure when Orrin suffered.

Cullen's fingers slid through her hair. He was everything that she had expected and more. His hands had played her body with skillful fingers, bringing her to heights she hadn't known existed.

The way they'd lain in each other's arms afterward had been amazing. It wasn't just because her body hummed with ecstasy. Something had happened. It hung in the air, surrounding them.

She worried that in that one night, he might have stolen her heart. Of course, she wouldn't say anything. It wouldn't be wise. Not now, at least.

Mia placed a kiss on his chest and sat up. His hand grabbed hers before she could rise. When she looked at him, his brow was furrowed in thought.

She waited for him to speak, to tell her what was on his mind. Finally, she rose to her feet. And this time, he didn't stop her.

While she showered, she wondered what he'd wanted to say. Had he wanted to tell her it was a casual thing between them?

It was how she'd pegged him from the start. Unfortunately, she didn't do casual. She was all in or not at all.

She finished her shower quickly. When she walked into the bedroom where she kept some clothes, she heard him up and moving about.

Mia found a pair of khaki cargos and a long-sleeved black henley shirt. After she'd put her hair in a ponytail, she returned to the living room to tug on her boots.

When she'd finished, she looked up to find Cullen holding out the jacket she had left in the cabin. She accepted it with a smile. While she put on the coat, he doused the fire.

She took one last look around the place, her gaze lingering on the floor before the fireplace while she tucked her guns and knives in place. She'd never be able to be here again and not think of Cullen.

"Ready?" he asked from behind her.

She turned to see him at the door, waiting for her. "Yes. Let's go."

They walked from the cabin into the stillness of the early morning. She saw a glimpse of soft gray sky as the sun began its ascent.

"Where do you think we'll find Yuri?" she asked a little later.

Cullen jumped from an outcropping of rock to the ground two feet below. "Sergei might know," he said and turned to help her.

She smiled at him, ignoring his hand as she jumped down beside him. "Are all you Texas boys so chivalrous?"

"Afraid so, darlin'. It's in the water."

Unable to help herself, she laughed softly. He really made her want to see Texas, specifically the Loughman Ranch.

They set off together again, winding through the trees, keeping far from any trails. Her thoughts turned to Sergei, and the potential problems a visit to him might cause.

"Sergei warned us not to return," she said.

Cullen briefly met her gaze. "If you can think of another option, I'm open."

"I can't."

"Then I can't see that we have any other choice. Sergei will either know how to get ahold of Yuri or can lead us to him."

"If he will," she added. "You're assuming Sergei will help. You saw him the last time. He wants no part in this."

Cullen moved a branch out of the way, ducking as he walked under it. "Sergei Chzov has a soft spot for you."

She shook her head. "Absolutely not. I'm not going to use that."

"The last time we visited, everyone saw us enter and

leave. This time, we need to get to him without any of the others seeing us."

He'd lost his mind. She was sure of it. "You were at the same building at the docks that I was, right? You saw all his men, the guns?"

"I did."

"How do you expect us to get past them without anyone alerting Sergei?"

Cullen's hazel eyes held a mischievous glint. "His home, of course."

"Of course," she repeated, shaking her head. "That's even more of a fortress."

Before she could blink, he'd stopped and had her pinned against a tree. His face lowered so that his lips brushed hers seductively.

Her body heated rapidly at the feel of his hard muscles. She gripped his arms, afraid that he would back away yet afraid that he wouldn't.

She wanted his kiss, longed for it with a hunger that startled her. Her sex clenched, aching to feel him inside her. After one night, she was addicted.

Completely, utterly obsessed.

"Do you trust me?" he whispered.

Her eyes met his. "Yes."

His response was a slow smile before his lips moved over hers. She leaned her head to the side and parted her lips. Their tongues met, danced as a groan rumbled in his chest.

The call of a hawk reminded her where they were. The kiss ended and he rested his forehead against hers. For several minutes, they remained that way.

"Damn, but I ache for you," he murmured.

It felt like a flight of birds had taken off in her stomach. She touched his face and leaned her head back. "Me, too."

He took a step away, clearing his throat. "We should keep moving."

"Yeah."

She wasn't sure what was wrong with her. She'd never acted like this with anyone before. The desire was so thick, so overwhelming, that it was all she could think about.

It only grew now that she knew what it was to be loved by Cullen. The idea that he could want her as frantically as she did him made her almost giddy.

And giddy was something she'd never been in her life. Even as a little girl.

He threw everything out of whack. She was off balance around him. He turned her world upside down and around, and she kept coming back for more. Was she a glutton for punishment?

She must be, because she couldn't get enough of him.

He moved ahead of her in a narrow spot, allowing her to get a look at his fine ass. She knew his body, knew the feel of those muscles moving beneath her hand, bunching and shifting. She'd felt the strength and tenderness.

Wearing clothes and without, there wasn't a man who could compare. Cullen Loughman was so different from any man she knew. Perhaps that was the appeal.

Or maybe she just had a soft spot for a Texas drawl. All she knew was that she liked being with him.

"You told me your secret last night," he said.

She frowned, wondering at the unease in his voice. "I did."

"You were right. Everyone has secrets."

"What's yours?"

He stopped and faced her, swallowing as he met her gaze. "It's one I've never told anyone."

"I'll never repeat it."

"It's not going to matter much longer, anyway. I'm sure in the time you spent with Orrin he talked about how every man in the Loughman family has served his country."

She nodded, slowly. "He did."

"Dad never forced it on us, but we all knew it was expected. At least, I felt that way. Both Wyatt and Owen couldn't wait to join."

"And you weren't so keen," she guessed as it all came together.

"All I wanted was to stay at the ranch and run it. I was good at it. You say being a pilot was your calling. Ranching is mine."

"You joined the Marines anyway. You didn't have to. Orrin wouldn't have said anything to you."

"I know," Cullen said quickly. "After I joined, I didn't even have to try very hard. It all came so easily. And when I did put everything into it . . . I didn't fail. Not once."

She closed the distance between them and linked her fingers with his. "How is it going to end soon?"

"I'm resigning my commission after we find Dad. I'm going back to the ranch where I've always belonged."

Hazel eyes searched her face. She smiled up at him, giving him her full support. "You've continued the tradition of your family and served your country with honor. There's nothing disgraceful about doing what you want to do now."

His shoulders relaxed, and a smile pulled at his lips. As if he'd been relieved of a thousand pounds upon his shoulders, he continued walking with a renewed purpose.

She couldn't imagine how long he'd been holding that secret. But he was free of it now. He was also free to do whatever he wanted.

Unfortunately, she didn't think she would be a part of his future.

They reached the Jeep. He tossed her the keys as they both climbed inside. She started the engine and turned on the heater. She rubbed her hands together for warmth before she put the vehicle in drive and drove over the rugged terrain for three miles until they reached the road.

"You weren't kidding that you hid the Jeep," she said with a smile.

He chuckled and held onto the handle above the door. "I wasn't going to take any chances."

"You did that in the dark in a place you hadn't been before. Impressive."

"Thanks."

She glanced at him, sharing a smile. She was impressed. Was there nothing Cullen couldn't do? She didn't like being told something was impossible, but to him, that word didn't exist.

They had been on the road for a few minutes when he said, "Is there a way you can get a message to Sergei?"

"I think so. Is that how you're going to get us inside his home?"

"Yes, ma'am. He won't refuse you. Once inside, with none of his men listening, he might help us."

She kept the Jeep at a steady speed as she navigated the sharp turns of the mountain. "I hope you're right."

"Me, too."

She looked in her rearview mirror and saw a fast approaching black Suburban. "I believe we have company."

He turned around and looked behind him. "Shit."

"What do I do?"

"Get us off this damn mountain."

She sped up, trying to keep distance between the SUV

and them. When a second Suburban joined the chase, her heart began thumping against her ribs.

The sound of a gunshot had her ducking her head. Cullen muttered curses as he drew out his gun and rolled down the window. Then he unbuckled his seatbelt and leaned out, his gun pointed behind them as he began firing.

The exchange of bullets only worsened the situation. She was a good driver, but the Jeep wasn't a plane. She couldn't control it as she did her aircraft.

The second SUV zoomed forward, coming even with them and slamming into her. She looked into the vehicle beside her and saw the gun pointed in her direction.

Cullen's hand grabbed her shoulder, pushing her back. A second later, her window exploded. She turned her head away from the flying glass while Cullen emptied more bullets into the SUV beside them.

When she righted herself, the Suburban had backed off, but the men in the first vehicle were still firing at them. It would only be a matter of time before a bullet found either her or Cullen.

"Fuck," Cullen muttered as he ducked back into the vehicle and ejected his clip before slamming another into his gun. Then he was leaning back out his window, trying to hit the Suburban behind them.

"Who are these people?" she asked.

He hurriedly ducked back inside the Jeep as several guns went off, spraying the vehicle. "The Saints found us."

That's what she'd suspected. Damn, didn't these people have lives? Was it luck that allowed the Saints to find them? Or did the group have men posted all around the mountain?

A third SUV pulled out as they raced past a secluded road.

"Watch it!" Cullen yelled in warning.

Mia saw the two SUVs come up on either side of them. They slammed into the Jeep on both sides. She tried to keep control of the vehicle, but the Suburbans had more power.

They suddenly pulled away just as the third SUV rammed the Jeep from behind. The second hit was directed at the left bumper, sending them spinning.

She saw the edge of the road coming. There was no way she would get control of the Jeep before they went over the edge. As if in slow motion, she turned her head and met Cullen's gaze.

And then they went over the side.

CHAPTER TWENTY-FOUR

For a second or two, Cullen stared at Mia, her dark eyes wide with fear. As the Jeep pitched forward, he saw the trees and mountain rushing past so quickly that it looked like a mix of black and green.

Then came the first jarring hit.

He was thrown forward against the dash, slamming his head into it. Pain exploded, but it was drowned out by the loud splintering of the windshield.

The deafening—and sickening—sound of metal crunching filled his ears from the Jeep landing on its nose.

He reached for Mia, trying to grab her hand. She was still fastened in her seatbelt, which kept her secure in her seat. He wasn't so lucky. Her arms were raised in an effort to block her face from the glass. His fingers brushed her hand, but he wasn't able to grab hold.

A creak of metal was all the warning he had before the Jeep fell to the side with a jolting thud. Glass rained down upon him once more. A heartbeat later, he was thrown about when the vehicle began rolling down the mountain.

He lost count of how many times he collided with something, helplessly flung this way and that. Until finally—blessedly—the vehicle came to a stop.

His ears rang, his head felt as if had been used as a

soccer ball, and there was blood dripping into his eyes. There wasn't time to think of his injuries because the men after them would arrive soon.

He blinked, wiping the back of his hand across his forehead. It came away covered in red. Damn.

A glance around showed that the Jeep had landed on its roof, and he was somewhere between the dash and windshield. He turned his head toward Mia and found her hanging upside down. Several small cuts were on her face from all the glass, but he didn't see any other blood.

That was a small comfort after what they'd just endured. With a grimace, he shifted, only to find that he had somehow held onto his gun. He tucked it into the waistband of his pants and made his way to Mia.

Her seatbelt was jammed. He blew out a frustrated breath because he wasn't moving as fast as he wanted or needed to. Reaching down, he pulled out the knife from his boot. Then he quickly cut the seatbelt, catching her in his arms when she fell. He checked her pulse, finding it steady and strong. Relief surged through him.

As expected, his door wouldn't open. It took him several kicks before it swung wide. He held her tighter and scooted out of the Jeep. Once free, he looked up to see how far they'd tumbled.

The distance was vast, making it difficult for the men to reach them. That would give them some time. He stood and hurried to some trees where he laid Mia on the ground. There was no way he could cover any type of distance in his condition while carrying her.

But he wasn't going to allow them to be caught either. He reached for his phone, but his pocket was empty. He hurried back to the SUV and found his cell smashed to pieces. Hopefully, Mia's was around somewhere.

He began to search but heard distant voices approaching,

speaking both American and Russian. His mind raced with different possibilities, various methods of getting away. That's when he heard the sound of something dripping onto the ground.

A quick look confirmed that the gas tank had been struck by a bullet, which compromised the integrity. The tumble down the mountain had only made things worse.

Cullen looked to the front of the vehicle when he spotted smoke and saw that the engine was on fire. It was only a matter of time before the flames and the fumes from the gas tank collided.

He turned and ran to Mia, slipping on the uneven terrain of the sloped earth. Cullen paused long enough to grab her and turn to shield her.

The explosion was deafening, giving him little time to prepare before the blast slammed into his back, pushing him forward. He shifted at the last minute so he didn't land on her. When he caught his breath, he lifted his head to see the fire flaring high into the sky.

He covered Mia with his body to protect her from the debris that had begun to plummet back to Earth. It was over quickly, but then came the sounds of men rushing toward the Jeep.

Cullen pushed himself to his knees, and once more lifted Mia into his arms. Pain shot through his arm and side, but he ignored it and staggered to his feet. Then he put one foot in front of the other.

He didn't know how long he walked. The sun was bright, blinding him, even through the trees. He no longer heard the men, but that didn't mean the Saints had stopped looking.

It only meant they had a reprieve.

He found a secluded spot of boulders and trees. There,

he dropped down to one knee and set Mia down. It worried him that she still hadn't gained consciousness. He touched her face with bloody, dirty fingers.

With a twist of his lips, he sank to the ground and rested against one of the trees. For several minutes, he simply sat there, giving himself time to rest. Gingerly, he felt along the top of his right shoulder and gritted his teeth when he found the wound.

Since he couldn't look at it, he hoped the bullet had gone through. Otherwise, someone was going to have to dig the slug out. His gaze swung to Mia.

If she didn't wake soon, they both would need medical attention. As long as they could find a car soon, he would be able to tend to his wound with just a stop at a store.

Then he recalled the pull in his side. He looked to his left side and saw his shirt soaked with blood. Carefully, he tugged it away from the wound, the sucking sound sickening. The sight of the laceration made their situation more precarious.

He pressed against it, hoping to staunch the flow of blood. He hissed in a breath at the sting. The cut needed to be stitched immediately. The more blood he lost, the weaker he'd become.

They had passed homes on their blistering ride down the mountain before the crash, but that was farther up than he wanted to climb. Not to mention the danger of the men after them.

Russian and American. The Saints. Who were these fuckers? They were relentless, which meant they would look for bodies at the crash site. When they didn't find any, the hunt would be on again.

He just needed to rest for a little bit more. Then he would carry Mia out of there.

* * *

Mia grabbed her head as soon as she regained consciousness. She curled in on herself, trying to stop the hammering. Had she crashed her plane?

Her eyes flew open as it all came back to her. She'd crashed all right, but not her plane. The Jeep.

With her heart slamming against her chest, she jerked upright, her hand on her head. She looked around. Her vehicle was nowhere in sight, but she was still on the mountain.

She dropped her hand and moved her legs to get to her knees, and that's when her foot hit something. Her mind went blank when she spotted Cullen lying half on his side. She went to touch him but hesitated when she saw the blood.

"Oh, no. Nonononononono," she said with a shake of her head.

He must've carried her from the crash. And that meant the men were still after them. There was no way she could lug him very far.

The injury on his side was bleeding badly. She jerked off her jacket, wincing at the pain. Every time she moved, it hurt, but her injuries were minor compared to his wounds. The pains of her body were ignored as she turned her full attention to Cullen.

She pulled off her shirt and used her knife to cut it in half. With one side, she looped the shirt under his arm and up and over his shoulder to tie it. Then she cut part of the other half of the shirt into a long strip.

The rest she bunched together and put against the cut on his side. Using the last piece of her shirt, she managed to get it underneath him and around to tie tightly.

It wasn't perfect, but it would help to staunch the blood

for a little while. There were supplies for just such an event at the cabin, but they couldn't go back there now.

She put her jacket on and zipped it. She stood and moved out of the shelter of the grove of trees and the boulders to get an idea of where they were.

Cullen had walked them west instead of south. Hopefully, the Saints would assume they were on their way down the mountain. That would give them some more time, but not much.

She turned and felt something in her coat. When she searched, she found the burner phone. Her gaze went to Cullen.

They couldn't stay on the mountain. Nor could they remain where they were. The men would find them soon enough, and quite frankly, she didn't want any of them near her.

There was only one decision. She looked at the cell phone in her hand and blew out a breath. Then she dialed a number. It rang twice before the call was answered.

"Hey," she said. "It's me. I need your help."

There was a long pause. Then Sergei said, "This is not your phone."

"I had to get another. I was being tracked."

"By who?"

She licked her lips, unwilling to say the name over the phone. "You know who."

"Where are you?"

"Somewhere on Backbone Mountain." She blew out a breath. "We were run off the road. I must have hit my head when we went over the side."

Sergei began bellowing for Lev. Then he brought the phone back to his ear. "Are you hurt?"

"Some bruises and a bump on the head. It's Cullen

who's injured. He's been shot, and there's a cut that won't stop bleeding. He's unconscious now." She swallowed and turned to face Cullen. "I know you didn't want to be involved, but I didn't know who else to turn to."

"Are you hidden?"

"Yes."

His voice became muffled as he spoke to Lev. Then Sergei told her, "Stay where you are. I'll be there as quickly as I can."

"They're here," she warned.

"They are everywhere, *Dochenka Moya*."

The line disconnected. She glanced at the time on the phone. It had only been two hours since they'd left the cabin. At least she didn't have to worry about being on the mountain during the night.

She returned the phone to her pocket. Her plane was several miles on the other side of the mountain. There was no getting to it. Besides, the Saints probably had it surrounded so she couldn't get to it.

Mia walked back to Cullen and sat beside him. She saw the glass in his hair and began to pick it out. Then she touched her hair and felt the shards.

Not only had he not been wearing his seatbelt during the crash, but he'd also managed to carry her away even after sustaining serious injuries.

She couldn't imagine the pain he'd been in while doing all of that. He'd saved her life. And now she was going to save his.

Taking out the gun, she rested it on her thigh. She wasn't going to be caught off guard by the Saints again. They'd gotten lucky earlier. Had she been in the air, her plane under her control, it would've been them who crashed.

Three SUVs had been waiting for them. General Davis and Sergei were right. The Saints were everywhere. She was taking a chance that Sergei wasn't one of them, but she didn't have much of a choice.

Cullen needed to be patched up. She was going to see to that as soon as they were off the mountain.

"Hurry, Sergei," she whispered when she brushed Cullen's forehead and felt the warmth beneath her palm.

CHAPTER TWENTY-FIVE

Danger! There's danger approaching!

Cullen came awake, instantly alert and grabbing for his pistol with his left hand. He lifted the weapon, aiming it at the area before him while he glanced around for Mia.

She wasn't there. Worry sliced through him, sharp and sizzling. Then he saw the trampled ground around him. She had moved about several times. Just how long had he been unconscious?

He recognized his makeshift bandage as her shirt, so at least she was all right. If only he knew where she was.

A look at his watch confirmed over five hours had passed since he'd lost consciousness. Five hours where anything could've happened. His arm began to shake. He lowered it, blood loss making it difficult to keep his strength.

It looked as though luck was on their side. For the moment. How long that would last, no one could know. He'd seen it come and go as fleetingly as the wind.

Perhaps Mia was looking for water. There was no way the men after them would take her and leave him behind. Unless she tried to lead them away from him.

That thought terrified him. He began to rise into a sitting position when he heard something. Immediately, he lifted his arm, ready to fire at anyone other than Mia.

The face that appeared wasn't her, but he recognized the bright blue gaze staring back at him. That didn't mean he was going to lower his gun, however.

Lev lifted his hands, his gun dangling from his middle finger. "Easy, Cullen."

"Turn around," Mia said behind Lev.

The Russian, and *Brigadier* to Sergei, flattened his lips in frustration. Then he slowly shifted to the side and turned his head to Mia. "You asked for help."

"I called Sergei."

Cullen frowned. She'd called Sergei? Of course, she had. With his injuries, and the Saints, she'd turned to someone who had the wherewithal to help.

Lev briefly swung his eyes to Cullen. "And Sergei sent me."

"He didn't tell me you were coming," she stated in an icy tone.

The *Brigadier* lifted one shoulder in a shrug. "He heard your fear and wanted you found quickly."

Cullen's arm began to shake. His breathing was labored, and he kept blinking, hoping the black dots in his vision would go away. Instead, they doubled.

He gave a little shake of his head to clear it. Mia knew just as he did that they should be careful who they trusted. Then again, there weren't that many options available.

"Do you have supplies?" Cullen asked before he blacked out.

Lev removed the backpack and dropped it. "Everything you'll need is in there."

Good. That was exactly what he wanted to hear. Now they could send Lev away and not have to worry about it.

It became more and more challenging for Cullen to hold

up his arm. The pistol felt as if it weighed a hundred times more than it really did. Sweat and blood rolled into his eyes, stinging them.

The blackness was creeping around the edges of his vision, but he fought to remain awake. He rolled to the side and felt thick, warm blood run down his back from his wound.

He looked to Mia. As he opened his mouth to tell her to send Lev away, the blackness took him.

Mia kept her gun trained on Lev as she rushed past him to Cullen. The blood was flowing in thick rivulets. A sick feeling began twisting her stomach.

"He needs attention now," Lev said.

A decision needed to be made right then. Because in order to help Cullen, she'd have to set down her gun. It was trust Lev, or let Cullen die.

With a sigh, she put her gun away and motioned to the backpack. "Hurry."

Lev jumped into action. He grabbed the pack and knelt on the other side of Cullen. While she pulled up Cullen's shirt encrusted with blood, Lev set out various items from the backpack.

She bit her lip when she saw the blood-soaked remnants of her shirt. It was too much blood loss. His skin was sallow, and his body burned.

"We'll get him fixed," Lev said matter-of-factly.

She wanted his certainty. She tried to hold it within her heart, but the worry smothered it.

Lev jerked his chin to the laceration. "This wound seems to be the worst. Let's get it tended before we move to his shoulder and the smaller cuts."

She didn't care what he did, as long as it got done. After Lev had cleaned out the deep cut, he handed her a package of Quick Clot. She hurriedly tore it open and poured it into Cullen's wound. Within seconds, it acted, slowing the flow of blood.

Meanwhile, Lev pulled out a field surgical kit. He readied things to stitch Cullen while she wiped away the blood to better see the injury.

Just as Lev began to make the first stitch, she stopped him with a hand on his arm. She took the needle from him and got to her feet.

"Switch with me. You can see to the bullet wound while I stitch him."

He gave her a nod and rose without a word. Once she sat on Cullen's left side, she drew in a shuddering breath and pierced his skin with the curved needle.

Time seemed to stand still while she slowly stitched the long gash. When she finally knotted the end, she was praying. It wasn't something she did often. She always thought others had bigger problems than her own, so why bother God.

This time was different. Because they were being hunted by men who had unlimited access to everything. Because other lives depended on them.

Because it was Cullen.

She tried to pretend that she cared as she would with anyone who braved this adventure with her. But she knew that for the lie it was.

"The bullet went through," Lev said. "I've cleaned the front, but his back needs tending."

Nodding, she helped roll Cullen toward her. Lev busied himself with the wound, and between handing him items, Mia found herself staring at Cullen.

She touched his jaw and wished that he would open his eyes. Maybe it was a blessing that he was unconscious and couldn't feel what they were doing.

Lev soon completed his task, swiftly and efficiently wrapping a bandage around both sides of Cullen's shoulder.

"You've had some practice," she replied.

He didn't look up when he said, "I thought about being a doctor."

Before she could respond to the startling declaration, Lev moved on to wrapping a bandage around Cullen's abdomen and the wound she'd stitched.

"He needs fluids, which I'll give him once we're safe," Lev said.

She looked around. "And how do you propose we get out of here? On your invisible jet?"

He threw a hard look her way. Then he took out his cell phone and pushed one button in a text.

"What was that?" she demanded.

"Sergei made sure the men after you went the opposite direction. That way, we can get the two of you out. I didn't know how severe Cullen's wounds were when you called. Precautions were put into place in case we couldn't all walk out of here."

She rubbed her forehead, feeling like an idiot. All she'd done was think the worst while Sergei and Lev had thought of things she hadn't.

"I'm sorry," she said. "I'm a little paranoid."

"It's better to be suspicious than trusting."

In all the time she'd spent with Sergei, she couldn't remember Lev speaking much—if at all. Now that she wasn't focused on Cullen, she noticed that there was very little accent in his speech.

Nor did he talk in the same patterns as Sergei and the other Russians. Lev spoke more . . . American.

He caught her staring. "What's on your mind, Carter?"

"You don't have much of an accent."

"That's because I was raised on the east coast."

Now that shocked her. Not only had he gone to college to be a doctor, but he hadn't been raised in Russia.

He gave a snort as he shook his head and climbed to his feet before gathering the medical supplies and placing them in the backpack. "Do you think everyone who works for Sergei grew up in Russia and came here just for him?"

"Well . . . yeah," she admitted.

Lev paused, a smile curving his lips. "Actually, that's true in every case except me."

"What's different about you?"

The smile faded quickly. "A lot."

She took in his wintery gaze, the firm set of his wide, thin lips, and the hard line of his jaw. There was a dark history he kept firmly hidden.

Lev was tall, muscular, and quite handsome. It was the ominous cloud of death that hung around him like a mantle that put everyone on edge.

Though it made him the perfect *Brigadier*.

Lev zipped the backpack and tossed it at her. "Sergei is putting his life at risk for you."

"Which you don't like."

"No. I don't. I told him not to get involved, but he won't listen to reason when it comes to you. There are dozens of women out there who would do anything for Sergei to give them the attention he does you."

She took immediate offense. "I never asked for special treatment."

"That and the fact that you look a lot like his dead daughter are what singles you out."

She saw the fury in his gaze. "You don't like me."

"If something happens to Sergei because of you, I'll kill you myself."

"If you do your job, nothing will happen," she retorted.

He didn't reply, simply checked Cullen's bandages before he got to his feet and looked around.

She took Cullen's hand in her own, feeling better just touching him. "If you hate me so, why are you helping?" she asked Lev.

"Sergei requested it of me."

His loyalty to the *Pakhan* was there in every syllable. Just as she'd started to warm to Lev, he'd let her know his true feelings. Now, she might not like him, but she respected him.

"They're coming," Lev said and turned toward her.

She stopped him before he could lift Cullen. "Do you trust these men?"

"Yes." Lev held her gaze. "If I find one of them betrays us to the Saints, the law, or anyone else, I'll rip their tongue out before killing them. Slowly."

There wasn't a word he said that she doubted. Lev hadn't gotten the position of *Brigadier* easily. He'd killed people. All in the name of loyalty and the protection of Sergei.

"Are you coming?" Lev asked.

She tightened her grip on Cullen's hand. She hoped she was making the right decision. For Cullen, for herself, and for Orrin. "Yes."

Without another word, Lev took Cullen's arms and pulled him into a sitting position. Then he lifted him over one shoulder.

She took Cullen's dropped gun and jumped to her feet, slinging the backpack over one arm. Lev's long strides ate up the distance, causing her to jog to catch up.

They came out of the trees just as a motorcycle came into view. Behind it was an ATV.

CHAPTER TWENTY-SIX

Cullen clawed his way from the darkness, struggling to reach Mia. He didn't know if she was safe. His aches didn't matter. The pain he could deal with.

But when his body wouldn't do as he demanded, that's when he wanted to bellow with rage.

He fought to open his eyes. The more he struggled, the more it felt as if someone had sealed them shut. Then he heard it. Mia's voice. It was from a distance, and thankfully, she didn't sound distressed.

If only he could see her.

If only he could touch her.

He came to again. The throbbing in his shoulder and side were the first things that assaulted him. He began to sink back into unconsciousness when he thought of Mia.

No matter how he strained, he couldn't hear her. Panic seized him. Was she hurt? Had they taken her? Did she need help?

He fought with everything he had to open his eyes. It was maddening to not be able to control his body as needed. The only other time he'd ever felt so . . . helpless . . . was the day his mother died.

He'd sworn never to be in that predicament again. And yet, here he was.

No!

As if the bellow that reverberated through his head had unlocked something, he managed to open one eye a slit. It was just enough to be blinded by a light, causing his lid to shut instantly.

That small fight cost him dearly as the darkness swallowed him once again.

Cullen didn't know how long it had been since he'd last regained consciousness. This time, he intended to do whatever it took to open both eyes.

It took a few tries, but finally, his eyelids parted. Once more, the light blinded him. He turned his head to the side, shutting his eyes for a moment to protect them.

Then he opened them again.

His chest heaved with the effort that took. It was several blinks before his eyes began to focus.

As things came into view, he saw a window covered with thick curtains of deep burgundy. In front of the window was a leather wing-backed chair with a small table next to it.

His gaze moved farther down the wall, and he spotted an armoire. Then he saw the thick wood of the four-poster bed at his feet.

Cullen's eyes slid shut on their own, the weight of them too heavy. But he forced them open again. His head rolled to the other side. He forgot about the room when he looked out the doorway and saw Mia.

She leaned over a table, looking at something sprawled before her. A map? He couldn't see who she spoke with. The only thing that calmed him was the knowledge that she hadn't been harmed.

Something moved to block his vision. He attempted to see what it was, but his body had other ideas.

"Easy, Loughman," said a male voice.

He recognized it, but couldn't place it.

"She's safe. For now."

It was the last thing he heard as he sank into oblivion.

Cullen's mind was much clearer when he came to again. He remained still, listening. It was quiet. There were no sounds around him, which led him to believe he was alone.

He took stock of his injuries. His shoulder twinged a bit, but the pain was manageable. It was the wound on his side that would make things difficult. Even so, he'd suffered worse.

No longer did he feel so lethargic. Probably due to the pain meds wearing off. It would allow him to move easier without having his reactions dulled. Approaching voices caught his attention. By the sound of footsteps, there were at least three people, possibly four.

His hands itched to have a weapon fitted in his palm. The comforting weight of his pistol would give him security in a situation like this.

"You do not know what you ask," came a voice with a Russian accent.

Cullen knew that voice. He was sorting through who it could be in his mind when he heard another voice that halted all thoughts. Mia.

"I know exactly what I ask," she said.

"*Dochenka Moya*, you just speculate," Sergei argued.

She blew out a breath. "We've been over this for the past two days. I know what I'm doing."

Cullen's eyes opened, and his head turned of its own accord toward the sound of her voice. Relief poured through him when his gaze landed on her.

She was in a new set of clothes. The white shirt molded to her full breasts, making his mouth water as he recalled holding them in his hands and teasing her.

Suddenly, her head swung to him. Their eyes met, and a bright smile lit up her face. "Cullen," she whispered and rushed to him.

The feel of her hand in his when she reached the bed caused him to grin. It felt amazing to be touching her again. He told himself it was because he'd feared she was hurt.

But he knew it meant something far deeper.

"Where I am?" he asked.

She looked over her shoulder as Sergei and Lev walked into the room. When she faced Cullen once again, the smile was still there. "This place is up for foreclosure. Sergei found it and thought it would be a good location to hide us for a bit."

Cullen's gaze shifted to the Russian. "Smart thinking. Thank you for the assistance."

"You needed it," Sergei said as he moved to stand at the foot of the bed. "If Lev had not arrived when he did, you would have bled out."

He met Lev's ice blue eyes. "I owe you thanks, as well."

"Not at all." Lev's mouth said one thing, but his gaze said something else altogether as he crossed his arms over his chest.

A silent exchange passed between them. One day, Lev would call in a favor, and Cullen was honor bound to do whatever he asked.

"How do you feel?" Mia asked.

He was happy to pull his thoughts away from Lev and focus on her face. "Good."

"That's all due to Lev. He patched you up on the mountain, but once we were here, he worked his magic."

Great. Cullen owed him even more. "Thank you," he said to Lev.

The *Brigadier* lifted one side of his mouth in a grin. "It was Mia who stitched you."

Cullen squeezed her hand. "Were you injured?"

"Only minor cuts."

Sergei made a grunting sound. "You had a concussion."

"What?" He searched her face, looking for any signs of illness.

She rolled her eyes. "I'm fine. Lev gave me the okay."

His gaze narrowed on the *Brigadier*, causing Lev's smile to grow.

"The seatbelt saved her," Lev said. "You might want to use one next time."

"He was shooting at the men chasing us," she stated in a chilly tone.

Sergei held up his hand, calling for immediate silence. "Mia tells me you both wish to speak to Yuri Markovic."

"We do," he confirmed.

"I do not think that is wise."

"He could be the answer," Cullen argued. "Yuri was at the base. It's no accident that he's here at this time."

Sergei clasped his hands behind his back. "Mia told me everything the two of you discovered. I agree that Yuri is involved, but I do not know to what extent. You could be walking into a trap."

"I have to find my dad. That means exploring every lead."

"Yuri is a powerful man. Even here in America. His ties to your father might only complicate things."

"No doubt they will," Cullen agreed. "If you were in my place, looking for your daughter, what would you do?"

Sergei's blue eyes clouded with sorrow and then admiration. "I would do as you are."

"Then you'll set up the meeting with Yuri?" Mia asked, her eyes widening hopefully.

But Cullen knew Sergei's hesitation. The thought of Mia walking into a potential trap wasn't something Sergei could condone.

"I go alone," Cullen announced.

Mia's angry gaze slid to him. "What? No. We do this together."

"If something happens to me, then you can pick up where I left off and continue the hunt. But you'll know Yuri isn't the key."

She was shaking her head the entire time. "Stop. I'm going with you. Besides, Yuri knows me. He'll talk to me before you."

"He'll talk to Cullen," Lev said.

It pained him to see her so upset as all three stood against her. The hurt in her beautiful black eyes tore at his heart, but he would rather she be furious than see her hurt or dead.

"This is bullshit," she declared.

Sergei put a hand on her shoulder. "It is the right thing."

She rose and walked from the room.

Cullen fisted his hand, instantly missing her touch. Long after she'd departed, his gaze remained on the doorway. In the short time he'd been with her, he understood why his father had taken such a liking to Mia, and why Sergei protected her as he did.

She was intelligent, strong, and brave. She stood boldly on her own in a world dominated by powerful men. Somehow, she persuaded others to trust her just by being the beautiful, kind, loyal daredevil that she was.

"For a long time, I have wanted to see Mia settled with a good man," Sergei said softly as he moved to the spot she'd vacated next to the bed.

Cullen looked at Sergei, wondering what the Russian was getting at.

"No one was good enough," Sergei continued. "And she did not seem interested. She has walked through life mostly on her own, as if she has been unknowingly searching for someone."

Cullen was locked in a stare with the old man.

Finally, Sergei sighed. "You could be that someone, Cullen Loughman. I see the way she looks at you."

It was on the tip of his tongue to deny it, but the words wouldn't pass his lips.

"You look at her the same way," Sergei said with a knowing look. "She is precious to me. I will not lose her."

"Then we're in agreement."

Sergei smiled. "That we are. I only met your father once, but I liked him instantly. I like you, as well. You are willing to go to extremes to protect Mia. Lev told me of the distance you carried her from the wreckage to the place he found you, all while you were injured."

Cullen shrugged.

"It showed me to what ends you will go for those you care about. I will set up the meeting with Markovic, but only if Mia remains behind."

"Deal."

"How soon will you be ready to travel?"

Cullen sat up and shoved aside the covers before he swung his legs over the side of the bed. Then he got to his feet, not caring that he was naked. "Now."

CHAPTER TWENTY-SEVEN

"She will be in good hands."

Cullen nodded at Sergei's comment. *But they aren't mine.*

"Lev will not allow anything to happen to her."

Unlike Cullen. He rubbed his cheek, feeling the scrape of whiskers. "Are you sure you can get Yuri to meet with you?"

"*Da.*"

Cullen tugged on the new shirt, grateful that it buttoned up the front. Even his jeans were new. His boots and weapons waited for him off to the side.

Sergei blew out a breath and set down the cell phone on the bed. "It is unlike Yuri not to answer."

"You've a new number," Lev reminded him.

Sergei waved away his words. "Yuri should still answer."

After he'd finished dressing, Cullen straightened, clenching his teeth as his side pulled. "Do you have another way of getting in touch with Markovic?"

"He will answer," Sergei responded and dialed again.

Cullen walked to Lev. "How well do you know Markovic?"

"Not very. Why?"

"I don't know. I feel like something is off."

Lev snorted. "You mean other than a secret organ-ization that we know spans at least two countries being after you?"

"Yeah." It was more than that. Much more. Though Cullen was hesitant to share everything.

Lev had helped them, but that didn't mean Cullen trusted the man. With just a word or look from Sergei, Lev would slit their throats in a second.

He felt Lev's cold blue eyes on him. Cullen turned his head and met the *Brigadier's* stare. For long moments, the two remained that way.

Finally, Lev asked, "What aren't you telling us?"

"As much as you aren't telling me."

Lev's grin was fleeting. "The Saints are killing with-out hesitation for the bioweapon. Why?"

"That's something I'd also like answered."

"To go to so much trouble and expense in killing and kidnapping for it . . ." Lev said, his gaze lowering to the floor as a thoughtful look filled his face.

Cullen watched him carefully. Lev might have gone to medical school and was now a killer for Sergei, but he thought and reacted much like any highly trained man in the military.

"The key is the bioweapon," Lev said suddenly. His gaze snapped to Cullen.

"I believe so."

Both looked to Sergei when he threw his cell phone on the bed and turned away angrily, muttering under his breath in Russian. That wasn't a good sign. If they couldn't find Yuri, they were back to square one.

The sound of a throat clearing behind him had Cullen turning around. There, he found Mia in the doorway, hold-ing out a folded piece of a newspaper. "What's that?"

"Read," she told him.

He took the paper, his gaze going to the picture of Yuri Markovic along with several other Russian and American military personnel walking into the Pentagon.

"He's in Virginia," she said.

Cullen handed the paper to Lev, who looked at it before passing it to Sergei. "It makes sense. If Markovic is here on official business, that will put him in the Virginia/DC area."

"With Dover only a two-hour car ride away."

"My dad isn't being held in Dover."

Mia smiled. "Orrin is in Virginia."

"Then you no longer have need of Sergei," Lev declared.

Cullen realized what the *Brigadier* was doing, and it was the same move he'd make in Lev's position. By the look on Mia's and Sergei's face, it wasn't going to be that easy.

"I need to find Yuri for them," Sergei said.

Lev patiently said, "You've put yourself in too much danger as it is."

Mia started to speak when Cullen put his hand on her arm. He leaned close and said, "Lev's right. The Saints are after us. We don't want them to turn their sights on Sergei."

"Yes. Of course," she mumbled.

Cullen wanted Sergei's help, as well, but he couldn't, in good conscience, endanger someone else's life to ease his own. "We'll find Yuri."

Lev unfolded the paper, but paused, his face tightening.

"What is it?" Sergei asked him.

Cullen watched Lev closely. Whatever the man saw, it didn't sit well with him. A moment later, Lev handed the paper to Sergei, his gaze meeting Cullen's.

A deep frown furrowed Sergei's brow. "Egor Dvorak's body was found in the water not far from Virginia."

Cullen read the paper over Mia's shoulder after Sergei had handed it to her. Was it a coincidence that the Russian consulate was dead? He highly doubted it. A man like Dvorak would be a part of the Saints. Why then was he dead?

"The way he was put in the water says that his killers wanted him used for food," Mia said as she tossed the paper to the bed.

"Dvorak wasn't a good man. He got what was coming to him," Lev stated.

"We'd better find Yuri before his body is used for bait, as well," Cullen said.

Mia turned her dark gaze to him. She was so close he could smell the lavender and mint of her hair. Without thought, he wrapped an arm around her.

Until that moment, he hadn't realized how much he'd ached to hold her again. It felt good to have her against him. It also felt . . . right.

She ducked her head and whispered, "You scared me."

He put a finger under her chin and lifted her face. "I didn't think anything frightened you," he teased.

But she didn't return his smile. "I couldn't stop the bleeding."

"You did everything right," he said and enfolded her in his arms.

He closed his eyes for a second when she rested her head against his chest. When he looked up, both Sergei and Lev were watching them. Sergei gave a nod while Lev's face remained as emotionless as ever.

Mia stepped back and out of his arms. "What do we do now?"

"Get to Virginia." It was their only move. Returning to

Dover was out of the question. "Hopefully, while there, we find Yuri or some trace of him."

"We won't stop until we have him."

He smiled down at her. She never gave up. He wasn't sure how she stayed so optimistic. "Exactly."

She then turned to Sergei. "We can't thank you enough for everything, but Lev is right. You've done enough. People depend on you. You need to be there for them."

"I've saved you only so you can fight another day," Sergei said, a hint of sadness in his voice.

"I've learned from the mistakes of my past. I know my limits. All too well," she added.

Cullen walked to Sergei and held out his hand. When the Russian clasped his palm, he gave a firm shake. "I owe you for all you've done."

"You owe me nothing," Sergei said. "Either of you. I did this because I wanted to."

"Regardless, if you ever need anything, I'll be there."

Sergei's smile was wide. "I'll take you up on that offer, Cullen Loughman."

Cullen released the Russian's hand and briefly shook Lev's. "We shouldn't remain any longer. The sooner we get moving, the sooner we find the Saints."

"Take this," Lev said, tossing him something.

Cullen caught it, glancing at the set of keys in his palm.

"The windows are tinted, which will help keep you hidden," said Lev. "Also inside, is a cell phone, still in the package."

Mia said, "Thank you both."

She began to turn away when Sergei called her name. Turning back to him, he waved her over. Cullen watched as the old Russian enveloped her in a brief hug before he walked past her and out the door.

Lev was right on his heels. In a matter of minutes, Cullen and Mia were alone.

He turned to see a shocked expression on her face. "I thought you knew how much Sergei cared about you."

"Up until recently, I've been terrified of the man. I always thought he'd be the one to have me killed."

"He'd be the one to save you."

"I think you're right. Why did he intentionally scare me all those years?"

"To keep you from making wrong decisions. And to keep you alive."

She swallowed and looked around the room. "I owe him a lot."

"*We* owe him a lot."

"Yes." She moved past him out of the room. "Let's get on the road, Captain."

It wasn't long before they were in the silver Ford Escape, heading toward Virginia. While Mia got out the burner phone, he set a course.

He realized it had been days since he'd spoken to his brothers. No doubt both had attempted to call him. He should check in with them while he still could.

As if reading his mind, Mia held out the phone. "I saw you eyeing it."

"I need to call my brothers."

"Tell me the number, and I'll dial."

He gave her Owen's cell. As soon as it began to ring, she handed it to him. Cullen put the phone to his ear. As it continued to ring, he began to worry that something had happened to his brothers, Cassie, or Natalie.

"Hello?" came the terse voice over the phone.

He smiled. "Damn, it's good to hear your voice."

"Cullen?"

"The one and only."

Owen let out a loud whoop. Then he shouted, "Nat! Cullen's on the phone."

Cullen's smile grew.

"Where have you been?" Owen asked.

He shook his head. "Everywhere it feels like. I have some information."

"So do we."

"You go first," he said and put the phone on speaker so Mia could hear.

Owen blew out a loud breath. "First, Natalie and I made a trip to Baylor University a few days ago. She has a friend who helped us get Ragnarok analyzed."

"What did you find out?"

"Hey, Cullen," Natalie said. "We found nothing, really. Your brother got into a fight with three Russians, though."

Cullen exchanged a look with Mia. "Sounds like him."

"Don't listen to her," Owen said, a smile in his voice. "It had to be done. All the chemist was able to tell us was that there was a different marker in the weapon that he'd never seen before."

"What does that mean?" Mia asked.

Natalie blew out a loud breath. "I'm no scientist, but I can tell you that based on his reaction, it isn't good. An unknown marker could mean anything, and with Ragnarok, I'm guessing it's something very bad."

"What's worse than what a normal bioweapon does?" Owen asked.

Cullen changed lanes. "My guess is that this is far from a normal weapon."

"It doesn't matter what it does. It needs to stay hidden," Mia stated.

Natalie replied, "Oh, it will."

"We also discovered who is running the Russians," Owen said. "Egor Dvorak."

Cullen and Mia exchanged a look. Then he asked, "And?"

Owen let out a snort. "We had a talk with him, and Nat got him to disclose some information."

"First, the scientist who developed the bioweapon is named Konrad Jankovic. Dvorak said they were looking for him. We discovered that Jankovic has defected to the States. Oh, and in good news, Dvorak gave up that Orrin is in Virginia," Natalie announced.

Cullen grinned as he sped up. "Good thing, because we're headed there to have a chat with a Major General Yuri Markovic."

"Looks like you got some information, as well," Owen said.

"In a roundabout way. First, did you leave Dvorak alive?"

Owen blew out a loud breath. "Unfortunately. Why?"

"Because his body was found in the water off Virginia," Mia said.

"Damn," Owen murmured.

Cullen said, "Natalie, do you remember any mention of the Saints on that document that put out a hit on you."

"I'll never forget it. Why?" she asked.

"The Saints are a clandestine organization that we know encompasses both Russians and Americans. And possibly Colombians. The Saints are the ones doing all of this."

There was a pause before Owen said, "Fuck me."

"That was pretty much our reaction," Mia added.

Cullen glanced at her. "It was General Davis at Dover who gave Mia the information. The Saints are well formed, with a very long reach."

"You make it sound as if they're after you," Owen said, his voice dropping a level.

"They are. We've eluded them for now."

"How injured are you?"

He didn't question how his brother knew. "I'll have a few more scars to add to the others."

"Do we need to come to you?"

"No," Mia said hurriedly. "These people are everywhere. All they want is to find one of you. It's better for you guys to stay at the ranch."

Natalie said, "Let us know if you need us."

"You find out anything else?" Cullen asked them.

There was a pause before Owen said, "Natalie has agreed to be my wife."

There was soft laughter in the background from Natalie. Cullen smiled, truly happy for his brother. It made him think of Mia. He glanced at her, but her face was turned away to look out the window.

"Congratulations," Cullen said.

There was a smile in his brother's voice when Owen said, "Thanks. Are you sure you're all right?"

"For the moment, the Saints don't know where we are. We're using that to our advantage."

"Make sure you stay safe. And Mia," Owen said. "Watch out for him.

She met Cullen's gaze. "I will."

CHAPTER TWENTY-EIGHT

Sklad . . .

Without a window, Orrin had no idea what time it was. With each minute that passed, he became more and more on edge. And he questioned whether Yuri would show.

Then again, even if he did, it might all be a trap. That was something Orrin would have to prepare for.

He thought of his sons. All three smart, courageous, lethal men. They excelled in their chosen branches. No father could be more proud of his offspring.

If only Melanie were there to see it.

He didn't allow himself to become morose as he usually did when he thought of his dead wife. Melanie had been gone for over twenty years. During that time, he'd held onto her memory and the love they'd shared.

And he always would.

He saw her every time he looked at their children. Whether it was a look, a smile, or something they said, she was always there.

The door to his room opened, and Yuri hurried in, closing the door softly behind him. Orrin got to his feet carefully.

"You look surprised, *stariy droog.*"

"I am," he admitted.

Yuri gave a shake of his head. "You will have to trust me for this to work."

"I know." That's what bothered him so much.

Orrin removed the clip in his pistol, checking it, before he slammed it back into place and tested the slide before shoving it in the waist of his pants. He motioned to the door with his chin. "Let's get the fuck out of here."

"Not yet."

Was this when Yuri would betray him? It seemed too soon for that. He remained in his spot, waiting for Yuri to explain.

"The guard change happens in two minutes," Yuri said and looked at his watch. "We will have to hurry. It will not take them long to realize you are missing."

"Or you."

Yuri shrugged.

"What about your family?"

"I warned them as best I could," Yuri whispered. "I can only pray they get somewhere safe."

"I thought you should know the doctor did not want to leave."

He frowned as his gaze met Yuri's. "What? Why?"

"I do believe she likes you."

"She was only trying to help."

"Maybe. Maybe not. It is time."

Orrin followed Yuri out of the room and into a hallway that stretched endlessly in either direction. Yuri didn't hesitate to turn left and stride down the corridor.

They took a set of metal steps down to another floor. There, Yuri hesitated. Flattening their backs against the wall, they waited for two men in suits to walk past.

By the way Yuri watched them, Orrin suspected they were part of the Saints. They wore no discernable uniform and looked the same as anyone else on the street.

It was no wonder Yuri was anxious. The Saints could be anyone, anywhere. For all Orrin knew, everyone he'd ever associated with was part of the Saints.

That thought set his teeth on edge. Who were these bastards? It was obvious they wanted world domination—or at the very least, to control whoever was in charge.

Releasing Ragnarok on certain countries could drastically change the powers that ran the world. The US could be toppled. Any country could.

It wouldn't be a quick change, but the Saints seemed to be fine with that.

Unless Ragnarok wasn't the only card up their sleeve.

Orrin was going to have to find out more about the group. That was the only way he was going to find a way to bring them down.

Yuri tapped him on the arm, the signal to move. They silently slipped around the corner and jogged to the door on the far end.

Just as they approached the door, a man stepped before them. He and Yuri held gazes for a long minute. Then he saluted Yuri, a silent message of good luck. The soldier's eyes then slid to Orrin. He gave Orrin a nod before he turned to the side to allow them to pass.

The next instant, they were outside. He drew in a deep breath of the fresh air, not even caring that it was raining. The storm would help them escape.

Orrin held his arm against his hurt ribs. The binding on his wrist helped with the jarring as they moved. His shoulder felt fine for the moment.

To fight the Saints, Orrin needed to be at his best. And he was far from that. It would take days of healing before he'd be fit, and that was time they didn't have.

"There," Yuri whispered and pointed to a large black SUV in the parking lot.

Orrin glanced around, looking for anyone who might be watching. He found first one, then two, who stood in the shadows near doors.

"They are my men," Yuri said.

Orrin sincerely hoped so, or it would be the shortest escape in history. Yet they made it to the Range Rover without incident.

Yuri got behind the wheel while Orrin climbed into the passenger seat. He took shallow breaths to combat the pain of his ribs.

The SUV's engine roared to life. They drove away, the warehouse's lights fading quickly in the rain. Although Orrin hoped to never see it again, he made sure to familiarize himself with the surroundings in case he ever needed to return.

It wasn't an easy feat in the dark with many of the street lamps out, but the signs and signposts for the docks off to his right helped.

"I have a lead on Jankovic."

Orrin lifted a brow and swung his head to Yuri. "You found the scientist?"

"He is in DC, holed up in a home with more security than your President."

"So the Saints have him."

"It appears that way."

Orrin twisted his lips. "That won't make getting to him easy."

"As soon as he sees me, he'll know why I'm there."

"And the Saints will know who I am. That doesn't leave us much."

Yuri flashed him a smile. "We've had less."

That was the truth. Then again, their families' lives hadn't been on the line before.

"Where did you put the formula?" Yuri asked.

He shrugged nonchalantly. "Somewhere safe."

"Are you sure the Saints will not find it?"

"Positive."

"Let us hope you are right."

Orrin hoped so, as well. He settled back against the seat. "If we can get to Jankovic, we'll strike at the Saints in a big way."

"It will get their attention. Ragnarok is still out there."

"Once Jankovic is dead and unable to formulate more of the bio-agent, we'll destroy Ragnarok and the formula."

Yuri gave a nod as he weaved his way through the streets. "I like that plan. But you and I both know it is only a matter of time before the Saints find another scientist who can produce another bioweapon of this magnitude."

"The public needs to know of them. Someone from our government needs to do the honors."

"I do not trust anyone in either of our governments."

That was the pickle, because Orrin didn't either. He wanted to think Mitch Hewett was on his side, but how could Orrin know for sure? It wasn't a chance he was willing to take.

"So, what do we do?"

He blew out a breath, hating the pain that it caused. "We find a way to get to the scientist. Or bring him to us."

"I like this idea," Yuri replied with a loud laugh. "Bring the *mudak* asshole to us."

Jankovic certainly was an asshole. What kind of human being could create such a thing as Ragnarok? And all for money.

If it were true that every man had a price, it looked as if Jankovic's wasn't so high. His soul, however, would pay for eternity. Right after Orrin made him suffer for a few days.

"Do you wish to contact your sons?" Yuri asked.

"No." Not yet, at least. Partly because he wanted to concentrate on keeping the Saints off their trail, but a large part was also because he wasn't sure how they would react to hearing from him.

It wasn't as if they checked in with him often. Orrin had stopped trying to call after they'd each joined the military because he had more access to them there.

They didn't know all the times he'd watched them from afar. It killed him not to talk to them and know what was going on in their lives, but he also understood why they wanted away from him and Texas.

"They blame you for Melanie's murder, do they not?"

"Yes. I blame myself, as well."

"You have no leads on her killer?"

"I got close about a year after she was killed, but the trail went cold. Then I was sent away on several missions that kept me out of the country."

"Curious, do you not think?"

He certainly did now. Why hadn't it raised red flags back then? Was the devastation of her loss so great that he'd allowed something like that to slip through without realizing it? What else had he missed?

"You said you got close to discovering who it was?" Yuri asked.

Orrin nodded slowly. "Apparently, too close. The question now is: did my own government take my wife from me and her sons? Or was it the Saints?"

"It is probably one and the same."

Orrin closed his eyes. The thought that his own government could do something like that to him left him chilled to his very soul. He'd given so much of his life to his country, and for what? To have some faction running it for its own agenda?

"I felt just as sick when I realized I was surrounded by the Saints," Yuri said.

Orrin opened his eyes, determination strengthening his resolve. "My family has been sacrificing their lives for this country since it was formed. I won't stand by and see it ruined by the Saints."

"Ah, now that is the Orrin I have been waiting on," Yuri said, slapping the steering wheel. "This may be our last battle, *stariy droog.*"

"Then we go out with a bang."

"And take those fuckers down with us."

Orrin turned his head to Yuri. "We're going to need help."

"Do you have people you can trust?"

He was about to reply that he did when he recalled that his murdered team had all been Saints—or so Yuri claimed. "If the men I vetted, trained, and trusted were Saints, I don't think I can trust anyone but my own flesh and blood now."

"Then we'll do this on our own."

CHAPTER TWENTY-NINE

"I've been meaning to ask. What is it that Sergei calls you?" Cullen asked as he drove.

Mia turned her head to him. *Dochenka Moya.* It means daughter of mine."

"And you thought he didn't care?"

"I assumed he meant it like some people say 'dear' or 'sweetheart' without the soft meaning to it."

Cullen shrugged. "I think he means it."

It made her realize how fortunate she was to have three strong men looking out for her—her father, Orrin, and Sergei.

"You had a weird look on your face when you discovered that Dvorak was dead. Did you know him?"

She turned her gaze to the road. "I know of him, and none of it's good."

"I know that evasive tone. What aren't you telling me?"

She shot him a surprised look. Damn him for learning her so quickly. "Dvorak has made waves throughout our country with his recent comments about US and Russian alliances."

Cullen raised a brow and glanced Mia's way.

She sighed heavily. "Also because he's had some dealings with Sergei."

That was all she was going to tell him. The rest was nothing.

But the longer he remained silent, the antsier she became. She tried to ignore him, but Cullen was patient as he waited for her to spill the rest.

She shifted in her seat, trying to ignore the expectant silence. No focusing on passing cars or the scenery helped. A quick look in his direction showed that he kept an equal eye on her and the road.

"Fine," she said. "One of the favors I did for Sergei was getting cargo to the docks for Dvorak."

"From Russia?"

"Yes, from Russia," she said, exasperated. "I had a job that took me to Germany. There were men waiting for me. They loaded up the cargo while my client did his business. Then we returned to the States."

"What was the cargo?"

"I was told not to look." But it was her plane, and her ass on the line.

Cullen issued a snort. "What was the cargo?"

"Art."

"You expect me to believe he used you to transport art simply because he didn't want to pay the import taxes?"

She gave him a droll look. "Underneath the art were documents. They were all in Russian. I can speak it enough to get by, but I don't read it well. Along with the documents were guns and ammunition."

"Shit."

That was certainly one word for it. "It isn't good news that Dvorak was in charge of things."

"He was well connected. Whether it was due to the Saints or not, doesn't matter. He was a brutal killer."

She crossed her ankles and considered Dvorak. "Don't you think it's odd?"

"What? That Dvorak was stupid enough to get taken by Owen and Natalie?"

"Yes, that. But also that he let Owen and Natalie know who he was. The Saints have remained in the shadows. Up until a few days ago, I didn't even know they existed."

Cullen kept with the flow of traffic so as not to draw any attention. "Dvorak might've been in charge of things in Texas, but he obviously isn't in command of the organization."

"I don't know whether to be relieved, or more worried."

"I'm more worried."

Her stomach roiled. "Me, too."

"We get just enough information to tease us, but never more. We know Ragnarok is dangerous with a marker that apparently is new, but we don't know what it does."

"And we know that Dvorak was part of the Saints, but not where in the organization he was," she added.

"Every layer we pull back exposes dozens more."

She wrinkled her nose. "I've been thinking ever since Natalie mentioned the scientist, Jankovic. I read the papers and get updates on the news, but I've heard nothing about a defecting Russian."

"Dvorak mentioned that they were looking for Jankovic. Which means the Saints don't have him," Cullen said.

She could see the frustration in the way he gripped the steering wheel, and could also hear it in his voice. "We're the hunters now."

"The Saints don't know that."

"Talking to Yuri will help," she added.

"What if we can't find him?"

"We'll find him." They had to. Because they needed some kind of win to gain the energy to keep hunting.

Cullen changed lanes to go around a slow car. "Groups like the Saints scare people. It's their secrecy, and not knowing how large the organization is or how far it extends that prevents others from trying to take them down."

"That's not us."

He turned his head to her for a moment. "It sure the hell isn't."

She reached over and put her hand atop his on the steering wheel. "How long do you think we have before they find us again?"

"If we're lucky, we'll get to Arlington. Once we start poking around there, it won't be long."

"We could use that to our advantage," she said with a grin.

His lips tilted in a smile. "There is normally bait when hunting mankind."

"Consider me your bait."

"Us," he corrected her. "We're the bait."

She dropped her hand from his. "You didn't mention Wyatt while talking to Owen."

"If there was something to tell me, Owen would've done it."

"You didn't talk to your father or brothers for years. This fiasco has brought you all back together. Don't let go of that opportunity."

His hand gripped the wheel tighter. "I said something very similar to Owen in regards to Natalie before I left."

"So take your own advice."

"That's easier said than done when it comes to Wyatt. He's . . . emotionally unavailable. He shuts out everyone and everything."

"Was he always like that?"

Cullen shook his head. "Things changed after Mom's murder. Wyatt became withdrawn. We all did for a time, but he never recovered."

"He stays that way to protect himself."

At Cullen's questioning look, she gave a half-hearted shrug. "I did something similar when I was younger in regards to my dad and his 'plans' for me. It's easier to stay withdrawn than to allow yourself to feel or be hurt in such a way again."

"Wyatt is just an asshole to everyone."

"What of your theory about him and Callie?"

He lifted a hand helplessly. "Wyatt doesn't date."

"Is he gay?"

"I don't think so. Not with the way I caught him looking at Callie."

She was intrigued now. "Then Wyatt must be interested in her. Whether it's from something in the past or something new."

"She used to follow Wyatt around like a puppy. He was kind to her for a short time, and then he became his regular jerk self."

"Perhaps he began to feel something for her."

Cullen snorted, his lips flattening. "I can't imagine Wyatt caring for anyone."

"He loves you and Owen. You're his brothers."

"We're an obligation. He didn't want to find Dad."

Now that shocked her. She might want to throttle her father at times, but she would never consider not helping him if he needed it.

"Yeah," Cullen said with a nod as he glanced at her. "Exactly. That's the kind of man Wyatt is."

"There's more to it than that. There has to be."

"He makes it impossible to want to find out. Or to even care."

"But he's your brother, your blood."

"Because of that, I'll always be there. Honestly, I can't say he'd do the same for me."

She wanted to get all of the Loughmans in a room and slap some sense into them. "I think you'd be surprised."

He cut her a curious look. "Why is my family of such interest?"

"I don't have siblings. I think you and your brothers are fortunate to have each other, to be able to count on one another. To know that, no matter what, you will always be there for the other."

"I suppose so," he said with a frown.

"You should call Wyatt."

Cullen grunted. "Yes, ma'am. I'll call when we reach Virginia."

That made her happy. She settled back in the seat, her mind still on the Loughmans. What a unique family who had suffered tremendous heartbreak.

She'd never thought of herself as a "fixer," but that's exactly what she wanted to do for Cullen. Each of the Loughman men had scars from Melanie's murder, and those scars shaped the lives they led.

Cullen may not have seen his mother's body, but it didn't impact him any less. In some ways, it had changed him more than either Owen or Wyatt.

She turned her head slightly to better see Cullen. She wondered what went on in his mind.

"Why aren't you married?" he asked suddenly.

Shocked, she could only stare open-mouthed at him.

He grinned and gave her a quick wink. "I've been dying to know."

She licked her lips to give herself time to think of an answer. "I had other things to do."

"Did you ever come close?"

"Once."

"What happened?" Cullen asked.

She tugged at the sleeve of her shirt down by the wrist. "He wanted me to stop flying."

"Ah," Cullen murmured.

Mia then asked, "And you? Why aren't you married?"

"I never wanted it."

"So you never came close?"

He shook his head.

She frowned, thinking of her initial assessment of him as being a love-'em-and-leave-'em type. "Have you had a serious relationship?"

"I never felt the need for any kind of relationship with women."

Well, if she'd held out any hope of having something with Cullen, it was splattered like roadkill now.

Yet, somehow, his statement didn't shock her. With the way his mother had been killed, and how devastated Cullen had been by losing her, he would shy away from anyone who might hurt him that way.

"No more questions?" he asked.

She wrinkled her nose. "I think your last statement said it all."

"Don't be upset."

"I'm not," she hurriedly replied. "You're the one who started this conversation."

"So I did."

"Why?"

His hazel eyes met hers briefly. "You're the type of woman a man looks for to spend his life with."

It was too bad Cullen wasn't that type of man.

Her heart tripped over itself at her thoughts. She wasn't looking for marriage. But love? Yes. Who wasn't? Everyone craved finding the other half of themselves, the person who was made for them—their soul mate.

She had started to think no one existed for her. Then she'd met Cullen.

Her mistake was giving in to the desire and taking a taste of his wickedly delicious body and the pleasure he could give. But Cullen would never be hers.

The sooner she realized that, the better.

He'd all but spelled it out. She wouldn't be one of those women who hung on after there was no longer any hope for a relationship.

She'd seen it before. Hell, she'd done it before. But not with Cullen. She was older and wiser now. From the start, she'd known what type of man Cullen was. He would never change.

None of that made her stop hoping that she would find love however.

One day . . .

CHAPTER THIRTY

Ever since Cullen had asked Mia about her relationship status, he'd wondered at his sanity. He'd told the truth in regards to his thoughts regarding relationships.

So why did he want to know hers so badly?

She weighed heavily on his mind, his thoughts affected by her. He wished he knew what it was about Mia that kept him wanting more. What did she have that no other woman before her had exhibited?

What was it that made him crazy if she wasn't near?

The miles passed in a blur as they drew closer and closer to Virginia. She dozed in her seat, allowing him time to get lost in his thoughts. Which wasn't exactly a good thing.

Because she consumed them. Though she might be in new clothes, the aftermath of their crash was visible in the tiny cuts that had yet to heal on her face and the bruise at her hairline above her right eye where her head had slammed into the steering wheel and concussed her.

The sounds of the crash echoed in his head. They had both survived, and that in itself was a miracle. But that meant the Saints would only up the ante next time.

By the time he stopped to fill up the gas tank, he had yet to come up with a solution to keep her safe. She would fight him to be in the action.

It wasn't that she wasn't qualified to stand with him. No, him wanting to keep her out of it was for purely selfish reasons. The idea of seeing her hurt again, or worse— dead—left him shaken.

He pulled on the baseball cap he'd found in the back-seat. With it tugged down low over his face, he shut off the ignition and climbed out.

While the gas pumped, his gaze moved over each person at the station. Everyone was a potential threat. After the tank was filled, he locked the vehicle with Mia still sleeping inside and made his way to the store to grab some snacks.

Within minutes, he was back in the car. He looked at her to find her still asleep. Unable to help himself, he ran the backs of his fingers along her cheek.

She'd saved his life. He owed her so much now, and he wasn't sure how to even begin to pay her back.

Others had saved him before, and he hadn't felt such . . . uncertainty with them. Then again, none of them had been Mia. She was as unique and special as the stars.

He blew out a breath and started the car. Then he drove away, pulling back onto the road. He glanced at his phone, thinking of her words regarding Wyatt.

Yet he still didn't call his eldest sibling. Wyatt was his family by blood, but Wyatt had never made Cullen feel as if he wanted another brother.

There was a bond between Wyatt and Owen because they'd been the ones to find their mom. Before that, Cullen had been the irritating brother who always wanted to tag along while not quite keeping up.

Even after all these years, he still felt like that young, gangly kid. No one quite measured up in Wyatt's eyes.

With all Cullen had experienced and been a part of, he no longer felt the need to try. Wyatt didn't even want to be looking for their father. It was only Callie and Owen who were making him participate.

Perhaps that was the reason Cullen wasn't so keen on calling his eldest brother. The reason didn't matter in the end. No doubt Owen would fill Wyatt in when they spoke.

Cullen set down the cell phone and pressed the accelerator. He saw the welcome sign as they passed into Virginia. His hands gripped the steering wheel tightly. They would immediately begin hunting for the Saints.

It was going to be tricky. Hunting while keeping themselves hidden. No matter what they did, they wouldn't be able to keep away from the Saints for long.

Beside him, Mia let out a sigh as she woke. She stretched, arching her back so her breasts thrust forward. He bit back a moan, his blood heating as he imagined leaning over and wrapping his lips around a nipple.

"We're in Virginia?" she asked as she looked out the window, reading the signs.

"Just crossed the state line."

She sat straight and smoothed back her hair. "Where do we start?"

"I thought we'd head to the Pentagon and stake it out for a while. Markovic might show there."

"And if he doesn't?"

"That's the only place I can think of."

She was quiet for a moment before she put her hand into the pocket of her jacket. He saw her frown before taking out a piece of paper to read it.

"We'll need a place to stay," she said.

He'd been so wrapped up in everything else, he hadn't thought about where they would sleep. The car might work for a night or two, but nothing longer. Having a place where they could set up would benefit them.

"We'll find a motel somewhere," he said.

She made a face. "We take the chance of someone being a Saint."

"It's not like we have a house."

A smile formed as she turned her head to him. "Actually, I think we might."

"What do you mean?" he asked.

She held up a piece of paper with an address written on it. "Sergei must have put it in my jacket."

"Or Lev."

She snorted, her face clearly stating what she thought of that. "Lev doesn't want Sergei helping. Lev wouldn't do this."

"Let's go check out the address."

Her smile widened.

"We're going to owe Sergei a lot if we survive this."

She laughed, nodding. "I know. And Sergei will collect."

"Lev will be pissed."

"Let him be," she said. "He needs to have those perfect feathers of his ruffled."

He grinned at her statement. "He's only doing his job."

"I know, but that doesn't mean he has to be an ass."

"He's a dangerous man. Having him for an ally is a good thing, especially now."

She gave a half-shrug. "He's just so . . . cold."

"And calculating."

"Yes," she agreed. "But you're just as calculating. What makes you different from him?"

He glanced at her. "Do you find me cold?"

There was a brief pause. "Anything but."

It was a good thing he was driving, because if not, he'd have taken her in his arms and kissed her. The fire he saw in her eyes was electric.

He shifted his eyes back to the road. The desire in him

burned. Blazed. His balls tightened just imagining having her in his arms again.

With a mental shake of his head, he pushed aside such thoughts before they led him down a road he wasn't prepared to walk.

Then he recalled her question about what made him different from Lev. "I don't think I'm much different than Lev. I kill for the government that trained me. He kills to protect a man he owes loyalty to."

"He's murdered."

Cullen thought back to a previous mission—the small village in Kuwait and the house he'd entered with his team. "There are many things I've done in the name of freedom for my country. Make no mistake, Mia, I'm as much a killer as Lev."

"You and every man and woman in uniform kills in war. It's either that or be killed."

"Sometimes it isn't so black and white. Sometimes, things go very wrong."

She licked her lips, her gaze never leaving him. "Like?"

Why had he said anything? Why couldn't he just let it go? Was it because he didn't want her to think he was a good man? Perhaps he was trying to make her dislike him as she did Lev. Would that make it easier to walk away from her?

Because walk away he must.

Even though he longed to stay.

For the first time in his life, he'd found someone who called to him in ways he hadn't thought were possible.

"Cullen?" she urged.

"A few years ago, my team and I were sent to Kuwait to check out a lead we'd gotten on a top member of a terrorist group. We found the tiny village and made our way to the house. We busted down the door. Standing there was a four-year-old boy, looking up at us with big, dark eyes."

He saw the boy in his dreams sometimes, but the nightmares had lessened with the years.

"My hesitation got one of my men killed when the terrorists opened fire. The screams of the women were as loud as the gunfire. I could see the boy screaming, but I couldn't hear him over the noise.

"We returned fire. When it was all over, the stillness and quiet were thunderous. And at my feet was the boy. I don't know who killed him. If it was us or the terrorists, Just a few feet away there was a woman riddled with bullets. She lay with her hand outstretched to the child."

"His mother," Mia said.

He nodded. "I believe so."

"That wasn't your fault. You did your job. It's the terrorists' fault for staying in a place with women and children."

"I told myself exactly that. When we were sent to another house, I didn't hesitate as I had before. We kicked open the door and entered. The instant I saw a weapon, I fired. It wasn't until they all lay dead that we realized the house only held women and children. Not a single terrorist was in the place."

She shook her head as a frown deepened her forehead. "You said you saw a weapon."

"They were guns they'd found and were taking apart so the terrorists couldn't use them. Those women and kids were trying to help us."

"Oh, God," she murmured.

He blew out a breath. He'd lived with what he'd done for many years. If only he'd hesitated again. Maybe then he wouldn't be carrying the weight of those deaths, but he deserved no less.

"You did your job," Mia said.

He appreciated how she was trying to justify what he'd done, but nothing could do that. "I'm a killer. Same as Lev."

"You're nothing like Lev. You do what you do to save lives. He does what he does to keep Sergei on top. Those are two different things."

"I think there is more to Lev than you realize."

"Well, I don't want to know it."

Cullen wasn't so sure they'd seen the last of the *Brigadier*. Lev was exactly the type of person they needed to fight the Saints. Besides, there was something about Lev that Cullen recognized, something he saw in himself—regret.

Mia suddenly put her hand on his arm. "What happened with you and those kids was a dreadful, horrendous thing. But it wasn't done with malice. You didn't go in there looking to kill women and children. That was a mistake. You were fighting terrorists trying to kill you."

"Our intel was confirmed by a local we'd used several times. I found him in a brothel a few hours later. I beat him until my knuckles bled. He confessed that the terrorists had paid him to lie to us."

"What did you do then?"

He met her dark eyes. "I slit his throat."

"He deserved no less."

Cullen didn't bother to mention that what he'd done was murder because he could see in her eyes that she would never think of it that way.

And strangely, that healed a part of his soul.

CHAPTER THIRTY-ONE

Haunted. That's what Cullen was. Though he tried to hide it. He did a good job, but he'd allowed her to see some of it. Mia didn't wonder why. She just accepted that he'd opened up.

She may not have been in the midst of battle the way Cullen had, but she had seen her fair share of it from the skies.

She'd only been in a few dogfights, but with millions of dollars worth of metal around you, it brought a different perspective to things.

Besides, any fights in the air were self-defense. It was completely different from Cullen, who was on the ground, coming face-to-face with the enemy.

Mia was fairly certain she wouldn't handle things nearly as well as he had. She was amazed he didn't suffer from PTSD. Or perhaps he did.

She put the address from the piece of paper in her phone and used the GPS to give Cullen directions. To her amazement, it wasn't a mansion as she'd half expected based on Sergei's preferences.

It was a modest house in a neighborhood that few would dare to venture into. The house was just run-down enough to mix with the rest.

"Well, isn't this a welcome surprise," Cullen said with a grin as he slowed the car to get a look out the window.

She returned his smile. "Sergei is full of surprises."

"It'll be perfect for us." Cullen then drove off, turning in the direction of the Pentagon.

Nothing more was said as they cruised through the city and circled twice around the Pentagon. Everyone she saw was a Saint in her eyes. That's what made the organization so dangerous, because they knew very little about them or who was involved.

It wasn't just people with money and power. It was anyone and everyone.

She was thankful the windows were tinted to keep anyone from seeing her, because many looked. Several times, Cullen tried to find a place to park, but kept coming up empty.

"Let me out," she said.

He shot her a frown.

"I'll play the part of tourist and let you know if I spot him."

"And if one of the Saints sees you?"

"The security details won't ignore us sitting in the car."

Cullen took the next left and drove away. "We're going to need help."

"Who?"

"Callie."

Which meant he'd have to talk to Wyatt. Since Mia was an only child, she didn't understand why some siblings didn't get along. She'd always wanted a brother or sister. Family was family.

They were the only ones who could never turn you away because blood bonded blood. When her father and stepmother were gone, she would have no other family.

At least with a sibling, she'd know there was someone

else with her in the world. Cullen had that and didn't seem to understand how precious it was.

On the way back to the house, she wondered if he was mentally preparing to talk to Wyatt. It saddened her that the two brothers had such a rift between them.

At least Cullen talked to Owen easily. Maybe when all this was over, the brothers could mend whatever had pulled them apart. And she prayed that Orrin would be reunited with his sons.

"You think it's wrong that I don't want to talk to Wyatt, don't you?" Cullen asked.

She shook her head. "Not at all. You explained your reasoning."

"But?" he urged.

"I was an only child. I can't tell you how lonely that was. My father and stepmother were frequently gone, and though I had someone to take care of me, it wasn't like having a brother or sister. I have to admit, I'm a little jealous of you."

"I didn't think of it that way." He wrinkled his nose while he turned into the driveway of the house. "That was insensitive of me."

"You only know what you had. I've only known what I have."

He put the vehicle in park and shut off the engine. Then he looked at her. "I want you to meet my brothers."

"I hope I get to." She looked at the house then. "Shall we?"

"Let's."

They exited the SUV together, closing the doors almost simultaneously. She met him at the front of the vehicle.

"I don't suppose Sergei let you know how to get in?" Cullen asked.

"I only have the address."

He wiggled his eyebrows. "Let's try the back."

She took out her gun and followed him around the house. She looked beneath the old mat, a cracked pot with the dried remains of some plant, and everywhere else she thought a key might be while Cullen did the same.

It was while she stared at the door that she realized there was something wrong with the doorbell. It was bigger than any she'd ever seen. "Do you know anyone who puts a doorbell on the back door?"

"No," Cullen answered. "Then again, I haven't met many men like Sergei."

She walked up the two steps to the door and pushed the doorbell, listening. There was no sound from within the house. No matter how many times she pushed, there was nothing. She then wiggled the doorbell.

To her shock, it swung on a hinge from the top. When she pushed it to the side, she saw a keypad that lit up.

"Do you know the code?" Cullen said from behind her.

She eyed the keys. "Sergei would only send me without the code if he thought I could figure it out."

"Then you know it."

Mia lifted her hand, pausing over the keypad. There was only one time that Sergei had given her a code. It was after she'd been rescued from the sex slavers and needed a place where no one could find her.

It had been a beach house in the Florida Keys. Sergei had told her the code was a date, the first time she'd agreed to work with him.

She punched in 4-12-11.

There was a click as the door unlocked. She exchanged a look with Cullen, who gave her a wink. Then he opened the door and slowly stepped inside.

She replaced the outside of the doorbell and followed Cullen into the house. The inside was just as modest as the outside, but clean. She pulled the door shut behind her and heard the click of the locking mechanism.

"That's a steel door," Cullen said. "No one is getting in. At least not fast."

That gave her some relief. While he explored the upstairs, she checked the kitchen. The pantry and fridge were completely stocked. The produce looked fresh, as if someone had bought it that day.

"Two bedrooms and one bath upstairs," Cullen said as he walked down the stairs and into the living room.

She went out to meet him. "Everything we could want is in the kitchen."

"This must be a safe house. The windows are double paned with bulletproof glass."

"So we're safe."

He nodded. "I think so."

She smiled and sprawled on the sofa. "It feels great to be out of the car."

"Yeah."

She lifted her head from the pillow and saw him holding the cell phone, his face lined with apprehension. "I can call Callie."

"I need to do this." He drew in a deep breath and released it. Then he dialed a number before putting it on speaker and setting the phone on the wooden coffee table.

"Hello?" Callie answered.

Cullen smiled at the sound of her voice. "Hey, Cal."

"Cullen? Is that you?" she asked hopefully.

"It's me."

Callie let out a whoop. Then she asked, "Where's Mia?"

"I'm here," Mia replied.

"It's so good to hear from you both," Callie said. "We were getting worried."

Cullen rubbed a hand over his jaw, scraping his

whiskers. "Callie, unfortunately I don't really have a lot of time to fill you in right now. Suffice it to say that it's not just Russians after us. It's a group—the Saints."

"That's what was written on that paper Natalie took from the embassy," Callie said.

Mia sat up and scooted to the end of the couch. She clasped her hands together with her forearms propped on her knees. "The Saints are well connected. They have people everywhere."

"They're looking for us, so we're hiding," Cullen explained.

"Do you need us?" Callie asked.

Cullen licked his lips. "What I need is for you to use your magic."

"Where are you?" came a deep voice over the phone.

Mia knew without asking that it was Wyatt. Cullen's entire attitude changed. He stiffened, and his face hardened. Her heart hurt for both brothers.

There was a pregnant pause before Cullen said, "Virginia."

"Good. Based on information that Owen and Natalie got, Orrin is supposed to be there," Callie said.

Cullen sat in one of the chairs. "We're looking for a Major General Yuri Markovic. Mia saw him at Dover AFB, and I know he's been at the Pentagon."

"You think he took Orrin?" Wyatt asked.

Mia said, "We think he's a good place to start. I did some business with Yuri before, and I can use that as our way in to see him. We think he's part of the Saints. The problem is, we need to find him."

"Ah," Callie said. "Give me some time. I'll locate him. What number is this you called from?"

"A burner," Cullen answered. "Our phones were being tracked by the Saints."

There was some mumbling. Then Callie said, "That means they could be monitoring ours, as well. We'll have to get new ones. I'll call when I have something."

The line went dead then.

Mia smiled at Cullen. "That wasn't so bad."

"No."

She rubbed her hands on her thighs. "I know it's none of my business, and feel free to ignore this, but I can't imagine what it was like for your brothers to find your mom as they did. That event changed all of you, but I'm betting it affected Wyatt more than you or Owen.

"I'm not saying Wyatt isn't at fault for his actions in how he's treated you. What I am saying is that perhaps he doesn't even know he's doing it because of the pain he carries. The same pain you have."

When Cullen didn't reply, she wished she hadn't said anything. She got to her feet and started past him. His hand reached out and grabbed hers.

She halted, her head swinging toward him. Looking deep into his hazel eyes, she found that she wanted to soothe all of his hurts and wash away his pain.

The seconds stretched on as their gazes held. The air became fraught with desire as the coldness left his beautiful eyes to be replaced by blatant desire.

She waited for him to do something. Say anything. But the moment came and went. She swallowed and pulled her hand from his.

Perhaps it was better that nothing else happened between them. Because the longer she was around Cullen, the more she wanted to know about him.

Without a backward glance, she went up the stairs to put some space between them—and her heart.

CHAPTER THIRTY-TWO

Mia turned on the water in the shower. The house might be modest, but the one bathroom had been overhauled and retrofitted with all the amenities anyone could want.

There was a claw foot tub that she considered using. Instead, she opted for the large, glass shower with two showerheads on either side.

The large rectangular tiles on the floor of the bathroom were a soft slate gray. The bottom of the shower didn't have tile but large, smooth pebbles the color of onyx instead.

She shed her clothes while she looked at the two separate sinks. One with bright lights and a vanity for a woman, while the other had all the components any man needed to shave as well as an assortment of colognes.

Mia was eager to see what was on the woman's side, but the steam from the water beckoned. She stood in the middle of the spacious shower, the hot water hitting her front and back.

She allowed the water to soothe her aching muscles. Suddenly, an arm wrapped around her, drawing her back against a strong chest.

Her heart skipped a beat at the feel of Cullen's magnificent body. He turned her slowly, his large hands caressing her.

Once more, she looked into his green and gold depths and saw the desire sizzling there. Her blood pumped in her ears and pleasure coiled low in her belly.

He drew her closer, his head lowering to take her mouth in a kiss. His lips were soft and insistent. Then his tongue swept into her mouth to mate with hers.

She sighed and melted against him. As the kiss intensified, she ran her hands over his wide shoulders. The feel of the bandage caused her to attempt to draw back, but he only intensified the kiss.

With a rough shove, he pushed her back. A moan rumbled in his chest as he pressed her against the glass and kissed her as if there were no tomorrow.

As if he'd die without the taste of her.

She clung to him, her body aching to have him fill her again. His arousal pressed into her stomach as he rocked his hips. She shivered and moaned. Her sex clenched eagerly as her body remembered his loving all too well.

With the water sluicing over them, he grasped her ass and lifted her. Mia widened her legs, wrapping them around his waist as she did.

"Your wounds," she gasped between kisses.

He gave a shake of his head. "I need you."

The sensation of the cool glass at her back, Cullen's heated body at her front, and the hot water all around was an erotic combination.

She dropped her head back while his lips moved down her neck. Powerless, she swayed her hips forward. The need to be connected to him in an act as old as time itself consumed her.

His teeth nipped at the skin where her neck met her shoulder. She shuddered. This man had the ability to touch her in ways she never imagined.

It was as if his soul sang a song hers recognized.

Everything about him beckoned her, summoned her. And she was incapable of denying him—even if she wanted to.

She moaned loudly when his hot breath fanned her ear right before he took the lobe gently in his teeth and bit down before sucking. All the while, he shifted her so that his fingers moved closer to her sex.

The teasing was an exquisite, beautiful torture. She burned for him. Her body was at fever pitch, and she hoped to never recover from it.

Cullen watched the pleasure cross her face. She held nothing back, allowing him to see everything she experienced. He'd tried to ignore his yearning for her, but it had been impossible.

He'd always been able to walk away from women, but not so with Mia. She'd bewitched him somehow. And the surprising, truly alarming part . . . he liked it.

Hell, he craved it.

His gaze lowered to see her pebbled nipples with the water cascading over her lush breasts. He twisted and took a peak into his mouth, sucking hard.

Her nails sank into his neck while her legs tightened. There were so many ways he wanted to make love to her and explore her body while seeing how many times he could wring cries of passion from those tempting lips of hers.

His cock twitched. He ached to be inside her again, to feel her slick walls close tightly around him. Just thinking about it brought a bead of moisture to the tip of his rod.

He raised her so that her folds hovered over his arousal. Their eyes met. Her chest heaved, and her skin flushed.

"Please," she begged.

His cock brushed against her sex. Then he slid slowly inside. Her gasp was a mixture of sensuality and decadence. It shredded the last of his control with all the force of a whisper.

He released his hold and let her lower onto his cock until she was fully seated. Her eyes were closed, her lips parted. The beautiful carnal look on her face made his heart trip.

The voice inside him that allowed him to leave his previous lovers warned him that he was getting too close. But it was already too late.

It was too late the moment he first tasted her lips.

He began to move his hips. Slowly at first, but the tempo quickly escalated.

Their bodies slid against each other, their passion growing with each heartbeat. Her tight walls squeezed him as her breasts bounced prettily.

Her breathing hitched, and her body tensed. Then he watched the bliss cross her face as her climax hit. He thrust hard, wanting to prolong her pleasure so he could continue to watch.

But no matter how hard he tried, he couldn't hold back his own orgasm. It barreled through him, leaving him dazed and unnerved.

When he was able to lift his head, Mia's hands caressed his back and neck. He didn't even attempt to come up with an excuse to leave her.

Instead, he moved her near the faucets so she could shut off the water. Still holding her, he walked from the shower to the bedroom, where he placed a knee on the bed and lowered them both.

She wasn't sure what emotion was reflected in Cullen's hazel eyes. There was a hint of distress, but it was gone before she could wonder about it.

She sighed when he threaded his fingers with hers and

lifted her arms over her head. His chest scraped against her sensitive nipples.

She hissed, causing his lips to form a crooked smile. It felt divine to have him still inside her. He was semi-hard and becoming harder the longer he remained.

He placed a kiss on her forehead, another on the tip of her nose, and then on her lips before continuing down her body. Her lids fell closed.

When he pulled out of her, she wanted to call him back, but the words died on her lips when his tongue found her clit. She sucked in a quick breath.

Her arms moved out to her side where she clutched the comforter. She lay defenseless against such wicked pleasure. His tongue did wonderful, sinful things that had her gasping for breath and her back arching off the bed.

When his hands reached up and cupped her breasts, gently massaging them, she sighed. That sigh turned into a cry of pleasure when he pinched her nipples.

Already she could feel another climax building—and quickly. His hands moved from her breasts, sliding over her body as a sculptor might caress a statue.

She'd never felt more beautiful or more sensual than in Cullen's arms. She became a wanton, a creature that couldn't survive without his touch.

Just as the first waves of her orgasm hit, he rose up and entered her in one smooth motion. She cried out, clutching him.

He held himself above her, his hips rocking forward as he plunged inside. The ecstasy stole her breath as she was tossed about on the wild ride of pure rapture.

All the while, she was drowning in his green-gold depths. He refused to allow her to look away. The link that had been forged, that connected them, strengthened and grew.

As he watched her, she was able to see the pleasure fill his face when he climaxed. She held him as his body jerked from the force of it.

And then they were in each other's arms, their bodies tangled. She tried to keep her eyes open, but she was too sated. She drifted off to sleep with a smile on her face.

Mia didn't know how long she'd slept or what had pulled her so viciously from her dreams. She lay still, listening. Beside her, Cullen's even breathing lulled her.

She moved her hand from his side and felt something on her fingers. It wasn't until she lifted her hand and saw the blood that she realized he must have torn his stitches.

"Cullen," she said softly as she rolled him onto his back and got on her knees.

He blinked and frowned as he opened his eyes. "What is it?"

"Your stitches. Stay here. I'm going to find something to stop the bleeding."

He lifted his head to look at his side. He tentatively touched the wound. She hurried from the bed, racing naked down the stairs.

She searched the kitchen and pantry before rushing back up to the bedroom to look in the bathroom. It was there that she found the First-Aid kit.

Grabbing it and some towels, she ran to the bedroom. She tossed the box on the bed. Then she climbed next to Cullen and wiped away the blood. With the majority of it gone, she was able to see how bad the bleeding was. Three of the stitches had popped.

"I can't believe I forgot about your wound."

He grabbed her hand to still her. Only when she looked in his eyes did he say, "This isn't your fault."

He released her when she gave him a nod. She was mortified that she'd been so careless. Cullen needed to be at the top of his game. The longer he remained hurt, the harder that would be.

In no time, she had the replacement stitches in, the wound cleaned, and a new bandage in place. She closed the First-Aid kit and started to rise.

He stopped her, moved everything off the bed, and pulled her against him as he lay back. She was loath to hurt his side, but his other shoulder was also injured.

"I want you beside me," he said into the silence as she lay stiffly beside him. "You're not hurting me. I wasn't in pain before."

Slowly, she relaxed and rested her head against his good shoulder. Her eyes grew heavy again. She let them fall closed while enjoying being in Cullen's arms.

"Do you think we'll find Orrin?"

She shifted her head to look at him. "Yes. Don't you?"

"There are so many things stacked against us. I'm beginning to worry."

"I'm not."

He grinned. "Liar."

"Do I think we're going to have an uphill battle? Yes. Do I think our hunt will lead us to the Saints? Definitely. I'd feel better if I were in the air, though. I'm pretty useless on the ground."

"I wouldn't say that."

She smiled at his insinuation. "I don't have the ground training that you do."

"Unfortunately, I don't think a plane would help us right now."

"I wish it would, because no one can touch me in the air."

He gave her a squeeze. "I don't want you hurt."

"You mean the way you've been injured?" she asked, her voice laced with heat.

"Exactly."

"You're not leaving me behind." No matter how un-skilled she was for this, Cullen was better with her beside him than alone with no one to watch his back.

He put his finger beneath her chin and lifted it to place a kiss on her lips. "No. I'm not."

CHAPTER THIRTY-THREE

As much as Cullen enjoyed lying next to Mia, his mind wouldn't allow him to relax. He'd dozed a bit, but now he was thinking about finding Markovic.

Yuri was their best shot at not only finding the Saints but also Orrin. Without Markovic . . . they had nothing.

Cullen always had a backup to a plan. This time, he didn't. And that worried him.

With the manpower and money the Saints had, anything could be waiting for them. Mia was actively being sought by the group, which made it particularly precarious for her.

The only thing they had on their side was surprise. And even then, he didn't know how long it would be before the Saints learned they were in town.

He pulled his arm from beneath Mia and swung his legs over the side of the bed, sitting up.

"Weren't you the one who said you wanted me beside you?" came her sleepy voice.

He grinned and looked at her over his shoulder. "I did."

"Then where are you going?" She leaned up on an elbow and raised a brow at him.

"I can't sleep. We have very little in the way of a plan, and nothing beyond that."

She sat up. "I was thinking about that, as well. And if neither of us is going to sleep, we might as well get up."

He watched as she rose from the bed and returned to the bathroom to get her clothes. Cullen stood and dressed. Just as he walked from the room, he stopped and looked at the bed.

As a rule, he didn't have sex with the same woman more than once. He'd broken that rule with Mia, but he wasn't scared.

Well. Not very much, at least.

This was the very thing that he'd been terrified of his entire life. It was what kept him from allowing any woman too close. And yet, here he was.

It almost felt like fate had stepped in and put what he'd avoided in front of him. Maybe she had. He didn't know, and there was no use worrying about it.

He made it downstairs before Mia and brewed fresh coffee. With a large mug in hand, he walked into the living room to get his cell phone. There was a message waiting.

Cullen didn't recognize the number. He queued up the message when Mia came down the stairs.

"Did you hear from Callie?" she asked.

He held up the cell phone. "I was just about to play a message."

Mia made her way to him. "Go ahead."

He put it on speaker and hit play. There was a pause, and then he heard Callie's voice.

"It's me," Callie said. "I did as you asked. Your quarry attended an event yesterday, but there have been two missed meetings this morning."

Mia looked at Cullen. "Why would Yuri miss those meetings?"

"Perhaps he couldn't attend."

Callie's voice interrupted them. "There is a hotel I think you might want to look into regarding our *friends*. The Willard, in DC. I'll let you know if I come across anything else."

The message ended then. Callie had gone to great lengths not to say any names in case someone was listening. As long as the Saints didn't know he was searching for Markovic, they still had the advantage.

Mia turned on her heel to disappear into the kitchen. When she returned, she had a mug of coffee and a map. "I saw this earlier when I was looking through the cabinets."

She unfolded the map to show it was one of Arlington, Virginia, and DC. It didn't take him long to locate the house they were in on the map.

He put his finger on the location and then moved in a straight line to the Pentagon. It was Mia who found the position of the hotel.

"Markovic wouldn't take the time to travel around the city," Cullen said.

She shook her head. "Probably not. He has meetings that he has to attend so he'd want a location that was convenient."

"Here," Cullen said as he drew a circle around a business section.

Mia pointed to a spot not far from the one he'd indicated. "Or here."

He looked at the docks and had to agree. "It would make it very easy for them to move him quickly by boat. We'll have a lot of area to search."

"We know where Yuri is staying."

They had a guess, but he agreed with Mia. It was much more than they'd had a few minutes ago. And after everything they'd been through, he was happy for it.

"I'm starving. I'm going to cook something, and while

we eat, let's figure out how we're going to get into the hotel," Mia said.

He followed her into the kitchen and opened the fridge to find items to make a sandwich. "Let's skip the big meal."

In a few minutes, they were at the table, eating. After a couple of bites, he said, "If we go into the hotel, there will be cameras. Something Callie found made her think there were Saints there."

"I tend to think there are Saints everywhere. I can wear a wig to disguise myself. I'll just need to stop somewhere and pick up the items I need."

That could work. But that meant she would go in alone. Something he wasn't crazy about. "That will get you into the hotel and possibly by anyone working for the Saints. It won't get you into Yuri's room."

"It will if they think I'm his wife," she replied with a perfect Russian accent.

Cullen smiled and shook his head. Was there anything she couldn't do? "It'll be a huge chance."

"As if that doesn't describe everything we're doing."

All too true. "No matter how dangerous my missions, I always knew I had others I could contact in bad situations. We're on our own. Every time we exchange phone calls with Owen or Wyatt, we're putting them at risk."

"Then we limit those calls to important ones. As for the rest, we'll have to get creative."

"Meaning?" There was something in her tone that said she already had an idea.

She swallowed the bite of sandwich she'd taken and smiled. "Meaning that I know where we might be able to find things we could use. Say, like a device that can get us into Yuri's hotel room."

Just when he thought he had her figured out. Cullen ate

the last of his sandwich and wiped his hands. "Is the place safe?"

"The safest. Only a handful of people know of its location."

He was going to ask her where it was, but he had a suspicion that she wouldn't share until the right time. By the mischievous glint in her dark eyes, she was excited about the prospect of their next adventure.

In no time, they were back on the road, looking for a place to buy a wig. Oddly, it wasn't difficult to find. The shop was on the fringes of the seedy part of town.

He put the SUV in park. Mia wound her hair up and put on the baseball cap he'd worn earlier. As he went to turn off the ignition, she gave a shake of her head.

"There's no need for both of us to go in. I'll be in and out, quick. Leave the car running."

Since he was parked in front of the store with a view inside, he relented. She winked at him and opened the SUV door. His gaze followed her around the front of the vehicle and into the store.

He lost her amid the high shelves, and as the minutes ticked by without him seeing her, he began to worry. Then she came into view at the cash register.

No sooner was she in the SUV than he backed it up and drove away. The large bag set between her feet had more than just a wig.

She caught him looking and smiled. "I do have a part to play. Now, I need somewhere I can change."

It took some time, but Cullen found her a place that didn't have any cameras. Once more, he waited in the vehicle as she went to the restroom and changed.

He did a double take when she walked out. Her long, dark hair was gone, replaced by a short, blonde wig with blunt bangs. Heavy eye makeup and red lipstick took the place of her natural look.

Her clothes had also been swapped out for very revealing attire. The black and white horizontal-striped shirt barely held in her breasts as it dipped low in the front, showing ample cleavage.

Then there was the black mini skirt that showed off her long, lean legs. When he spotted the platform heels, he was amazed she could walk in them. A black jacket with a faux fur collar was the finishing touch.

She climbed into the SUV and turned her head to him. "What do you think?"

"I think you'd stop a blind man in his tracks."

She laughed, the sound filling the vehicle and making him smile in return. "I'll take that as a compliment."

"That's what it was."

"So, blonde is a good color for me?" she asked and touched the wig.

He gave a shake of his head. "You look the best naked with your black hair spread around you."

It hadn't been his intention to reveal such a thought, but it was out before he realized it. The way her lips curved up in a soft smile said she didn't mind at all.

"Are you sure about this?" he asked.

"I am. We need Yuri. Gaining access to his room is one way to do it."

Cullen wasn't so sure. "If he's a Saint, you'll face him alone. That's if he doesn't have men with him, which he probably will."

"I don't see that we have another option."

Cullen ran a hand down his face as he blew out a breath. "I want my father free of those bastards, but I also know that he won't reveal anything."

"They could kill him."

That was something he'd accepted from the moment he learned his father had been kidnapped.

Her eyes grew round with outrage. "And you're okay with that?"

"Of course, not," he retorted, letting his frustration be heard in every syllable. "Ragnarok is hidden. No one knows where the formula is."

"You're forgetting, Jankovic is still MIA."

"No, I haven't forgotten. I'm trying to keep us alive so we can finally get to the Saints and get information."

She looked out the windshield before returning her dark gaze to him. "Right now, the Saints need Orrin. Jankovic is in the country. We don't know where, but I'm guessing he'll be in the hands of your government, a.k.a. the Saints, by now. How long until he begins making more Ragnarok? How long until the Saints no longer need your father?"

Cullen wished he had a good argument against what she'd said, but he didn't. He knew better than most that not everyone came back from missions.

But he couldn't lose Mia. He couldn't hold her dead body in his arms. He couldn't attend her funeral.

He'd done that for many of his buddies. Though he mourned them—and always would—it was different with her. And he knew his father would side with him on this.

"Drive to the hotel," she told him. "I'll look around. If I see Yuri, I'll approach him. If I don't, then we'll leave. Going after Yuri was your idea, and it's a good one. Before we toss it aside, let's check it out."

Cullen knew she was right, but it didn't make it easier to accept. She would be heading into the hotel alone. Even in disguise, one of the Saints could spot her.

But he would be watching. Just in case.

CHAPTER THIRTY-FOUR

"It'll be fine," Mia said to Cullen as she got out of the vehicle in front of the Willard Hotel.

She sounded more confident than she felt. In truth, she was terrified. Her heart hammered wildly, and the air seemed thin each time she attempted to take a breath, preventing her from getting an entire lungful. Yet she knew what she'd told him earlier was the truth.

Their hunt for the Saints depended on tracking down Yuri.

Ignoring the stares at her skimpy outfit that showed an abundance of leg and cleavage, she made her way into the lobby. Her gaze searched faces for Yuri. But no matter how hard she looked, he was nowhere to be found.

"Damn," she mumbled.

Her next step was to convince the front desk to either take her up to Yuri or call him down. The hotel's concern was for their guests, which meant Yuri would be asked to come down.

The lobby was too packed for her to single out a man she hoped she might sway to take her to Yuri. Just as she about to go to the front desk, something stopped her.

Instead, Mia headed to the seating area and chose a

chair that allowed her to see both the entrance to the hotel
and the path from the elevators.

Her instincts had pushed her to come to the hotel. If she
were wrong, they would waste hours. But if she were right,
they could leapfrog over the Saints.

If Yuri cooperated.

The fact that they suspected the Russian also held Orrin had a lot to do with her decision-making, but she also
knew Cullen was right. Orrin was strong. He could withstand weeks of torture.

It was the Saints themselves who posed the biggest
threat. Not to mention that they were after her and Cullen. After her close call with them on the mountain, she
was more than ready to face the assholes and let them
know what she thought of their "secret organization."

The more she found out about the Saints, the more she
knew they needed to be taken out. With every day they
were allowed to exist, the entire world was put in more
danger.

As she watched people come and go from the hotel,
minding their own business and going about their daily
lives, unaware of the threat that hung over them, she felt
as if a clock hung above her, counting down at an incredible rate.

How much longer did any of them have? How did they
take down an organization that spanned at least two countries? How could they begin to dismantle the Saints without knowing their true agenda?

Because in order to stop an enemy, one must understand
them first.

And she knew next to nothing about the Saints.

That's probably what frightened her the most. They
could've existed for months or decades. Their network could
be so extensive that it might take years to dismantle them.

The one thing she knew for sure was that the Loughmans wouldn't stop fighting the Saints until the Texans had
breathed their last breaths.

She would be standing beside them all the while, fighting with everything she had. Even if that meant turning to
her father for help.

His influence was substantial, which meant he might be
able to help them in ways others couldn't.

She checked her watch. Nearly an hour had passed. The
waiting was getting them nowhere. She needed to get into
Yuri's room one way or another.

Her gaze caught on two men who walked into the lobby
from the street. One was dressed in a suit, his stomach pro-
truding over his belt and his face red with exertion. Drops
of sweat dotted his chubby face as his beady eyes looked
at everyone with contempt.

The second man was tall and fit, wearing black pants
and a dark gray dress shirt that barely fit over his thick
arms. His dark hair was thick and combed away from his
face. He walked as if he owned the world, ignoring everyone else around him.

Some people had a distinctive look about them, and
these two men wore the Russian mantle with ease. It was
in their bearing, their clothes, and even the way they stood.

By the way they searched the lobby, they were also
looking for someone. And she'd bet her father's company
that it was Yuri.

She glanced out the revolving glass doors and spotted
a shape across the street that she recognized. Cullen. A
smile tugged at her lips just looking at him. He might not
be beside her, but he'd made sure to be close.

It wasn't because he didn't think she could take care of
herself. It was because it was in his nature to protect.

She made a quick decision and rose from the chair. She

walked to the concierge desk near the Russians. Thankfully, there were a few people already there. She grabbed a brochure about the sights in the area and positioned herself near the men to hear them speaking Russian in quiet tones.

"He wouldn't be foolish enough to return here," said the chubby one.

The other snorted. "I warned you not to trust him. Markovic was too easily convinced to join us."

Mia bit back a smile. Just as she'd thought. They were looking for Yuri. Then she frowned. Why? Where was Yuri, then? And why was he running? When they began talking again, she moved closer so she could hear better, all the while hoping the little Russian she knew would help her translate it correctly.

"He was needed," replied Chubs.

"You thought his connection to Loughman would help. I had my doubts."

"When we find Markovic, you can kill him."

Slim smiled. "By then we'll have Ragnarok, and our plan will be in action."

Her stomach plummeted to her feet. Hearing them talk about using the bioweapon as if it were bug spray left her shaken. The fact that the Saints were maniacal enough to want to use such a weapon pretty much said it all.

It was a good thing she and Cullen had begun hunting the Saints. They could begin with these two.

The men moved away. When she began to follow, Slim's gaze met hers. She flashed him a flirty smile, hoping he'd think she was another tourist.

His annoyed frown as he turned forward again allowed her to release a relieved breath. The wig and clothes managed to hide her in plain sight. She replaced the flier and calmly walked from the hotel.

As she made her way across the street to Cullen, she spotted a woman staring at him as if she'd seen a ghost. The woman stood about twenty feet from Cullen, unmoving.

"What?" Cullen asked when Mia reached him.

She jerked her chin in the direction of the woman. "She looks as if she recognizes you."

"I've never seen her," Cullen replied when he turned toward the woman.

Mia suspected the woman was in her late forties. She was thin, and by her name-brand clothes, she had money. Her shoulder-length red hair complimented her pale complexion.

Finally, with slow steps, the woman closed the distance between them. She never took her eyes off Cullen. He faced her, waiting.

Mia moved closer to him, curious as well. No one said anything. It was Mia who broke the silence. "Hi. Can we help you?"

The woman gave a little startled jerk. She swung gray eyes to Mia and smiled briefly before looking back at Cullen. "This may seem incredibly forward, but is your last name Loughman?"

Cullen's entire demeanor changed. He glanced about before he took the woman's arm and walked her away from the throng of people. Mia hurried to catch up.

When they stood in an alley, just out of the light of a streetlamp, he took a menacing step toward the woman. "How do you know who I am?"

"Because you look like your father."

Mia closed her eyes for a moment. "He's alive."

"Tell me everything," Cullen demanded.

The woman licked her lips. "My name is Kate Donnelly. I'm a doctor at a nearby hospital. I was taken from my home and forced to help an injured man."

"Orrin," Mia said.

Kate nodded, glancing at her. "He was badly beaten. Broken ribs, dislocated shoulder, broken wrist, black eye, and multiple contusions and lacerations."

Cullen ran a hand down his face as he turned away and took a few pacing steps.

While he digested that information, Mia got Kate's attention. "Did you speak to Orrin?"

"I did. He told me to get help for him. I wanted to, but they had my son."

"You did the right thing," Mia assured her. She glanced at Cullen, who had his back to them.

Kate said, "I helped him. I gave him a combination of vitamins that accelerated the healing process. The Russian that took him, Yuri, only wanted me to bring him back from the brink of death."

At that, Cullen whirled around. "My father nearly died?"

"Yes," Kate replied. "Yuri acted fast, though. I was able to get Orrin on the mend quickly."

"They obviously let you go. Why?" Mia asked.

Kate fidgeted. "Something changed. There were men patrolling everywhere, but once, while Yuri was gone, a camera was installed in Orrin's room where I tended to him."

"Who was in charge?" Cullen took a step closer to her, his gaze focused.

She gave a shrug. "Yuri. But not all of the men there were his."

"Were they all Russian?"

"As far as I know."

Mia touched Kate's arm. "How did you escape?"

"I didn't," Kate said. "Yuri let me go. It was only yesterday when Orrin claimed he was well. Yuri agreed and ordered Orrin to return to where he'd been held before.

The next thing I knew, I was released. One of Yuri's men returned me home and told me not to speak of it to anyone or they'd kill my son."

Mia met Cullen's gaze. "It makes sense now."

"Does it?" He raised a brow. "Please elaborate because I'm confused."

"Inside the hotel, two Russians were looking for Yuri. I overheard them talking. They said he joined the Saints too easily."

"We're close, then," Cullen said with a wry twist of his lips.

Mia scratched at the wig, wanting it off. "Yes, and they want Yuri. If he let Kate go, and he's running—"

"Then he might've helped Dad," Cullen finished.

Mia turned back to the doctor. "Do you think you could find where you were held?"

"They blindfolded me, but I know it was on the docks. I caught a glimpse of a faded fish logo, though."

"That helps immensely," Mia said.

For the first time, Cullen was smiling. They knew where Orrin was. Once they had him, they would have another asset in the hunt for the Saints.

Mia's joy dimmed as she turned to the hotel. She pointed out the Russians for Cullen, who glared at them as if just by staring they could kill them. "We should go now before those two go to the docks, as well."

"I'm coming," Kate said.

That got Cullen's attention. He turned back to her. "You're lucky to have gotten out with your life. Leave while you can."

"You're going to need me." She pointed to his shoulder then.

Mia leaned over and saw the blood seeping through his shirt from the bullet wound.

"What if Orrin needs medical attention?" Kate asked. "Will there be time to get him to a hospital?"

Cullen gave a shake of his head and glanced upward. "The last place you should be is in the middle of this."

"I know."

"Do you even know what all of this is about?" Mia asked.

Kate shook her head. "It doesn't matter. I want to help Orrin."

Mia looked at the doctor differently. Did she have feelings for Orrin? It would make sense. A handsome American held against his will and tortured. . . .

"You like him," Mia blurted out.

Cullen frowned while Kate looked away nervously.

Mia smiled at Kate. "Anyone willing to risk their life for Orrin is perfect in my eyes."

"Thank you," Kate said.

Cullen blew out a breath. "You're going to regret this, Doc."

"I risked my life, and my son's, to help Orrin while I was being held. I'd do it again in a heartbeat," she stated with a lift of her chin.

Mia had never thought it was right that Orrin was alone. He needed a special woman, and she was beginning to think that Kate was just what Orrin needed.

"Let's get moving," Cullen said and turned on his heel.

She waved Kate to follow. "Where's your son?"

"On a trip with his father. I thought it best he leave the city for a while."

Mia looked down and saw no wedding ring on Kate's finger.

The doctor leaned over and said, "I'm divorced. Six years now."

When they reached the SUV, Cullen got behind the

wheel while Kate slid into the back seat. Mia hurriedly removed the wig and shook out her hair.

Then she kicked off the platform heels as Cullen pointed the vehicle in the direction of the docks and began driving. Mia took off her jacket and the skimpy shirt.

She wadded them up, returning them to the bag as she dug out her old clothes. She caught Cullen's grin when she sat up. With a smile she couldn't hide, she put on her white shirt. Cullen's eyebrows rose as he looked pointedly at her skirt.

Mia laughed and pushed his face forward. "Watch the road, Casanova."

The tension lessened for a bit. Once Mia was changed, she glanced in the back seat to find Kate wearing a knowing smile. The two exchanged grins. Mia gave her a *what do you do* look.

Then all laughter ceased as they reached the docks. Cullen slowed the SUV as they drove past warehouse after warehouse. Large ships were anchored, and containers were stacked at the port and on the ships.

Men milled about while bright lights shone everywhere, illuminating everything as if it were daylight.

"There," Kate said, her arm pointing through the seats.

They looked to where her finger was aimed and saw a warehouse with a faded logo of a swordfish twisting. Cullen parked and turned off the engine as he looked at the building.

"Let's go kill some Saints and get Orrin," Mia said.

He palmed a knife and gave her a nod.

CHAPTER THIRTY-FIVE

The lack of guards at the warehouse doors spoke volumes to Cullen. For one, the perimeter was most likely monitored by surveillance equipment. Which meant the Saints would see them coming.

Second, they didn't care who came in, because once inside, the Saints didn't intend to allow anyone to leave.

The absence of guards kept them low profile. The dockworkers would take notice of men standing in the doorways. The Saints had thought of everything.

Cullen wanted to meet whoever ran the faction. He was either extremely smart, or he had a group he trusted explicitly that gave him advice. Either way, the individual was a foe that kept Cullen on his toes.

There had been few of those. In any other situation, he'd welcome such an adversary. Now, all he wanted was to kill the son of a bitch who had murdered his aunt and uncle, taken his father hostage, and tried to kill Mia.

"What are you thinking?" Mia asked, breaking into his thoughts.

"If they don't already know we're here, they will as soon as we walk to the door."

Kate leaned forward. "There's a side entrance. To the left."

Mia turned sideways in the seat toward him. "I'll take the front. You go to the side."

"All right." He was really going to have to work on this feeling of having to be beside her to protect her all the time.

She was more than capable of taking care of herself. Why then did he believe he was the only one who could safeguard her? Each time he thought of her facing the Saints alone, it twisted his gut.

Perhaps it was the sound of crunching metal and the feeling of helplessness as they'd rolled down the mountain. It wasn't an emotion he wanted to repeat ever again. His nature demanded that he exact his vengeance.

A knock on Mia's window had them all jerking their attention to the right. She lowered the glass an inch and peered outside.

A big, burly man with a long, dark beard and beady eyes looked inside the vehicle. "You have business here?"

Cullen gave a nod. "Is that a problem?"

"Seen some odd things this past month. You Feds? You have the look of Feds."

"What odd things?" Cullen asked, ignoring the question.

The man crossed his arms over his wide chest. "Expensive vehicles rolling up all hours of the day and night. Men in uniforms I don't recognize. And I heard a few speaking what sounded like Russian."

"We appreciate the information," Mia said.

The man's gaze shifted to her. "I wouldn't go in there."

That got Cullen's attention. "Why?"

"The last man who went in didn't come out."

"We've got this," Cullen told him. "Though I'd suggest you and everyone else steer clear the rest of the night."

The man walked away without another word as he pulled out a walkie-talkie and began speaking.

Kate sighed. "The two of you are going to be outnumbered."

"How many of them did you see?" Mia asked.

"About thirty."

Cullen caught Mia's gaze. "You go to the front. As they begin questioning you, I'll sneak in the side."

"I don't know where they kept Orrin," Kate said. "The room I treated him in was on the second level. They locked me in a space on the first floor."

"We have a lot of ground to cover," Mia said.

Cullen took her hand when she started to open the door. "If they detain you, don't fight. I'll find you."

"We've got the Saints to deal with as well as searching for Orrin. I'll be fine."

"How long do you think it'll take them to realize who you are? They're after you."

She shrugged, her black eyes gazing into his. "We set out to hunt these jerks, and we've found them. Luck has also given us the very place your father is. Don't pass this up."

"I'm not leaving without you."

"I don't intend to be left behind."

He'd learned that it was pointless to argue with her. So he smiled in response, and silently vowed to make sure she left the warehouse in the same condition as she walked in.

"Be safe," she said.

He put his hand on the back of her neck and pulled her forward as he leaned toward her. Their lips met, and he kissed her deeply. Reluctantly, he released her.

"Don't get hurt," he warned.

She touched his face, a soft smile lifting her lips. "The same goes for you."

He wanted to tell her . . . what? What did he want to say? He wasn't even sure. He was still coming to grips with the idea that he wasn't nearly finished with her.

And he was beginning to suspect that he never would be.

There wasn't a woman alive who could hold a candle to her. She outshone them all—in every way.

If he found his father inside, would she leave? Would that be the end of whatever this was between them? He didn't want that.

"Let's go find some Saints," she said.

He watched as she got out of the car and started toward the warehouse.

Kate shifted in the back seat. "If you want her, tell her. Life is too short."

He briefly looked at the doctor. "Stay here. We'll be back as soon as we can."

Cullen exited the SUV and started running, making a wide path around the warehouse to reach the side entrance. He looked at Mia often. She walked with sure steps, as if there were nothing in the world that frightened her.

He'd been like that once. Right up until he met her. Now she was his Achilles heel. There wasn't much he wouldn't do for her.

Surprisingly, he felt comfortable with that knowledge.

He kept to the shadows when he could find them. Letting his gaze search the side of the warehouse, he looked for cameras.

In the distance, he heard the sound of cranes and the *boom* as containers were stacked. No dockworkers were near the warehouse, leaving the area almost ghostly quiet. He'd have to be careful about whatever noises he made.

He bent at the waist and made a dash for the door. His knife was in his palm, ready to take out anyone who attempted to get in his way.

No one threw open the door and stopped him. He flattened himself against the side of the warehouse and waited.

A few seconds later, he softly tried the handle. As expected, it was locked.

The sound of a hand banging against a metal door echoed around him. Mia. He sent up a quick prayer for her safety. Then he waited until he heard the sound of her voice.

Though he couldn't hear what she said, it was enough that she was talking. He jabbed his knife into the doorframe and broke the lock.

Quietly, he opened the door wide enough to squeeze through and let it close behind him. He looked around, waiting for an attack. None came.

A quick skim of the area showed metal stairs near him and farther away. Several closed doors down one side of the interior. Everything was old and rusting; what paint was left on the walls was peeling.

The warehouse was huge, but the part he was in left him claustrophobic—everything was so tight. It also left many hiding places for someone to lie in wait.

No sooner had that thought crossed his mind than he walked past a piece of large machinery. A man lunged, the tip of a knife coming close to Cullen's eye.

Cullen raised his arm, blocking the attack while twisting away. Then he turned and came up behind the man, locking an arm around his neck.

Two quick stabs to his heart later, Cullen put the dead man back in his hiding spot. Then he continued onward.

He grinned when he heard Mia talking from somewhere in the warehouse. She seemed to be putting on a show to attract more of the men to her.

The longer he heard her without the sound of bullets, the better he felt. Whatever she was doing allowed him to check rooms without being seen. Except with each one that was empty, he became more worried. It was the tenth door that he opened that revealed where they must have kept Kate.

There were charts lying about with Orrin's name on them. Cullen didn't stay. The discovery only made him eager to locate his father quicker.

He turned a corner and came face-to-face with a large man with eyes as cold as death wearing Russian military camouflage. His blond hair was kept short on the sides and longer on top.

By the way he stood, he'd been waiting on Cullen.

Cullen halted, taking in the scar on the man's left cheek that ran from his cheekbone down to his jaw. With some it was obvious that they had seen a lot of death.

This was such a man.

He was also the type that doled out death effortlessly. Except Cullen wouldn't go down easily.

"It took you long enough."

That caused him to pause. Cullen eyed the soldier. "It's a big place."

"So it is."

Cullen frowned. There was an accent there, it was faint, but he heard one. The only problem was that it wasn't Russian. Just who was this man?

"Shall we get on with this then?" Cullen asked.

The man raised a brow. "So eager to die?"

"Eager to find my father."

"You're too late."

No. That couldn't be possible. Cullen couldn't have come all this way to find Orrin dead. "Where is his body?" he demanded.

The man raised a brow. "I never said he was dead."

"Then what. He's gone?"

Silence met his words. Cullen's mind raced. Mia had said two men were looking for Yuri at the hotel. Could his father and Yuri have taken off together?

He focused back on the soldier. "I can't let any of the Saints live."

"Good thing I'm not a Saint, then." With that, the man pivoted and walked away.

Cullen waited a few moments to make sure he wouldn't return, then he hurried toward Mia. He heard her long before he saw her.

She stood on the first floor, surrounded by men. Some were in uniform, some weren't.

"Seriously?" she said. "I've got Girl Scout cookies to sell for my niece. Thirteen huge boxes of these cookies. Everyone on the docks buys them. Surely I can sell at least a box of Thin Mints to one of you."

Cullen noticed how the men in uniform were eyeing the others. While the plain clothes men stared at Mia as if she were a mouse and they the cat.

"Anyone?" she asked.

"We'll take you instead," one of the Saints said in a Boston accent. "You've taken us on a merry chase only to drop right into our laps."

Mia smiled at the man. "You really think I'd come alone?"

No sooner were the words out of her mouth, than Cullen came up behind one of the non-uniformed men and knocked him on the back of the head with the hilt of his knife. As soon as the man fell, all hell broke loose.

Mia pulled out her gun just as two men rushed her. Three quick shots, and they were dead at her feet. The uniformed men were attacking the others.

Except more of the Saints' men came pouring out. Cullen used his knife and his gun, working his way toward

Mia. The floor was littered with bodies and slick with blood.

Gunfire blasted around them, mixing with shouts of pain. He felt his shoulder pull and blood run down his side, but he paid none of it any mind.

Mia was in the mix with their enemies. The Saints were all around them, killing the Russian soldiers. When Cullen saw a break, he grabbed Mia's hand and ran.

The corridor was narrow as they raced down it and then up a set of stairs. There were easily fifty Saints in the building. It was a hefty number to overcome.

The reality of their situation settled over Cullen like a blanket of iron that threatened to choke him.

CHAPTER THIRTY-SIX

Mia flattened herself against a wall after ducking into a room with Cullen. She released her empty clip, letting it drop to the floor before sliding in a new one.

"We're outnumbered," Cullen said.

She looked into his hazel eyes. "It appears that way."

"I can distract them."

So she could get away? She shot him a withering look. "The ones in uniform turned against the Saints. I believe those were Yuri's men."

"They're all dead now. But the soldiers managed to take out quite a few Saints in the process."

"The only reason for those men to turn against the Saints would be if Yuri left as we suspected."

Cullen peered around the door. "I've known men to inspire that kind of loyalty, so I suppose that's a possibility."

She thought back to the two Saints at the hotel. "Yuri wanted in the group."

"What are you thinking?" Cullen asked as he glanced at her.

"What if Yuri joined the Saints to get to something?"

He rested his head back against the wall and blew out

a breath. "If Markovic wanted to get to Dad, there were other ways to do it. He didn't have to join a fanatical organization."

"Right," she said with a nod, thinking. Then it dawned on her. "Yuri joined to get Ragnarok."

"Now that is a definite possibility," Cullen replied. "Except my father screwed things up by sending the bio-agent away."

She twisted her lips. "And the formula."

"The question is, does Yuri want Ragnarok to use for himself? Or to destroy it?"

She saw something out of the corner of her eye and raised her gun, firing when she saw one of the Saints. The bullet slammed into his chest, knocking the man backward.

"Come on!" Cullen shouted and pushed her into the hallway as he began shooting at the approaching Saints.

She ran, glancing over her shoulder as she heard shots. Cullen had stopped and turned to fire off several more rounds. She stepped into a shallow puddle that sprayed water onto her leg. The yellow lighting hurt her eyes. She was beginning to hate the warehouse.

"Turn right," she heard from behind her.

It registered just as she reached a junction. She turned to the right and ran as fast as she could. The floor was damp, causing her to slip on the concrete several times.

Then someone stepped out ahead of her. She knew she'd never stop in time. She bent her legs, falling to the ground and sliding feet first toward her opponent as she raised her gun, sighting down the barrel.

She fired three quick bursts, watching as they tore into his chest. His body jerked with the impact while he stumbled back and fell, unmoving.

The sound of gunfire behind her had her rolling to her stomach as she came to a stop. She took aim and waited.

Her heart hammered against her ribs, but her hands never wavered. She paused when she saw Cullen rushing toward her. When he caught sight of her, he ducked into a room, leaving her time to fire several rounds into the three men chasing him.

She jumped to her feet and looked back at the man she'd shot to make sure he was dead. He was the slim one from the hotel. Where was Chubs?

"Mia."

The sound of her name on Cullen's lips eased her, comforted her. She turned to him and gave him a half-smile to let him know she was unhurt. Pointing to the man over her shoulder, she said, "He's one from the hotel. I think he's in charge. We need to find the other one."

"Perhaps with those two gone, it'll end the Saints."

Her smile widened at the thought. Then she spotted someone behind Cullen. It was Chubs. And he held a gun pointed at Cullen's head. There was no time to warn him. All she could do was look at Cullen as she raised her gun.

A heartbeat later, Cullen whirled around and lifted his gun. Chubs smirked as he motioned for both of them to drop their weapons.

It irked her to lose her pistol. She grudgingly bent and lowered it to the floor. Meanwhile, Cullen glared at the man for a long moment before he did the same.

"Kick them to me," Chubs ordered in a Russian accent. After they'd complied, he asked, "Did either of you really think you would win?"

She lifted her chin. "Well, I got one of you."

Chubs looked around her to his dead comrade. He slid his gaze to her and shrugged. "It matters not. Tell me where they are."

"Who?" Cullen asked.

"Do not play stupid," Chubs angrily bit out. "Yuri Markovic and Orrin Loughman."

Cullen smiled smugly. "Lost them, did you?"

"I do not believe I need your father anymore. Now that I have you."

She shot a look at Cullen, but he didn't seem the least bit fazed by the statement.

One Saint leader was dead. All they needed to do was kill Chubs, and it would end. One more death. In theory, it was easy. But with him holding a gun, things looked vastly different.

She eyed her pistol, but it was too far away for her to reach. Chubs would get her before she was able to reach it. But she did have her knife.

Cullen laughed and took a step sideways, edging closer to her. "You couldn't hold one Loughman. Do you really want to try with a second?"

"You walked right in," Chubs said with a smile. "As if you wanted me to hold both of you captive. Though, I'll kill the bitch."

She glared at Chubs. How she wished she had her gun. She'd aim it right at the bastard's eye.

"You can certainly try." Cullen shifted nearer.

She was wondering what he was about when his hand touched her leg. Her knife! Of course. How could she have forgotten? With a glance at Cullen, his subtle nod confirmed what she suspected.

"Why don't you come and get me?" Cullen asked with a cocky grin.

When Chubs took a step toward them, she slowly turned to the side. His gaze was locked on Cullen as if he'd forgotten her completely.

By the time he stood two feet from Cullen, she had her

back against the wall and had scooted away. There would be precious time between her bending over, lifting her jeans, and taking the blade from her boot before Chubs realized what was going on.

"You should check me for other weapons," Cullen said.

She shook her head, wondering what he was doing. Time seemed to stand still as she waited.

"Give me your weapons," Chubs ordered.

With a grin still in place, Cullen bent at the waist and pulled out an eight-inch blade from his boot. He flipped it end over end. "You mean this?"

"Hand it to me."

It was Cullen's hesitation that put her on alert. Then his gaze met hers. She rolled, reaching for her knife. When she came to her feet, she was behind Chubs with the weapon in hand, aimed to slide it between his vertebrae.

She tried to stab him, but he turned. Still, the blade cut into his suit jacket and shirt to his skin to leave a long cut that immediately welled with bright red blood.

He bellowed and fired the gun. Mia saw Cullen drop to his knees after the retort. *No!* her mind screamed.

She drew back her arm and was ready to plunge the knife into Chubs when his meaty fist slammed into her forearm. Her fingers went numb, and the blade dropped to clatter to the concrete.

Chubs turned the gun on her. She jerked as she heard the shot and waited to feel the pain. Then Chubs' face went white as a trail of blood ran from his forehead to his nose and down his right cheek.

She spotted the single bullet hole in the center of his forehead before he fell forward. Mia moved aside and watched him hit the ground, Cullen's knife in his spine. She looked to find Cullen standing, his eyes filled with cold determination. And she knew she was witnessing him at his most lethal.

He blinked and raised his gaze to her. He held out his hand. She eagerly took it as he pulled her against his side. She checked him for wounds, but only found his previous injuries bleeding.

"Who shot him?" she asked.

He looked down the corridor. Mia followed his gaze and saw a man in a Russian uniform lower a sniper rifle. Cullen took her hand and began walking.

When they reached him, Cullen asked, "Where are Markovic and my father?"

"I don't know."

She narrowed her gaze on the man. He might be in a Russian uniform, but there was something about him that didn't fit with the others she'd seen.

"Did you help them escape?" Cullen asked.

The man raised a blond brow, his gaze unyielding. "I follow orders."

Which didn't answer the question. Whoever the man was, he was good. Mia rubbed her bruised arm. "Thank you for the assistance."

"You didn't need my help," he said and turned on his heel.

Mia and Cullen watched him walk away until only silence greeted them. She had never felt so tired in all her life. She rested her head on Cullen's chest when he threaded his fingers through her hair.

"We did it," he said.

That brought a smile to her face. "The Saints are finished."

When he didn't reply, she lifted her head. "What is it?"

"We took down two obvious leaders, but were they the top ones?"

"If they weren't, the Saints will be gunning for us with everything they have now."

"As well as my father and Yuri."

"We need to find them."

He nodded and began walking to the front of the warehouse. "That we do. I'm not done hunting the Saints yet."

"Me either."

They made their way to the entrance hand-in-hand. There was no other sign of the blond Russian. The dead littered the warehouse, and the smell of blood filled the air, making the already unpleasant building fouler.

She was glad when they walked outside, and she was able to take a deep breath. The back door of the SUV opened, and Kate stepped out.

Mia faced Cullen. "I'm sorry we didn't find your father."

"Killing two Saints' leaders is nothing to sneeze at," he said after a brief pause.

She lifted one shoulder in a shrug. "I know, but I wanted to find Orrin. I wanted the two of you to be reunited."

"We will be."

She saw the determination in his hazel eyes. Whatever happiness she felt dimmed when she realized he had no more need of her. "I suppose you'll be heading back to Texas to meet up with your brothers now."

"I don't know where I'm going, but wherever it is, I want you beside me."

Her heart skipped a beat at his words. She couldn't catch her breath or even get any words past her lips. Hope spiraled through her, bursting in an array of brilliance at the mere suggestion that they not part.

"I'm not going to lie to you," he said. "My longest relationship was a week. In high school. I'm used to doing things my own way, and I can be stubborn. I never expected to ever feel anything for another, and yet, here it is."

He touched his hand over his heart for a moment. "You did that. I don't know when or how, and it doesn't matter. All I want is to have you beside me."

"For how long?"

"A month, an eternity. I want it all. As long as you're with me, I can face anything."

She swallowed past the lump of emotions in her throat. This was exactly what she wanted, but it was fear that held her tongue. "You have such a hold over me that I know you could shatter my heart if I gave you the chance."

"Never," he vowed. "My father once told me that if I ever found the woman that was my other half, I'd know. It's you. That wandering spirit that I've always had is gone. I . . . I love you."

Her eyes clouded with unshed tears that she hastily blinked away. One escaped and fell down her cheek.

Cullen caught it on his finger. "I know you doubt me. You have every reason to. I didn't realize my feelings until the crash. I tried to deny and ignore them, but I can't. I won't do that to either of us.

"I know how to fight and stay alive. What I don't know is how to be the kind of man you need. Teach me."

She laughed through her tears. "Oh, you silly man. I don't need to teach you anything. You already know what to do."

"Does that mean you'll stay with me?"

The hope that shone in Cullen's eyes was blinding. She nodded, and the next thing she knew, she was pulled against his chest, his strong arms holding her tightly.

She squeezed her eyes closed. It was too good to believe that she'd finally found what her heart had searched for. The fact that she hadn't been looking for it made it even more special. To have such a horrific event bring such a man into her life made her wonder at the plans of the

Universe. But then she didn't care because Cullen was kissing her.

Suddenly, he pulled back, a frown marring his forehead. "You did hear me earlier, right? The part where I said I loved you."

"I heard you," she said with a smile.

He raised a dark brow, concern lining his face. "That's all you have to say?"

"I love you, too, Cullen Loughman."

His face split into a wide grin. "We're going to have a wonderful life, darlin'."

"Right after we take down the Saints and find your father." Because they couldn't truly be happy until those two things were done.

Cullen drew in a deep breath and released it. "With you by my side, we can do it."

He held out his hand. She took it, and they walked to the SUV where Kate waited. Another night was coming to an end, and they were going to enjoy the victory they'd gained that night.

Tomorrow was another day.

EPILOGUE

Two days later . . .

Cullen frowned at the surveillance from the city's cameras. It was like his father and Markovic had simply disappeared. There was no sign of the black Range Rover they had used to drive away from the warehouse.

"Where are you, Dad?" he asked the screen.

Arms came around his waist from behind. Mia kissed his bare shoulder and laid her head against his back. "Still nothing?"

"No."

"Orrin is smart. I believe he and Yuri are working together. Why would your dad do that?"

Cullen turned around in her arms and cupped her face as he gave her a quick kiss. "Because they're going after the Saints."

"Or Jankovic."

The scientist. Of course! He gave a nod. "I know Wyatt and Callie are trying to find a way to get to Jankovic."

"I bet that's where we find your father."

"To go there means we'll be gathering, just as the Saints probably want us to do."

Mia smiled. "The one thing the Saints should fear is all four Loughmans fighting as one."

He snorted and gazed into her black eyes. "You're pretty smart."

"Took you long enough to realize it."

"Oh, darlin', I always knew it."

Her smile was wide. "I talked to my father. He was shocked about the Saints. He's going to see what he can find out for us, and he's demanded we come for dinner as soon as this is all finished."

"You called your father?" he asked, running his fingers along the side of her face.

"I knew he could help."

"We're going to need all the allies we can get." He bent his head for another kiss when his new burner phone rang.

Mia leaned to the side to look at it. "It's Callie."

Their reprieve was over. It was time to go into battle once more.

Mia's lips turned up in a smile. "I'm ready, cowboy. Are you?"

"I was born ready," he said before he picked up the phone and answered it. "What's our move, Callie?"

Orrin stared at the stately home where Konrad Jankovic hid. For days, he and Yuri had staked out the house, watching who came and went.

"There is more activity," Yuri murmured from beside him as they peered through the window of a house for sale across the street.

The Saints checked the house often, but not once had they found him or Yuri. Nor would they. The Saints may have numbers, but Orrin had experience.

"Something must've happened," Orrin said as he looked through the lenses of the binoculars.

Yuri peered out the window. "Whatever it is, they are not happy."

Orrin snorted and set the binoculars down. "Good." He noticed then that Yuri looked upset. "What is it?"

"I heard on the news that Davis is dead. A heart attack."

Both of them knew that Davis didn't die of such a thing. The Saints learned that he'd helped Mia and killed him. Davis had been in a position where he'd had no choice but to help the Saints.

It was too bad Davis hadn't confided in Orrin before his trip to Russia. A lot of this could've been avoided. But Davis had felt as Orrin did now, that there were few people he could trust.

"It is someone in his office," Yuri said.

"Most likely. The Saints were probably monitoring him, as well."

"I am ready to end the *mudak*, assholes."

Orrin glanced out the window to the house. "Definitely."

Because he wasn't going to lose any more of his family to the Saints. It was going to end once and for all.

"He's gone? Is that what you just told me?" asked the male voice over the phone.

Mitch Hewett winced at the cold anger he heard through the line. "Orrin won't get far."

"You said Markovic was with him."

"We think that's the case," Mitch corrected him.

There was a long pause. "Do you realize how much is at stake?"

"Yes, sir, I do."

"I think you've forgotten."

Mitch shook his head. "Sir, I can find Orrin. I've been his handler for years, and I was his friend before that. I know how he thinks, as well as the moves he'll make."

"You've seen what we can do to those who fail us."

Mitch swallowed, recalling witnessing such an event years before. It was how he knew just what kind of power the Saints wielded. "Yes, sir. I won't fail."

"Let's hope you don't," came the reply before the line disconnected.

Mitch lowered the phone to his desk. Then he walked from his office into the outer room where his people worked. "Listen up," he called. "I want everyone looking for Orrin Loughman. He's turned traitor. Every resource we have needs to be focused on finding him. Forget everything else for now. Turn your full attention on him. And his sons," he added.

Because there was one thing he'd learned about the Loughmans—they stuck together.

Read on for an excerpt from the next
Sons of Texas novel by Donna Grant

THE LEGEND

Coming soon from St. Martin's Paperbacks

He wanted her.

He craved her.

No longer could Wyatt pretend otherwise. The truth had become painfully evident when they had been locked together, their bodies rubbing against the other.

Had the alarm not gone off, he would've kissed her. It was the thought of tasting Callie's lips again that caused him to look at her.

She was staring into the fire. As he gazed at her profile, he wondered what she was thinking. Did she long for his touch once more? Did she remember the pleasure they found in each other's arms?

Or had he burned that bridge once and for all?

He held out hope. It was slim, but her reaction to him couldn't be denied. Not the way her breathing had changed or how her lips had parted. Most definitely not the way her blue eyes had filled with need.

His balls tightened thinking about it. And when her lids had slid closed, his only thought had been to claim her lips, to let her know how he'd hungered for her kiss all the years they'd been apart.

But the damn alarm had interrupted everything.

Now he might never get that chance again. Callie was a

master at remaining just out of his reach. Perhaps if he were more of a charmer, like Cullen, or even as open as Owen there might be a chance for him.

But he wasn't either of those things. He was hard, cold, and closed off to the world.

Callie had been the only one to get close to him, the only one to ever touch his heart and make him long for a life that could never be his.

This was where Owen would urge him to let Callie know that secret, but Wyatt didn't dare. It would leave him too exposed. Admitting it to himself was one thing, but no one—absolutely *no one*—could ever know.

His thoughts came to a screeching halt when Callie's head turned and their eyes clashed. The palpable desire he saw made his body pulse with a yearning he hadn't dared to give into. But there was no turning away from it now.

From the very beginning, Callie had a hold over him. She swayed him with a smile or a look. He didn't know if she grasped the power she had back then—the power she still had.

Because if she did, with just a few words she could make him invincible—or break him.

She rose from the couch and stood facing him. There was no other choice for him but to go to her, to go to the only woman he'd ever wanted.

When he reached her, she turned to him, shoving him back onto the sofa. He looked up at her and was consumed with lust. Callie stood between his legs not as the young girl he remembered, but a woman who knew what she wanted—and got it.

Her head tilted to the side, blue eyes shamelessly looking over him. He swallowed a groan and grabbed her wrists. A seductive, teasing smile pulled at the corners of her lips before she placed one knee on the outside of his hip.

His mouth went dry as she straddled him, her breasts even with his face. Before him was a temptress who would accept nothing less than all of him.

She slid her hands up his arms and over his shoulders before sinking into his hair. Then she arched her back and rolled her head to the side before letting it fall backward.

The moan he'd been holding back rushed past his lips. He gripped her on either side of her ribcage and leaned forward. His lips touched the space just below the neck in the middle of her chest.

"Wyatt."

His name whispered in that husky voice of hers stirred something deep and primal within him. He wrapped an arm around her while he yanked at the neck of her sweatshirt to expose a slim shoulder.

He nipped and kissed the skin there before moving across to her neck. All the while the long silky strands of her hair teased his arms and hands with whispered touches.

Her head shifted to the side to give him access to her neck. Slowly, he worked his way up the column of her throat to her ear and licked the spot that always drove her wild.

Just as he expected, her response was immediate. Her nails sank into his scalp and her hips rocked against his cock. He gently sucked on the delicate skin until her breathing was as erratic as his heart.

Only then did he return his lips to her throat and kiss his way up to her chin. But he didn't take her lips. Her head lifted and their eyes clashed.

For several seconds they stared at each other, the longing, the hunger growing with each second. The only sound was the popping of the fire. Without realizing it, they moved toward each other.

Her hands came around to caress his jaw as her gaze lowered to his mouth. Her thumb swept across his lower lip. He hesitated in kissing her, because once he did, there would be no turning back. He only had so much self-control, and she was quickly sapping him of what was left.

She lifted her eyes to him. Then she leaned forward and placed her mouth over his.

For a heartbeat, Wyatt didn't move. He was afraid that it would shatter the moment. But when her tongue slid along the seam of his lips, he couldn't hold back.

Gripped with desire so overwhelming, so consuming, he had no choice but to succumb. He held the back of her head, his fingers tangled in her chestnut locks, and kissed her—letting her feel and taste the years of longing, of aching to have her again.

He had to feel her skin, her warmth. Her softness. No longer could he wait. He took her arms and moved them above her head. Then his hands slipped beneath the hem of her sweatshirt and impatiently pushed the cloth upward.

As soon as the shirt was gone, they were kissing hungrily again. With just a twist of his fingers, he unhooked her bra. The garment was tossed aside. He wrapped an arm around her before shifting them so that he lay atop her.

Her warm flesh against his palm as he caressed upward from her waist was exactly what he'd longed for. But that wasn't all. Not by a long shot.

He broke the kiss and rose up enough to look down at her. The sight of her hair spread around her with her lips swollen from his kisses caused his cock to jump. His gaze moved lower to her breasts.

His mouth went dry when he saw her dusty nipples already hard. Callie always had the most amazing breasts.

There was a rough intake of breath from her when he cupped her perfect globe and massaged it.

Her eyes rolled back in her head, her lips parted on a silent moan. He rolled one tip between his fingers while leaning down to tease the other with his tongue. Her answering cry was just what he wanted to hear.

Just as he was about to get settled to feast on her breasts, Callie surprised him again by once more taking control and pushing against his shoulder to roll him. He tumbled off the sofa onto the floor with her still in his arms.

She leaned over him, her hair falling in a curtain around him. He was so turned on by her aggression that he was more than willing to see what she would do.

Her lips brushed against his, but when he tried to kiss her, she pulled away. Then she sat up, giving him a view of her bare chest in the light of the fire.

"Take off your shirt," she commanded.

He eagerly complied. This new side of her was something he could definitely get used to. Callie had always known what she wanted, and had never been afraid to ask for it. But this was a whole new level.

With her hands spread wide, she leisurely caressed his chest, gliding over his muscles and lingering at his wounds. His gaze never left her face as her eyes followed her hands. He couldn't tell what she was thinking, and he hated that.

Suddenly, she rolled back onto her feet and stood. Wyatt rose up on his forearms, afraid that she'd changed her mind. He should've known better.

Callie removed her shoes, then shimmied out of her jeans before slipping her underwear off. His gaze swept her naked form from her breasts to the indent of her waist to her flared hips then lower to her muscular legs.

He held out a hand. As soon as she placed hers in his, he pulled her down beside him. Then he rolled to his side and let his hand move over her body.

"Have I changed much?" she asked.

He touched the swell of her hip. "You've filled out more in all the best places. Have I?"

"I don't know," she replied saucily. "You still have your clothes on."

The smile formed before he realized it. Not one to disappoint, he stood and removed the rest of his clothes. When he finished, he let her look her fill.

"Well?" he prompted after several quiet minutes.

She got to her knees and began to touch the scars on his legs before moving to the ones she'd already investigated on his upper body and arms. Then she climbed to her feet and walked to his back.

His wounds were proof that he had survived. He barely noticed them anymore, but he began to wonder if she found them offensive. Did she think them unsightly?

When they were younger, she had often commented on the beauty of his body. He'd laughed about it then, but that memory returned, putting doubts in his head.

Her hand trailed behind her over his butt as she walked to stand before him. "Yes, you've changed. Your stronger than before, more filled out." She reached up and ran her middle finger along the outside of his eye. "You have lines from squinting in the sun."

"Is that all?" He didn't know why he asked. He should've just left well enough alone.

A slim brow lifted. "You're a warrior, Wyatt. Your body proudly carries the marks of battle—and victory."

With one hand, he yanked her against him and claimed her mouth in a savage fiery kiss.